Maria Soltera

The Fat of the Land

A novel. Part 2

Maria Soltera

The Fat of the Land
A novel. Part 2

ISBN/EAN: 9783337052027

Printed in Europe, USA, Canada, Australia, Japan

Cover: Foto ©Andreas Hilbeck / pixelio.de

More available books at **www.hansebooks.com**

BY

MARY LESTER

(MARIA SOLTERA)

AUTHOR OF 'A LADY'S RIDE ACROSS SPANISH HONDURAS'

IN THREE VOLUMES

VOL. II.

WILLIAM BLACKWOOD AND SONS
EDINBURGH AND LONDON
MDCCCLXXXVIII

CONTENTS OF THE SECOND VOLUME.

THE FAT OF THE LAND.

CHAPTER I.

L'HOMME PROPOSE.

"How did you manage to get into this field?" was Mrs Fanshawe's first exclamation to her new visitor, as Sikes, loudly protesting, and croaking like a bird-fiend, scuttled away in the direction of his harem. "Miss Clavering—Mr La Touche; I believe you have not met before. You have really had a rough reception. Did none of them warn you about the gander?"

"The fault is entirely my own," the young lady replied. "I espied some blossoms of the cuckoo-pint flower close to the hedge on the other side, and so stayed behind the rest to gather them. I found that the flowers were farther off than I had thought, so I went into the meadow itself, never, of course, expecting any attack. As I stooped the creature rushed upon me, inflicting a stab in my foot, and at the same time tearing my dress very savagely. As he raised his head to make a second onslaught, I seized him by the neck, twisted him round, and made him march on the extreme tip of his toes as you saw."

"I wonder you managed to retain your grasp," said Mrs Fanshawe. "Sikes is a very powerful bird."

"It was hard on my hand and arm, I assure you, and he very nearly wriggled away, but the sight of you encouraged me to hold on. Thanks for your aid," Miss Clavering added, turning to Stephen; "like the Prussians at Waterloo, you helped materially to secure the victory."

"You caught your enemy at a disadvantage," said Stephen, gallantly ignoring his own share in the achievement. "Were you, may I ask, carrying out a special code of tactics in gander training, or was the method you employed with such signal success the work of inspiration solely?"

"The work of inspiration solely, if you will put it in that light," Miss Clavering answered with a gentle laugh; "the motive power within always prompts me to grasp my nettle. There is nothing like facing a difficulty at the outset; promptitude is more than half the battle."

"I, for my part, am very much obliged to you," said Mrs Fanshawe,—"that is, if Sikes does not pick himself up presently, and rush at the next comer with renewed malignity."

"He seems pretty well cowed now," said Mr La Touche, surveying that part of the field whereon the gander lay sprawling, and evidently quite exhausted, for the time being at any rate. Meanwhile the females of Sikes's flock gabbled and wobbled, and revelled and exulted at the prostrate condition of their tyrant: it was an ungracious thought, but Stephen could not help likening the geese to a party of women over the reputation of a fallen sister. Here, however, the victim was masculine, and so the parallel was not exact. In the like situation, as affecting human beings, those who rejoice in the downfall of the man who is erring are certainly geese—though, as a matter of fact, he rarely obtains unqualified feminine reprobation.

Wisely keeping his thoughts to himself, Stephen turned to the younger lady with the remark, "I think you have acted like Rarey the horse-tamer: in future, there will be no more trouble with Master ﹒ Sikes."

"Sikes! what a name for a gander;" and thereupon Miss Clavering was supplied with all information respecting the antecedents of this bird, together with the reasons why the Fanshawe family had put up with him so patiently. "I believe the rector is quite proud of him," said Mrs Fanshawe in continuation, "so we must hope that his spirit is subdued but not utterly quenched."

"The reputation he has by all accounts acquired will stand in good stead," said Miss Clavering; "still, I should be sorry to put Mr Fanshawe out of conceit with his friend. I have been quite close enough to him to discover that Sikes is a magnificent specimen of his kind."

Here the sweet jocund laughter of early youth broke on the air,—the boyish shout, and the ripple of young girls' voices, now rising, now falling, and anon flooding the calm evening with spring's own melody,—freshness and flowering life, ever changeful music, but all its notes in tune.

They call, they whistle, and the sweet carillons of united happy voices bring smiles of sympathy to those whom these sounds are intended to summon. Then some one among them looking through a hedge espies the ramblers, and the lost Miss Clavering is proclaimed to be safely walking with the Mater and Touchy. " Now for it,—who is to ask first ? " says Harold Fanshawe.

" Not I,—it is your place ; no, no, you go on," say the boys the one to the other : then at length a bold spirit suggests, " Let Mary Leppell ask—she's more grown up ; besides, she's a beauty."

So Mary is pushed to the front, stimulated by the moral support of "brick," "trump," "duck," and "dear," which terms are liberally applied to that young lady on all sides ; and it turns out, as she proclaims her " mission," that a game before high tea is in contemplation, which game means a run down the terrace-walk bank, and a trial as to who will reach the bottom of that all but perpendicular declivity without fall or foot-trip. It appears that majestic-looking Willina Clavering, regarding whom some doubts had been expressed, would enjoy the fun as much as the youngest of them, and off they all go to test their prowess. Mrs Fanshawe, meanwhile, is glad of the opportunity, and improves it, to return to the house for the purpose of seeing that a noble ham, roast-fowls, milk-puddings, sweet fresh bread and cake, and good pure ale are all to the fore, to be presently served by the handmaidens in the noble old hall, which is used as a dining-room when the party is large. It is all very country and very simple, but Mr and Mrs Fanshawe are not of those who entertain grandly for a month in the year, and starve and pinch themselves and family for the other eleven to make up for the one month's feasting.

A part of the old Court had to be shut up for want of means to maintain the large establishment which the mansion in its entirety would demand, and Mr Fanshawe had determined, like a wise man, that if he was to reside in the house of his ancestors, he must do so by cutting off every luxury, together with the outward style in which these were wont to live.

" Their friends," the rector had said to his wife and children, " must accept the best they could give, and if they did not like it, the other course was available, and that was to go their ways and leave Pinnacles Court behind them."

The game begins, and the player who can run up and down three times faultlessly is adjudged to be

king or queen of the following day, and to order all
the sports and occupations, if it so please him, of
his playfellows for the space of twelve hours. A
recusant may get off by paying twopence to the parish
poor-box; or the victor not taking his or her privileges, which in this case are doubtful, contributes
threepence to the same laudable object.

The rules being settled and proclaimed, they begin,
but Stephen La Touche is requested to stand on the
lawn in the capacity of umpire, it being ascertained
that he is likely to achieve victory without trouble.

Francis Clavering of course insists upon giving his
hand to assist Miss Leppell, but he is repulsed by that
damsel and informed that his overtures are mean, and
that he had better mind his own running, for the performance is not so easy as he seems to think. The
boys Fanshawe scream with exultation, as, after a
movement betwixt a skate and a scuttle, Mr Clavering
comes down a "whopper," sprawls on his back, and
objurgates. Two boys have flown like arrows from
summit to base, but having put on too much steam at
the outset, they arrive on the lawn head over heels,
and gasp, "Well I never! there goes one to the bad,"
as they rise disgusted. Sweet little Clarice, who is
already established as "Touchy's" pet, walks carefully
sideways, for the grass is slippery as an eel or as glass :
she pauses, goes back again, tries zigzag, and finally
gives it up, calling to Stephen to come and take her,
for she is "deffel frighted." The two friends of Harold
both take to the sitting position and slide, using their

hands as oars ; but this device comes to nought, and they are hooted back to the point from whence they started.

Etta Fanshawe manages fairly well, but she does not run quite straight, and betrays symptoms of a clutch at the grass here and there to steady herself in the descent ; still she passes muster. Now comes Miss Clavering's turn : holding her body slightly backwards, she swims rather than walks, and has arrived on the lawn without change of poise in a single graceful and firm movement. Evidently the young lady is acquainted with the secret of descending an abrupt elevation ; and as many of her sex fail most signally in performing this feat, and generally look to the worst advantage whenever they attempt it, a hint may as well be given here as to the mode of progression which is necessary to achieve success. It is this simply : keep the feet well together, the one foot almost within the other, and as close to the ground as possible ; walk in short steps in the third position, the body being at the same time a little thrown backwards ; above all, move in regular time.

Miss Clavering finds it more difficult to ascend, but she manages well, using this time a striding motion in zigzag direction. Mary Leppell and Etta degenerate into a scramble ; and Mr Clavering, trying "scientific dodges," as the boys declare, is nowhere. Harold falls prone on his face in one ascent, and it is popularly opined that he will never do for the Alpine Club. So they come and go, and this with remarks complimentary or the reverse, and the peals of laughter, make a joyous and innocent scene.

At last comes Stephen, and he performs his task both up and down in accurate style. "He is best, and Miss Clavering is next best," was the general verdict, the rigour of the game not admitting of any palliation on the score of sex. So the young people assert to Stephen that he is king, and ask him what he means to do with himself and with them.

"*Place aux dames*," replied that gentleman, explaining at the same time that this was French for ladies first ; "the honours of royalty belong to Miss Clavering."

Then of course there was a pleasant little altercation as to whom these honours did legally belong to. Miss Clavering solved the difficulty.

"They are yours, Mr La Touche, by all manner of right," she said; "is not your first name Stephen— that noble Christian name which means a crown ? "

" What a beautiful meaning ! " said Mary Leppell ; "till now I have thought the name of Stephen—well, not pretty ; now I shall always like it,—Stephen, a crown."

"You remember the first martyr who wore the crown ? " said Willina. " I like the name,—it is associated with so much that is noble. Stephen Langton helped greatly to give us Magna Charta ; King Stephen of Hungary was a crown of goodness ; and our own King Stephen was renowned for manly beauty. St Stephen also gives his name to many beautiful chapels and gates all the world over; I could multiply many instances besides."

"Here is a Stephen, who, though unworthy to be named with the majority of those whom you have mentioned, still aspires to be your knight, Miss Clavering," said young La Touche, his handsome face lighted up with a smile which only needed the fire of the "refiner's gold" to be declared ethereal, for as yet the physical beauty of all the family of La Touche was of the earth earthy. "Let me be your knight, and I shall indeed reckon myself no longer Stephen, but a crowned king indeed!"

"Then Crown La Touche, come along," said Francis Clavering; "there's a warning bell, and we are hungry. Come, my heavenly Moll," said he, as he handed fair Mary towards the steps which led down from the garden to a side entrance into the Court. It occurred to Stephen that Mr Clavering emphasised "my heavenly Moll," in a jealous misgiving that he might claim the honours of Beauty for Willina; but he was magnanimous enough to consider that it is but seldom brothers can discern the attractions of their own sisters, however expert they may be in this particular with regard to the sisters of other people.

"You are prepared to pay that threepence to the poor-box?" called out Harold Fanshawe, who it appears was responsible for the collection of the tribute.

"I pay thankfully," said Stephen, handing the lad a shilling "to get rid at once of the dangerous privilege of regulating such a party as this, even for half an hour."

"Here is my contribution," said Willina, as she presented the like sum ; "now I think our consciences are clear."

"Well, girls are a blessing sometimes ! " exclaimed the eldest hope of the Fanshawes; "if it had not been for you, we should only have got twopence out of Mr La Touche, and not a fraction more. Yes or no," continued the young gentleman, appealing to Stephen.

However, Mr La Touche seemed disinclined to answer this question, and Miss Clavering drew herself up, the colour of her cheek at the same moment rivalling the scarlet curve of her beautiful lips. "Have I said too much, or gone too far," thought she. The thought pained her, for upwards of twenty years ago a Frenchman could not have written of the English race that the female courts the male ; it is owing to the "progress" at which the year of grace eighteen hundred and eighty-eight has arrived, that a popular author makes this assertion, and lays it down as an axiom which neither admits of challenge nor question.

Meanwhile the conscience of Master Fanshawe smote him as having taken a liberty in speaking of Miss Clavering as a girl; the youth felt that she was one of nature's queens, and on this conviction he got himself out of the way with all convenient speed.

Then, after making a slight evening toilette, the whole party flock into the old hall and stand in reverence as the rector asks a blessing on the good gifts bestowed upon them by the Father who careth for us all. Now the hospitality and courtesy and all the bright flowers of social intercourse burst forth in the full tide of happiness, and a red-letter day is afterwards chronicled in the modern records of Pinnacles Court.

And Lillian, the unloved daughter of this house, how fares she? Do her thoughts wander, or even willingly turn in speculation as to what may be going on in a home which, in its usual course, is certainly somewhat dull and uninteresting? Does she wonder if this infusion of new blood will widen her mother's heart, or strengthen her father to show outwardly those marks of regard which only in private he ventures to display towards her? Will the attention which she feels sure will be paid by the grown men, and even by the boys, to the girls of all ages then at Pinnacles, modify the undefined yet subtle jealousy with which Mrs Fanshawe ever seemed to entertain any distinguishing marks of attention shown to herself by strangers male or female?

Has she hope that any but Mary Leppell will feel her absence, or wonder if she would like to be among them?

No, certainly no, must be answered to all these queries. Mrs Fanshawe is thankful that Lillian is out of the way, because her pretty second daughter quite pales before the calm beauty and high-bred manners of the elder born.

Etta is good - pretty, to coin a word; but the astute mother knows that this kind of attraction requires much propinquity, and the stimulus of money present or in prospect, to prompt the generality of men to make an alliance with a family wherein daughters abound, and where the strain of making clerical sobriety march with the ways of the world is felt in full force. In the present mould of society, the daughters of the dignified clergy, at least, should be well dowered.

Truth to say, also, Mr Fanshawe recognises freedom in his elder daughter's absence, for his wife is invariably sharper and more unkind to Lillian in the presence of strangers than at any other time. The rector feels that he cannot take part with the child without coming to an open rupture with her mother; and the boys, following suit with their elders, are persistently troublesome to their eldest sister, safe in the conviction that no word of reproof will fall upon them for their turpitude,—they were privileged, as it were, by Mrs Fanshawe's habitual injustice towards their sister Lillian. Lillian, on her part, is also well satisfied with the present state of things. At Hunter's Lodge she sees Francis Clavering with more satisfaction, probably, than she would have done had they been living beneath the same roof. He comes and goes easily enough, for there are only eleven miles of train service betwixt Yarne and Pinnacles, and the young man is naturally very anxious about Lady Asher on Mary's account, and makes it his business to run over to Blythe to inquire for the old lady pretty frequently.

The health of Lady Asher at this time neither advances nor retrogrades, and she may continue in this state for months; Mr Clavering inwardly hopes that she may, though he benevolently wishes the old lady no harm. The present time is a halycon time for him, and he makes good use of it, never heeding nor looking to the future.

His cousin, Mr Glascott, also enjoys a walk to Hunter's Lodge, and becomes wonderfully interested in the young lady who so strikingly resembles what Mrs Leppell was in her palmy days; and he lavishes attentions upon Miss Fanshawe which, in a younger man, would have promptly led to the opinion that he aspired to a nearer connection than that of a friend.

The presence of Miss Fanshawe also served to mitigate any awkwardness which Mrs Leppell might probably have felt had she been obliged to receive Mr Glascott alone. Clara was not yet introduced, and nobody belonging to Hunter's Lodge could be found for drawing-room purposes when they were wanting; so the visitor paved the way for the elderly gentleman to drop in whenever he liked. Nothing loth, Mr Glascott came in the morning hours, stayed to luncheon, played with the babies, and fell, *con amore*, into the privileged attitude of old friend of the family,—the intervening past being summarily bridged over by the magic touch of the genius of oblivion.

Lady Asher was really unconsciously contributing

an active share to this pleasant state of things, and it must be further allowed that the absence of the master of the house was borne with fortitude. As there was no reason to hurry home, Colonel Leppell had concluded to prolong his stay in London, whereat the adjutant of the Yarneshire Militia, who acted as Ralph's *locum tenens*, was also well pleased.

Though the cares of a sick-room were the ostensible reason of Miss Fanshawe's visit to Hunter's Lodge, it was more the help that Mrs Leppell obtained from the young girl's forethought, and her general adaptation to all departments of household management, that made her presence so agreeable to her hostess, and thus left time to the latter to avail herself of the opportunity to take the rest which she so much needed. Adelaide, no doubt, was nearly worn out ; she felt it a blessing to have one near her who knew all her trials, and who, without ever appearing to invite confidence, met it half-way, and who, besides, possessed the rare tact of not appearing to know the things which were not supposed to be known,—and further, that were not intended to be known.

Miss Fanshawe was supremely happy in the knowledge that she was appreciated, and that she was allowed to be of use : her coldness of manner relaxed, and she spoke the truth when she said that she was always happy at Hunter's Lodge.

Francis Clavering now brought his science and laid it at her feet ; and Mr Glascott was ever bestowing those tender courtesies which men of his age and of the old school were wont to render to youth and beauty, because to them youth and beauty were sacred things, and were ever accounted as pure in their sight, unless the possessor betrayed the trust.

The modern worship of wealth and contempt for simple competence, together with the yearning for the vulgarities of soft living and glitter, is daily wrecking this high chivalrous creed; youth, alas! has its market price, and beauty sells itself openly at the highest rate at the gates of Mammon. Legal prostitution bids fair to become the vice of the age, and the world's whole litany to lie in the axiom, "Gardez les convenances, et puis, Dieu vous gardera." *Miserere Domine.*

Meanwhile the days passed by, and all went merrily as the proverbial marriage-bell at Pinnacles Court. The elder Fanshawes were satisfied with everything; the weather, too, was wonderfully fine for the time of year—so much so, that an archery party was projected, and it was with great difficulty that the rector had his say concerning east wind and the varieties presented by the English climate. The party were, however, pressed to prolong their visit, much to the satisfaction of Mr Stephen La Touche, who had discovered somehow that his aunt's affairs required more of his supervision than he had at first imagined.

Mrs Kemble, with the pertinacity which often characterises persons similarly afflicted, became much attached to the kindly handsome girl whom the house of Fanshawe was then delighting to honour as Mary Leppell's future sister. The poor lady felt that in consequence of the attention paid to her by Willina, the inmates of Pinnacles no longer regarded her as a dangerous person, but held her to be what she really was,—a sweet nervous soul, tormented to frenzy often by the stupidity of her own kind, and to whom human sympathy, properly directed, must, like the touch of an angel's wing, bring reason as well as healing by the contact. Thus it fell out that, from having been on the whole very miserable at Pinnacles, Mrs Kemble became loth to leave it, because it had given her Stephen back, and brought Willina Clavering to her heart.

Gladly then did she hail the news that her stay was to be prolonged for a week at least; these two dear young people, she said, were to her strength and the happiness of life.

This pleasant state of things was not, on the whole, quite satisfactory to Mr Percival La Touche. The prolonged absence of his brother seemed strange to him, as he did not believe for a moment that the alleviation of their aunt's condition could be the sole motive for Stephen's visit to the county of Yarne. Both he and Marcia were totally unaware that Lillian was at the time a guest at Hunter's Lodge; and jumping together at the same conclusion, they convinced themselves that this young lady was in reality the magnet which drew this particular loadstone from its sphere, and that the time was come which required some elucidation of the proceeding on their part.

A little *contretemps* also in the Brighton *ménage* had somewhat upset Percival's convictions with regard to the "liberty" said to be enjoyed by those who look upon marriage as a superfluous ceremony; his head, in lieu of his mouth, had become acquainted with the contents of a soda-water bottle, and he had been at the same time frankly informed, in the most literal rendering of the English tongue, that he was lower than the beasts, and that his future "habitat" would be a fiery one.

A fear that his personal safety might be threatened, or even endangered, was, to a moral coward like Percival, a most serious apprehension, and in his terror and excitement he poured all his woes, without reservation, into Aunt Marcia's ear. A remedy by what she was pleased to term a "safe marriage" was quickly proposed by that lady, who, foreseeing the inevitable, determined, if possible, to manage the inevitable in her own way.

"Why not marry Lillian Fanshawe?" she asked, as if impelled by a sudden inspiration; "she has everything but money, and you don't want that, happily. You need not add to your expenses for a year or two; you could live here, for Laurence is going to pay a round of visits, and then he'll be off to India. Besides, if you do not want to be cut out by Stephen, you must act promptly, my dear. Stephen admires Miss Fanshawe, and down in the country he has nothing else to do but stump about green lanes and make love! His letter of this morning is full of the delightful time he is having; you had better go to Pinnacles at once."

"But I can't present myself there without some pretext for so doing," said Percival, ruefully ; "all Aunt Arabella's affairs are now in Stephen's hands, confound him ! "

"You can invent some business matter to account for your being in the neighbourhood : it would be a compliment to say that you wished to call and see Aunt Kemble and the Pinnacles people before the former finally leaves that part of the country. Why not take a case of wine for Mr Fanshawe as an acknowledgment of the interest he has taken in Arabella ? He really behaved very handsomely in taking the old rectory off your father's hands without the customary notice—in a moment as it were ; very few people would have done that, you know."

Percival stroked his chin, and without heeding the last part of his aunt's exordium, inquired who was going to pay for the case of wine.

"You and your father between you," replied Marcia, undauntedly ; "I am sure my brother would not object. But I think, coming from you, it would be a nice way of opening negotiations, and it would be an attention to Mr Fanshawe——"

"And a nice little surprise for him," interrupted Percival, with his horrid leer and grin.

"Well, that is all arranged," said Marcia, thinking she was following up an advantage ; "and you can say that little Anna is still in such an unsatisfactory state that we are obliged to have her home, so that it will be impossible for me to go to Pinnacles and accom- .

pany Aunt Kemble to her new abode. You could say that you have offered to represent me,—this will be doing the thing in the best style, and fits everything in the most natural manner possible."

Percival agreed that it was a very feasible plan, and submitted, without demur, to his aunt's advice; and as the natural amenity of his disposition always caused him to gloat over the annoyances of other people, he in perspective enjoyed the confusion with which he imagined Stephen, and certainly Miss Fanshawe, would be overwhelmed when his descent upon Pinnacles should take place.

His former misgivings and hesitation as to the advisability of the Fanshawe connection having vanished under the pressure of his uncomfortable "domestic relations," Percival now worked himself up into the conviction that he was desperately enamoured of Miss Fanshawe, and that it was imperative that he should go down to the country and bring matters to a decided understanding, and that without loss of time. His brother Stephen to be poaching on *his* preserves! Perish the thought!

So Mr La Touche promptly managed a business excuse, opened his heart, moreover, to procure the case of wine and pay for it on his own account, and set off for the county of Yarne, full of triumphant expectation, and expedited by the good wishes of Aunt Marcia.

These last were genuine and sincere. Although it might, in some respects, be advantageous to the family

to keep Percival among them, Marcia, with the fear
before her eyes that the Brighton *ménage* might eventually, through her nephew's means, acquire a legitimate head, had of late contrived to have always one
nice girl or another domiciled as a visitor at Hinton
Square. Pleasant, good-looking women were also
frequent casual guests at their quiet dinners, and
the "small and early" evening parties. Nothing
had hitherto come of this diplomacy, for Percival's
inordinate vanity led him to regard himself as
irresistible, and it was his pleasure to pit (as he flat-
tered himself) one lady against another in his good
graces. The consequence of this was, that the nice
girls, and the eligibles, and the fascinating women,
deserted to the camps of the younger brothers, and
were quite *au mieux* with these young gentlemen, who,
on their side, were content to be the objects of passing and innocent flirtation.

Marcia then tried "girls with money," but none of
these would even look at Percival; and the handsome
Stephen, having given out that he would not be bought
up by any woman, was at the time a very forlorn hope
in Aunt Marcia's sight.

It was in the midst of these difficulties that Lillian
Fanshawe paid her first visit to Hinton Square, and
the general admiration which she commanded drew
Percival's attention to her for the first time. Till
then he had merely regarded her as one of the quiver-
ful of the Rector of Pinnacles, and had perhaps wondered how she and her numerous sisters would be

disposed of in matrimony,—arranging in his own mind that Miss Lillian would eventually marry her father's curate, and that the Fanshawe interest would ultimately secure a living for the provision of the pair.

The visit that Miss Fanshawe paid to Hinton Square very soon dispossessed Percival of this idea. The quiet self-possession of the young lady, her cool tact, and the easy manner in which she fell into the style of London society, with its ways and habits, at first excited the amazement of Mr La Touche, and ended by securing his admiration.

He delighted to inform his friends that the distinguished-looking girl with whom he had been seen at the Botanical *fêtes,* or at the Rose Show at the Horticultural, was the guest of his family, and was leaving them to pay a visit to her aunt Lady Hautenbas.

Judging from some of Percival's remarks, Miss Fanshawe drew the inference that both he and his family looked, if not with actual contempt, still with depreciation upon persons of all grades who live entirely in the country; and it was rather in a spirit of defiance that Miss Fanshawe played the town lady with much greater *aplomb* in Hinton Square than she was wont to do when in the mansion of Lady Hautenbas.

When Percival La Touche showed himself especially purse-proud and insolent, Miss Fanshawe had a quiet retaliative way of alluding to the wonderful manner in which persons of all degrees made their fortunes in trade. She spoke of some as "mere *merchanticles;*" and nearly sent Marcia into a fit one day by assuming to believe that Percival had begun life as a commercial traveller.

"Do you not know," exclaimed Miss La Touche, "that Percival is sole heir to Mr Squash, his granduncle! and when the old man dies my nephew will have at least seven thousand a-year, independent of his share in the business?"

"Yes, I have heard that often enough," the girl replied, looking as unruffled as a snowflake, and with a voice quite as icy; "but you know heirs as well as other folks must subsist and possess the wherewithal to live. I meant no offence; indeed I think it very honourable to your nephew that he should have earned his living with such expectations as his."

"But he never was a commercial traveller, never," insisted Marcia, with great emphasis.

"I don't suppose it much signifies," returned the visitor. "Why, Mr Dyson, a man of good, poor family, weighed out tea for years in an apron and white sleeves in a warehouse in St Paul's Churchyard. He was never thought the worse of for so doing. A fine handsome man, who is now rich through his own common-sense, and who is proud of his antecedents in commerce. We have all a high respect for Mr Dyson."

Not knowing how to carry on this incipient warfare, Marcia remained silent. She, however, reported the conversation to Percival, with the intimation that it would not do for him to play grand with Miss Fanshawe,—"it may do very well with the Dowager of Cauldkail and the Slocombes, and even with those poor rags of nobility the Ladies Varnishe. The girl has an opinion of her own, and can, or thinks she can, pick and choose," insisted Marcia.

A very few months after Miss Fanshawe's visit, Percival came into his fortune; and as London and Brighton life had at that time especial charms for him, and his father's house was both comfortable and convenient, he elected to reside there still, and to let the principal part of his property for a term of years.

His aunt's proposition that he should still make Hinton Square his headquarters in the event of his marrying, had acted as a powerful stimulant in Mr La Touche's intentions towards Miss Fanshawe. An undercurrent of jealousy of his brother Stephen also became a very decided motive power, and caused him to depart for Yarneshire with all convenient speed. The possibility that his proposals might be rejected by the lady in question or her father, never crossed his mind. His wardrobe was packed, the case of wine was on the carriage-seat, and Percival went his way, Marcia wishing him good speed. *Væ victis!*

CHAPTER II.

A HEARTY COUNTRY WELCOME.

THE whole of the party at Pinnacles were under the cherry-trees, then in full bloom,—for it was one of those delightful phases of the English spring, when the afternoon sun is genially warm and sheds his radiance for a short spell, as if to give an earnest of the fair summer which is in his wake,—and a grand discussion was going on as to the advisability of there and then setting up targets for archery practice.

Mrs Kemble had been induced to leave her house, and to come and sit on the lawn in a cushioned old-fashioned chair, which Miss Clavering had dragged out for the afflicted lady's especial benefit. And there she sat, quiet and happy, at times nodding her head and smiling at the young people who passed to and fro discussing their projects, and severally trying to bring the rector round to the opinion that it was just the weather for an archery party, and that it was so delighful to gather people together in out-door amusements, and the like.

The rector, however, presented a stubborn and opposing element to the machinations of his young friends. His *bête noire* through life had been east wind; and as he got a good deal of this ingredient, both in his physical and domestic relations, he had come to air it as his own particular grievance, and to drag it forward as an invincible argument against garden-parties and *fêtes* of every kind. The very word *fête* had a light zephyr-like sound which was repulsive to his British ears : it brought with it a flavour of sunny, warm, and dulcet airs, in which, in the common order-ing of things, no Briton had a right to indulge; it smacked of French frivolity and Italian sloth, and the enjoyable *dolce far niente* was a relaxation which he never permitted even to the over-worked of brain or the sorrowful of heart. Now he must have his say about the proposed archery party.

"You think because it is rather warm for an hour now," said Mr Fanshawe to Miss Leppell, "that we are beginning a course of fine genial weather. It will snow to-morrow, most likely, and perhaps rain the day after. Yes, the cherry-trees look splendid now, but every blossom will be cut off in a week. I don't believe we will have a cherry this year, and I am sure the wind will bear round to the east as soon as the sun goes down."

Mary, who from long experience knew the value of the rector's weather-forecasts, returned no remark concerning the elements, but asked humbly if they might be allowed to have an inspection in the barn on the morrow. "You have got a lot of targets there, Mr Fanshawe," she said, "and the boys might dust them and mend them up. We have always to do a good deal of this kind of thing at Hunter's Lodge before the targets are ready for company; might we not just look through the—the stock, and see what materials are available? You are so well off for stands and other things that, I think, you could well set up targets for three sets of archers without any expense. I can mend and paint and stuff a target with any one."

The rector was on the brink of refusal. But who can resist the pleadings of a sweet young face, and that accompanied by the courteous deference of the young girl to the elderly man? Had Mary been endowed with the sharp "bounce" of the girl of the period, which is so fatal to beauty, and so offensive in itself, not an arrow would have been shot for months on Pinnacles lawn.

"Well, yes, there's no harm in looking through the archery gear," the rector replied; "and you Leppell girls seem to know how to do all work that's not needle and thread. I've seen you stuff a target, Miss Moll. You shall have the key of the barn to-morrow; there are some good arrows, never used, somewhere—I'll rout them out—but we won't talk of an archery-party till we see it;—too early in the season,—east wind."

"Oh yes; and we will want to practise a little for a few days," returned this young diplomatist; "and I must teach Mr Clavering a little: he has no notion of these out-of-door sports—not even cricket."

"A mistake, my dear Moll,—every Englishman should play cricket;" and then the rector walked away and invited Mrs Kemble to pace up and down in the sun. "Sitting in that chair would only cramp her limbs," he said; and offering her his arm, they went here and there, and Mrs Kemble was so happy, and discussed so easily, that the good man became convinced that another mistake had been committed of a far graver import. Mrs Kemble had been allowed to remain too much alone, and had not been treated with sufficient kindness. This was the truth concerning the whole matter.

There was just the sharp dart through the air and an occasional uprising of the wind as the afternoon fell into evening, which confirmed Mr Fanshawe's prognostications, and during the next half-hour complaints of "chill" were unwillingly extorted from the most juvenile lips—so transient is the early spring-time in mid England.

Presently a pile of home-made cake and flagons of good mulled elder wine (prepared in the orthodox silver saucepan of our ancestresses) made its appearance on the lawn, and inspired no doubt by its influence, a game of "Bank," as this pastime was now called, was universally proposed wherewith to conclude the pleasures of the out-of-door day.

Just as all had been arranged for a start, the deep-toned bell of the hall-door rung a fretful, nervous peal, which seemed to tell of itself that the visitor was either of an irritable temperament, or that time was pressing and demanded immediate attention.

" I hope it is no one come to call," exclaimed Mrs Fanshawe, with the hospitable candour of the British matron when she is unwilling to be disturbed in her avocations.

" It's the Wigginses," volunteered Master Horace. " They have heard we have got visitors, and wish to give us an opportunity of asking them to join us."

" Hold your tongue, sir," said the rector; " what business have you to speak of any parishioner in that manner ?   Go round and see who it is.   Don't show yourself.   It may be Mr Sproggles on business,—I rather expect him."

Harold hied away, and from some invisible coign of vantage he espied a small gentleman clanging at the front door,—"at least I think he is small," this observer remarked, on his return to report what he had seen ; " but I could only make out his left leg, and half of one of his shoulders, for he turns to the thirty-two points of the compass in a moment, I do believe : any way, he fidgets as if he had an early bee about him."

" Show whoever the visitor is into the drawing-room, and be sure and say that the family are all out in the garden," said Miss Etta, who had pelted after the parlour-maid as the latter was well on her way to answer the summons of the bell.   This caused her young mistress some difficulty in getting out of sight before the visitor was admitted within the house.

There was some little bustle as a portmanteau and a large wooden case were brought in from the vehicle and deposited in the porch. "The case will remain here, and the portmanteau can be sent down to 'Esperanza' presently,—I shall sleep there," declared a voice which Etta fancied she recognised, though at the moment she could not recall to whom it belonged. "I hope the family are all well."

"Please to walk in, sir," replied the maid, who, recognising Percival, and flurried by the way in which he had installed his baggage, neglected to answer Mr La Touche's inquiry most completely. Ushering him into the drawing-room, she closed the door of that apartment with a bang in order to apprise Etta that she might issue forth in safety.

Dismay was legibly depicted on the face of the domestic as, after securing the new arrival, she confronted that damsel. "Mr Percival La Touche, Miss," said she in a stage whisper ; " what can have brought him here ? and his Haunt setting in the garden, so sensible like ! I had not better tell your Mar before Mrs Kemble," continued the girl wisely ; "the old lady can't abear Mr Percival, and it might frighten her, his coming so promiscuous like."

" You are right," said Etta ; "go to Mr Fanshawe and tell him that a gentleman is in the drawing-room who wishes to see him, but don't say anything to Mr Stephen, unless he is quite out of Mrs Kemble's hearing. If Mr Stephen is quite away from his aunt, tell him that his brother is here."

Mr Fanshawe had deposited Mrs Kemble in her chair after their little promenade, and persuaded her to take a glass of the mulled elder wine; after presenting this beverage he turned to walk into the house.

To him the waiting-maid, who announced that a gentleman on business was waiting to see him in the drawing-room. "Ah, as I thought, Mr Sproggles;" and the rector, without waiting to hear the visitor's name, went into the house at a rapid rate. Rhoda, seeing that Stephen was standing before his aunt, went no further, but followed her master into the hall with the vain intention of communicating the visitor's name. The door of the room closed on Mr Fanshawe before he could be caught, and it was therefore with much surprise that the rector had the honour of receiving Mr Percival La Touche.

"I have some business at Bath," Percival said, in explanation of his sudden visit; "and as I have a little time to spare, I have devoted it to calling here, and also to take leave of my aunt before she finally leaves this part of the world. Although my brother is staying with her, I dare say I can be accommodated for one night at 'Esperanza.'"

The rector's answer was to invite Mr La Touche into the garden, wherein, he told his visitor, all his family and some guests then were, including Mrs Kemble, who, Mr Fanshawe said, seemed not only more composed, but also much more cheerful and talkative than formerly. This improvement he attributed to Mr Stephen's visit.

"No doubt—very likely," returned Percival, with a sarcastic intonation of voice; "he's been away for some time, and variety is charming. My brother Stephen quite serves to illustrate this axiom."

The rector did not know why, but he did not relish the tone in which Percival spoke: whether the "variety" mentioned consisted in the visit to Pinnacles, or to the enjoyment of Mrs Kemble's society solely, on Stephen's part, he could not quite understand, and therefore he took the discreet way of solving a difficulty by answering with the neutral, "Hum, haw; we all like a change."

Though of a quiet and undemonstrative temperament, Mr Fanshawe was by no means so devoid of penetration as many persons elected to believe. He had ever regarded the elder Mr La Touche as a kindly selfish old humbug, who made the best of both worlds, and Marcia as a thorough worldling, whose backslidings were in a great measure redeemed by her warmth of heart, and the undoubted sincerity with which she devoted herself to her brother's family. Mr Fanshawe also entertained a shrewd suspicion that the world in general had Marcia to thank for the many whims and absurdities which distinguished the eldest scion of the house of La Touche. She had uniformly pampered his appetite to keep him in good humour, and had set him up on a pinnacle and glorified him mightily, in deference at first to his expectations, and more lately in deference to his position and actual possessions, and often at the expense of his own kith and kin. All this Mr Fanshawe had noted on the occasions whereon Mrs Kemble's business had brought him in contact with the La Touche family; and now that the young people were interchanging visits, the rector convinced himself that his early impressions of Mrs Kemble's relatives were thoroughly correct.

Though of a mean higglety nature, which he certainly did not inherit from his parents, Percival was not altogether a person to be overlooked, much less to be lightly esteemed. He was well educated, and he also took much interest in many of the scientific enterprises of the day; and when he could divest himself of the notion that the man entertained some design upon his commercial influence, and that the woman held snares for entrapping him into matrimony, no one could be more agreeable or diverting than Percival La Touche. He added to a certain graphic method of imparting information, a vein of sarcasm which was amusing in its way, although it never attained to the confines of wit.

The misfortune was that, in common with many underbred persons, Percival never knew where to stop; and his utter want of sympathy for others often led him to indulge in personalities which always gave great offence, and very often gave great pain. He imagined, in his presumption, that to indulge in personalities was a sure evidence of his own insight into the character of those with whom he chanced to come in contact.

Here it was, if the expression may be permitted, that Mr La Touche broke down. What sense was there in especially alluding to courts-martial when in conversation with an officer who, at one time of his career, had suffered the annoyance of being censured by one of these tribunals? Why remind Mr Gravéy that his mother had been Dr Gravéy's cook? What object was served by informing the Protestant bishop of Soapisande that Roman Catholicism was steadily on the increase, when he knew full well that the prelate's only daughter and her husband had joined the Catholic Church, and attributed this step to the teaching and preaching of the right reverend ecclesiastic then dining at the same table?

These and the like solecisms Percival frequently and knowingly committed; and as they were in some cases indulgently passed over from the firm belief of the affronted ones that the man was "cracked," and in the greater majority from the latitude which the world, in its worship of wealth, ever allows to the possessor of its honours and its gold, this glaring offender escaped scot-free in situations wherein an impecunious man would have encountered a withering glance, if not a sharp rebuke. He certainly could steal society's horse when another man dared not venture to look over the hedge at that animal.

Mr Fanshawe had delayed some moments in conducting Percival into the garden,—for the latter, with a mysterious sign, had beckoned his host towards the hall porch as they left the room. Drawing himself

up before the case of wine, he said, "It's the very best
I could get—*real* Marsala; and I have put in a couple
of bottles of brandy and four of whisky, all good
brands—drop of comfort, you know; cold nights now
and then, even——"

"You had better place this at the discretion of Dr
Williams," Mr Fanshawe said, mistaking the destination of the case. "It's very good of you, and very
right to add to Mrs Kemble's comforts; but I fancy,
at present at least, that the rules of the asylum would
not allow such items as wine and spirits to be entirely
at the command of the patient."

"Oh! it's not for Mrs Kemble," replied Percival,
hastily; "such luxuries must come out of the board
she'll have to pay. It's for you, Mr Fanshawe—little
remembrance—gratitude for taking the house off our
hands——"

"Very kind of your father," said the rector; "will
you——"

"But it's not from the governor," interrupted
Percival, with a triumphant cackle; "it's from me.
You see I know how to do the handsome thing. No
thanks—I take those as said; all I want you to do
is to be particular about returning the case. Send
it as a 'returned empty,' and the carriage will be but
a trifle; be sure and address it to me. It is a private
package, with which the firm has nothing to do."

Mr Fanshawe felt inclined to kick the case into
space, and the donor of its contents for company; but
he swallowed his indignation in the conviction that

Percival meant well by the offering, and that he really knew no better how to present it. So he accepted the wine very much in the manner of a chief who receives tribute in kind, and undertook to return the "empty" according to directions. "Now come into the garden," he urged, as he was beginning to feel that he had enough of Percival; "the young people are at high jinks, and you may like to join them. As your brother has not come into the house, he very probably expects you on the lawn."

Percival seized his umbrella; this article was as necessary to him as a broomstick to a witch. His brothers declared that he slept with it; and there was another legend current in Hinton Square that a Frenchman in Vienna, discerning Percival as a spot upon the far horizon, had unhesitatingly pronounced his nationality: "Ah, voila! c'est un véritable Anglais; il n'a pas oublié son parapluie."

Arming himself therewith, Mr La Touche followed his host through the hall, and up the flight of low broad steps which led out upon the lawn and terrace walk, and so into the open air.

The disposition of the group had somewhat altered, as twilight had begun to sober the sky, and the game of "bank" could be put off no longer. The young people were, therefore, collected at the foot of the terrace walk, and Mrs Fanshawe had vanished to superintend some domestic arrangements. A few of the nursery children were running here and there, but Mrs Kemble was alone, looking with great interest from her cushioned chair upon the game which was going on directly in front of her seat.

So absorbed was she that she did not perceive Mr Fanshawe and his companion until they were within a few feet of her. The kindly smile on the rector's face literally froze there, as Mrs Kemble, upon recognising them, rushed with a bound upon Percival, threatening him with instant death, and, in addition, using such language as is popularly supposed to be the sole property of the lowest order of people. This was interspersed with cries and shrieks, and naturally these last more particularly attracted the players from their game.

"You wretch! you villain!" called out Mrs Kemble, as, after exhausting her strong appellatives, she fell back upon a milder vernacular; "just as I am getting happy and sane—quite sane—you come back to torment me. But you can't frighten me any more; you can't shake your fists and make me say what you please—oh, no! Heigh cock-a-lorum! Stephen is going to protect me, and somebody else—ah, a pretty girl! Dr Williams is going to marry me—his mother does not know he is out; but I must wring your neck, my dear, before that.

"'Froggy would a-wooing go,
Heigho! says Rowley.'

But I must have a clutch at Froggy"—and she again darted towards her nephew, with the evident determination to inflict some injury upon that gentleman.

He meanwhile, pale as death, stood his ground, using the umbrella as a weapon of defence, — now twirling it round with great rapidity, and again pointing it in full front of his relative, thus keeping her at bay, whilst she danced round him in a wild maze which was truly horrifying. It certainly was marvellous how Percival managed to foil his assailant at all points, with the intervention solely of so slight a defence; and it is probable that the steadiness with which he fixed his eyes upon Mrs Kemble's face, and maintained his gaze without swerve or shrink, was the means whereby she was at length reduced to exhaustion, if not to quietude, in three minutes of time.

It was a sad scene: the rector writhed under the knowledge of an open scandal committed in his very presence. Stephen could have knocked his brother down for his wanton intrusion: he would rather have cut off his right hand than Miss Clavering should have witnessed such an exposure. It must be patent to all that the affliction of his aunt was somewhat more than an indisposition that is passed off as a "nervous" or "peculiar" affection. The girls fled in all directions; it was only Emma Fanshawe who preserved a stolid bearing, and stood open-mouthed, witnessing the gyrations of the umbrella in a mixture of wonder and interest, which on a less trying occasion would have been ludicrous in the extreme.

A sensation of relief was experienced by all when the poor lady, exhausted by her exertions, came to a sudden stand-still, and exclaimed, "I am tired out; but I will catch that villain another time, when I am in the vicinity of a poker, my dears—nice handy weapon! No more Heigh cock-a-lorum to-day; I am tired out now. Oh where, where is Miss Clavering? I know she won't desert me. Do come, Miss Clavering!"

The last words were spoken in a tone which was almost inaudible, and Willina was just in time to support Mrs Kemble as she stumbled forward, faint and rigid, into her strong young arms. Delicacy, rather than fear, had kept Willina somewhat aloof: her time for action was now come, and she commenced operations by warning Percival off the premises.

"You had better keep out of sight, had you not?" she said in a suggestive tone to this young gentleman; "it would be so dreadful if Mrs Kemble were to recognise you when she comes round. Pray, keep out of sight; and Emma, like a good girl, run and get some wine and water."

Percival mechanically did as he was requested, feeling somehow a strange pleasure in obeying the behest of this fair stranger. As he moved aside, he could not help looking with admiration upon the graceful form and earnest speaking eyes of the girl,—eyes which by their expression seemed to appeal to his common-sense, and at the same time to exonerate him from the imputation that he might be responsible for this sudden outbreak. There was too, he thought, something of compassion in her glance. Certainly a more embarrassing situation could scarcely be imagined, and it was a consolation in its way to perceive that there was one person among the number present who understood the position, and who could, moreover, sympathise with the annoyance with which it was fraught.

The rector had vanished: his mission was to find his wife, and consult with her what was best to be done. The outcome of the consultation was the appearance of an old bath-chair in which invalids at Pinnacles were wont to be dragged short distances when their locomotive powers were out of order, or temporarily suspended through illness or some of the accidents to which our earthly tabernacle is heir.

" Don't let her into the house," Mrs Fanshawe had insisted rather than implored — " you never know where these attacks may end. As it is, our party is very much disturbed. Mary Leppell is frightened out of her senses, and Mr Clavering must needs take to swearing by way of relieving his feelings: you see it would never do. Besides, Mrs Kemble has got her two nephews."

" There's the difficulty," answered Mr Fanshawe; " it will never do to let Percival La Touche sleep at the old rectory as he proposed and intended, nor even to go near it—she'd murder the fellow; and all our rooms are full. But I don't like sending the poor soul back to her house without some lady to look after her; indeed we ought to have her within, if only to lie down on the sofa in my study."

" There's the bath-chair," answered the lady; " when she is better Stephen can get her into that, and Horace can push at the back. I suppose I must go and see her into bed," continued Mrs Fanshawe, ungraciously; " Etta and Emma are both too nervous; besides, we have no right to frighten young girls. Well, get out the bath-chair, and I will see what can be done; perhaps Stokes is clean,—if so, I'll send her."

Now Stokes was the girl in the kitchen, not a kitchen-maid proper, and had fate sent Stokes in attendance upon Mrs Kemble, the chances were that, betwixt ignorance and fear, Mrs Fanshawe might have had the management of two " peculiars " on her hands that night.

" I wish Lillian were here," suggested the rector, with some slight misgiving as to how the remark would be received; " at any rate she would have accompanied Mrs Kemble at once, and smoothed all difficulties with the guests."

" Mrs Kemble doesn't like her," said the rector's wife shortly; " will you go and get the bath-chair? I suppose I had better go out and see how matters are going on: dear, dear, it's very inconvenient having people subject to attacks! Of course the nephews will communicate with Dr Williams at once; as to Percival, I can put him up in the spare attic."

The rector sped his way to the coach-house wherein the vehicle was laid up, if not in lavender, yet dry and serviceable amid straw and hay. Mrs Fanshawe appeared on the lawn, and, summoning Stephen, laid out the plan of action that was to be pursued.

" Your brother must stay here," said she, " and must on no account be seen near the old rectory. It would be advisable to persuade Mrs Kemble to keep within doors, or at least not to go beyond her garden till she leaves the place. The bath-chair will be here directly. Put her into it, Horace will help you to propel it, and I will come with you to see your aunt safely into the house, and into her bed. You had better stay with her till she goes to sleep; then the woman at the house can look to her, and you can come here as fast as you can. Mr Percival will excuse an upper chamber here for to-night under the circumstances.

" Here is the bath-chair,—put the cushion into it, Horace. Are you better? don't you think you would like to go home, and get into bed?" continued Mrs Fanshawe, turning round suddenly, and addressing herself to the patient.

" Yes, oh, I'm very well—rather tired, perhaps, but thank you for a very pleasant afternoon," Mrs Kemble answered feebly. " Stephen will take me home. I am to go in that thing, am I?" she continued, looking doubtfully at the vehicle. " Miss Clavering, you are there; give me your arm, my dear. That little villain has gone, has he?"

" Quite gone," replied poor Stephen, who, good fellow as he was, felt rather rueful at the part Mrs Fanshawe had assigned to him. He, however, accepted his responsibility without remark; but he made a mental determination, and that was, that the woman at the house should attend to his aunt, and that he would return to the Court as quickly as he decently could. He was not going to allow Percival to make all the running, which, as Miss Fanshawe was absent, he felt his brother would attempt to do in the direction of Miss Clavering. He was not blind, and he thought he had perceived some very furtive and enamoured glances already cast by that relative in the direction of the lady.

Considering the circumstances, and the shortness of time, it must be confessed that both the La Touche brothers had improved their opportunities with a celerity which was quite electric · in its working.

Mrs Kemble was with some little difficulty inveigled into the bath-chair; a misgiving had seized her poor weak brain that this was a prison on a small scale in which she was to be for ever shut up: it was only on the promise that Miss Clavering would stay with her, and hold her hand till she should be disgorged from the vehicle, that she could be persuaded to enter it. The presence of Mrs Fanshawe was in consequence an absolute necessity, and it looked well for her humanity as well as for her sense of propriety that she accompanied the *cortège*, and remained with Mrs Kemble until she could be safely left to the attendant's care. As a supplementary precaution, the gardener's boy was enjoined to remain in the house, to be ready to run up to the Court, should the necessity for further help arise. This would be hardly necessary, for Mrs Kemble, as soon as she was laid in her bed, fell into the heavy sleep of utter exhaustion.

The convoy returned to the Court, together with the bath-chair, into which the young gentlemen insisted on placing Mrs Fanshawe. Everything was necessarily late, owing to the *contretemps* of the afternoon. The supplementary dishes of the evening meal were spoiled, and the rector, if he did not actually refuse conversation, was snappish and out of sorts. Nobody would play or sing; in fact, everything appeared jangled and out of tune. Percival seemed to be the only person who was thoroughly unconcerned and at ease; and his brother, who knew him well, felt convinced that he was privately exulting over the embarrassment which his unwelcome advent had occasioned, and that he would make a fine story of the affair, even though it told against himself, when he should return to Hinton Square. Mrs Fanshawe, for once in her life, wished that her elder daughter had been at home; for Etta was too shy to cope with Mr La Touche, and Mr Clavering seemed to take care that Mary Leppell should have nothing to do with that gentleman. In consequence, Miss Clavering exerted herself to alleviate the annoyance which she felt sure Mr La Touche must feel, in spite of his apparent indifference; and this provoked Stephen into abandoning the young lady to her decided preference, as he

was pleased in his own mind to regard her well-
meaning offices.

It was therefore with the most cordial sincerity that
the members of this party, at ten o'clock, wished the
one the other " Good night."

CHAPTER III.

THE apartment which had been assigned to the use of Mr La Touche was veritably an upper chamber, lighted by a large dormer-window, and of the shape of a highly irregular triangle, the apex of which dashed laterally into a corner, and terminated in a commodious dressing-room.

This room was formed partly by the stone-work of the outer wall, but the inner partition was of wood. It was evident that a similar construction existed on the other side, and that this was the junction of one of the corners of the slanting roof.

Percival, true to his habits of caution and precaution, engendered perhaps by his experience of insular and Continental travel, bolted the door; and then, taking up the candlestick, he surveyed the apartment with rather more of scrutiny than is usually employed in a private house.

His horror of catching cold always prompted him to examine the bedding provided for his use, wherever he might be. He would have done so even in Buckingham Palace. So he thumped the mattresses and smelt at the sheets, and snuffed for damp with all the apprehension of a valetudinarian of ninety years.

This inspection being concluded, he proceeded to the dressing-room and took a look around therein. It presented the usual appearance of a boarded-off compartment, made serviceable for a second person who might chance to share the sleeping accommodation of the principal room. A chair, a full toilet apparatus of homely kind, and some hanging-hooks, composed the furniture of this sanctum, from which Percival withdrew in haste, feeling as he imagined a cold draught: he, however, left the door partially unclosed in his retreat.

The inspection proving satisfactory, the visitor set down the light and plunged into the depths of one of those easy-chairs with high circular back and stuffed elbow-rests, covered with white dimity and generously flounced below, which are yet to be found in the bedrooms of old-fashioned houses.

How comfortable, how homely these are! Percival was right in his assumption that this piece of furniture had formerly been the house-mother's haven of refuge in the early days of her weakness, subsequent to the advent of the several scions of the house of Fanshawe.

It had fulfilled its duty in that state of life into which it had been at first called, and was now destined to end its career in the higher regions of the house, and impart an air of respectability and finish to the room which was dedicated to male chance visitors from without, and to casual invalids of that sex from within.

Percival, from this coign of vantage, now mentally surveyed his position; and as he had arrived at his destination with the full intention of proposing for one lady, and had in her absence become desperately enamoured of another, his mind was naturally in rather a perplexed condition.

The possibility of his being rejected by either of these ladies never crossed his imagination: his present dilemma was how he could best attract and secure Miss Clavering's regard, and yet not appear to desert Miss Fanshawe.

The absence of the latter appeared to be a most fortuitous circumstance, as things turned out; but this did not prevent his coming to Pinnacles being rather a marked thing to do, for which anxiety concerning Mrs Kemble's removal was hardly a sufficient pretence. All authority on that affair had been delegated to Stephen, and the Fanshawes collectively must be fully aware of the fact.

True, he had alleged, with his usual habit of self-defence, that business in a neighbouring county was the cause of his making a detour in the direction of Yarneshire, added to his desire to take leave of the family at Pinnacles. Now that Mrs Kemble was to be finally removed, it was a chance, said Percival to

Mr Fanshawe, whether he should visit that part of the country for some time to come.

Mr Fanshawe probably believed all this. His wife had her doubts, possibly also her fears; but Percival felt sure that his brother attached very little credence to this assertion.

There was one thing, however, of which Percival was positively certain, and that was, that metal more attractive than poor Aunt Arabella induced Stephen to prolong his stay in Yarneshire; and with the elation of a little mind, he grinned and exulted at what he considered to be his own astuteness in at once discovering his brother's secret.

Percival further reflected that, as he had brought himself into its neighbourhood, he must call at Hunter's Lodge. This he had certainly intended to do, as a visit of congratulation on the part of himself and his family on the approaching marriage of Miss Leppell.

This projected event had been formally announced to Marcia, so all was plain sailing in that direction.

Further, to give a fair colour to his previous assertions, this diplomatist had informed Mary Leppell that he contemplated doing himself the honour of calling upon her parents, either immediately or upon his return from his business tour.

The young lady, thinking to do Lillian a good turn, and with an excellent opinion of her own powers of manœuvring, enjoined Mr La Touche to go to Hunter's Lodge forthwith.

"Papa is in London," she said, simply, "and he hates visitors; so you had better take an early train and go over and lunch there to-morrow. Mamma and Clara will be glad to see you; and, you know, Lillian is filling my place at home, now that grand-mamma is so ill. Would you mind taking a note and a tiny parcel for me if you go?"

Percival undertook the commission; and as no in-vitation to prolong his stay over the night had been tendered by Mrs Fanshawe, and the antagonistic atti-tude of Mrs Kemble rendering it unsafe for him to take even refreshment at the old rectory, he decided to depart on the morrow, stay at the Red Lion at Yarne for the next night, and so proceed on his tour.

All this was very nicely arranged for getting rid of Miss Fanshawe; but on reviewing his programme, Percival became aware that it in nowise furthered his prospects of improving his acquaintance with Miss Clavering.

The idea that his brother might prove a serious obstacle to the success of his plans, Percival rejected almost as soon as it occurred to him; but he was in difficulty as to how Miss Clavering was to be culti-vated. He solved the enigma in this way: Mr Glas-cott and Miss Clavering were coming to London on their journey to Brydone. He would make Marcia call upon the lady, and invite her to stay a few days in Hinton Square.

Then he fell to thinking how advantageous from all points of view a match with Miss Clavering would be for himself. No sisters; no herd of unmarried females for him to entertain or *chaperon* about — an only brother, and that brother affianced to a lady who, if not a fortune, possessed that high connection which commands many of the advantages which fortune brings. Again, Miss Clavering had a little of her own, and it was but fair to assume that she would be handsomely dowered by her relative and guardian whenever she might marry.

So, putting aside the personal attractions of the lady, Percival found out at last that there was one woman in the world who was thoroughly eligible to occupy the position of his wife. But what of Lillian Fanshawe?

Well, she might be disappointed, but that need not matter: he had never committed himself in that direction. A few *petits soins* here and there were all the latitude he had ever allowed himself, and these *petits soins* meant nothing, as all the world knew.

Lillian, Mr La Touche assured himself—and rightly — was not of the stuff to cry or mourn over spilt milk. Her good looks would always ensure her a mate if she cared to marry; and, after all, Marcia might ferret up some city man with money who might like the Fanshawe connection, and thus matters would square themselves and no harm be done.

The course of these ruminations was arrested by a shimmer of light which Percival descried upon the floor of the dressing-room, through the half-open door.

Presently he heard voices, and it soon became evident that two of the young ladies of the house were denizens of the opposite gable, and that one of them was then speaking from her dressing-closet to her companion in the room into which it opened.

At first, what was said was conveyed in broken and indistinct sounds, which, however, made Percival aware that the girls had come up-stairs from some household duty which had been required of them in preparation for the morrow. Then the voices became louder, and on approaching nearer, Percival had the satisfaction of hearing Miss Etta and Miss Emma discussing him, their guest, and that freely.

"Tiresome little man!" exclaimed the occupant of the dressing-room, giving her hair-brush a rattle as if she were shaking him. "It seems he can't eat mutton-chops, and he won't eat cold beef, and veal-cutlets don't agree with him; so I have had to cut up all that nice boiled fowl that was left at tea, in order to have it ready to curry for his breakfast. Mind you don't take any, Emma, for there is only just enough for the visitors."

"I suppose there will be some devilled kidneys," returned the sister. "Papa and the young La Touche like them."

"Yes; but this old one won't touch them unless they are cooked as splendidly as he gets them done at home."

Percival winced at the estimation of his age : at the moment he forgot that the speaker numbered but sixteen years.

" Marcia, the aunt, has a dreadful time of it, especially when Mr La Touche gives a state dinner. The cook has been there eighteen years, and takes things more easily."

" Ah! you see," said Etta, sagaciously, " she does not hear the fault-finding and grumbling: all that comes upon the lady of the house. I heard old Mr Chivers say, the other day, that nine-tenths of the men *dare* not speak to their cooks in the way they speak to their wives or female relations about the dinners. Bless you! the cooks don't lie awake all night thinking over the dishes, and trying to remember about the right sauces and all that."

" They are supposed to understand all particulars of cookery," said Emma; " it is part of their business."

" I know; but if they do make mistakes, it never troubles or upsets them. Lillian has often made me laugh at the cool way in which the La Touche cook ignores all Percival's messages. Sometimes she sends the dish complained of in another form to table; and Percival never finds out that the same kidneys he raved against in the morning form part of a savoury pie at dinner, of which he partakes with great gusto."

" What fun!" exclaimed the other girl.

" I'll pitch into Marcia," vowed Percival, as he listened to these revelations. He never thought, however, of tackling the cook, who really was the sinner; for Miss La Touche was thoroughly ignorant of more than half the metamorphoses which went on in the kitchen to save appearances and avoid a row.

"Suppose he does not like the curry," suggested Miss Emma, after a pause.

"That contingency has been provided for," answered Etta: "we are going to have a nice little piece of rump-steak, nicely grilled, and surrounded with a ring of mushrooms. It seems Percival is very fond of mushrooms, and they are always sent up from Wheatley in the season for his private eating."

"Little glutton!" exclaimed the sister. "Private eating, indeed! he deserves to live on bread and water!"

"Fortunately," Etta went on, "there are a few very young mushrooms to be found in one of the meadows, and some of the boys will have to turn out and find them to-morrow morning. The season is rather early, and there will be scarcely enough to put round the dish: mind you don't attempt to eat any of it,—it's a visitor's *plat*,—not for country maidens like ourselves."

"*Plat* — that's French," said Emma; "why don't you speak plain English?"

"*Plat* is the correct term for a little *recherché* dish. Lillian says that Percival is a *gourmet*—that means a person who is more particular about the quality than the quantity of the food; what you call a glutton is a *gourmand*."

"And so this little man is to have the best of everything," said Miss Emma. "Pray, what will happen if the *plat* goes wrong, or is not cooked to his fancy?"

"If he can't put up with the dressed dishes of the country, he will have to fill up with eggs," returned Etta, sententiously. "You know we should not take so much trouble, only Lillian has been visiting at Hinton Square, and mamma thinks we ought to set before Percival what he likes best. Well, we have done our best; and, as I said before, he can fill up with eggs."

Here the girls laughed loudly, and Percival, on the other side of the boarding, grinned for sympathy: they had entirely forgotten the proximity of a neighbour, and were again in full swing in their conversation.

"Miss Clavering seems a nice girl," called out Miss Etta, from the bedroom.

"Yes; and her eyes are just like two stars: do you know, she says that we are all too hard upon little Mr La Touche, and that he is very agreeable and well informed. Fancy that!"

"You young monkey!" muttered Percival, under his breath; "how I hate bread-and-butter damsels."

"So Lillian says—that is, when he chooses to waste his sweetness on the desert air. You know he is dreadfully afraid of people wanting to marry him; and to prevent this, he affected to be very rude and disagreeable when he was young. Now that he has got his fortune, I suppose he can't help himself; and the being disagreeable is now the nature of the beast."

Percival's face was now a "study"; but he kept perfectly still, as the girls were talking again.

"I should not like to live in Jersey, if I were Miss Clavering," said Emma; "she will find it very dull—worse than this, because there is the sea to cross."

"Yes; but they will often be in London. I think Mr Glascott has a small house somewhere in that neighbourhood; it has been let until lately. I think they are going to it for a month, whilst they buy new furniture for the Jersey place."

"Brydone?"

"Yes; Brydone. If Lady Asher gets better, Miss Clavering is to return to Hunter's Lodge with Mary, and pay them a visit; then I suppose the time of Mary's wedding will be fixed. I hope Lady Asher won't die; it would really be very inconvenient," remarked Miss Emma, with the utmost coolness.

"She'll do now," said Etta, with an air of superior wisdom; "but I don't mind her being rather ill, if that keeps Lillian away and Mary here. It is not that I do not care for Lillian; but it is so uncomfortable to be with her and mamma together, and now that our sister is from home, mamma is so much nicer in all ways. I wonder how it is that these two have never got on?"

"I believe Lillian was intended to be a boy," said Emma; "but as she isn't, I wish she would marry. Do you know, I fancy Stephen La Touche comes here more on her account than for his aunt. I would like him for a brother-in-law; he is handsome, and quite a gentleman. Now there is a dash of the snob in the old man; and this Percival, in spite of his money, looks like a bad style of commercial traveller."

Here the individual in question objurgated Miss Emma as an impertinent little beast, without, however, naming the genus.

"You don't mean to infer that Lillian would look at the old man!" exclaimed Etta, aghast.

"Oh dear no—I was thinking of the family style, and how different Stephen is. I do wish," continued the girl, with great enthusiasm in her voice and manner,—"I do wish that Stephen and Lillian Fanshawe would make a match of it."

"That will never be — never!" answered Etta. Have you no eyes? don't you see that Stephen La Touche is over head and ears in love with Willina Clavering? I don't know much of these matters, but I am not wrong in my conviction of this: however, don't make any remark to any one else."

"Oh no; what is said up here between you and me is sacred," said Emma; "it is the only place where we are safe. But I fancied that Stephen La Touche was very much disappointed, the day he arrived, to find that Lillian had gone to the other side of the county."

"Yes; that is true enough. You see, he hardly knows the rest of us, and Lillian having stayed in his father's house, they seemed to be more like old friends; but when Miss Clavering came, he brightened up considerably, and he always manages to get near her. Besides this, Percival is supposed to be rather an admirer of Lillian."

"He has lots of money," said the elder girl slowly.

"But what would Lillian say?" demanded Miss Emma; "what does she think of him?"

Percival here screwed himself close to the partition; he was strangely interested in the answer that was to come.

"Who can tell what Lillian thinks of anybody? She is as mute as an oyster,—one of those who, like the goose, says little but thinks the more," replied Etta. "Of course she would only take Percival for his money. He is not so very old—twenty-nine, I think —but papa says he has got the ways of a man of fifty."

"Very much obliged to Mr Fanshawe, very," thought Percival. "I wonder if the family have been discussing me in the privacy of their domestic life. However, the money seems to smooth all objections, even with these unsophisticated country innocents." He suspended his mental comments, for the girls were speaking again.

"You see there is a drawback to the La Touches, and one that papa would never get over," said Etta; "they are all—well—cracked."

"Oh, not all," returned the sister. "Stephen is right enough, and the old man and the aunt are weak, perhaps,—at least papa says so."

"Yes; but I have heard mamma say that if the complaint were to attack Percival, it would be something dreadful: she says he has got it in his eye"—here Mr

La Touche opened and shut his visual organs with great rapidity—"got it in the look of his eye, I should say; and it would be something more than weakness or peculiarity with him — it would be raging madness."

"How dreadful!" replied Emma, her visions of a brother-in-law becoming toned down by this assertion. "But then," she added, "if he went very bad suddenly, he could be put in an asylum at once, out of harm's way, and he is rich enough to be a first-class patient."

"Yes, that is all very fine; but suppose Mr La Touche murdered Lillian (if she got him) first," said Miss Etta, with the maturer reasoning of an elder sister: "you never know what lunatics will be at."

"But he is not a lunatic yet," said Emma; "and if he were to marry Lillian, it would keep him sane, I am sure it would; and as to violence, just look how Mrs Kemble, quiet as she is, broke out upon him when papa brought the poor little man out on the lawn. That was raging madness, if you like,—if Aunt Arabella could only have got at him then, we should have had to pick up some of the pieces of the eldest hope of the house of La Touche," and the girl laughed merrily at this vision.

"What I admired in Percival," volunteered Etta, " was the cool and scientific way in which he received Mrs Kemble's onslaught. Miss Clavering quite agreed with me that he showed great presence of mind."

Percival brightened up at this, and breathed more

freely : it was comforting to find that Miss Clavering had remarked him with approbation.

"I don't see what there was particularly to admire," said Emma. "He turned very pale, and then he made passes at the poor old lady with his umbrella."

"It was not that," the sister said; "it was the beautiful play he made with the umbrella. Pointing at all the four cardinal points of the compass, and working in a circle with the accuracy of a teetotum, he never touched his aunt, and yet he managed to keep her at bay until Stephen came up. She danced round him like a dervish the whole time, yet he never gave her the slightest advantage."

"Self-preservation," returned Miss Emma, decisively: "he's an awful little coward. Now you see, when the other brother came up she became quiet directly, and only said that she was afraid of Percival, and that he was always unkind to her."

"I am afraid he has been that," said Etta slowly; "but then, you know, people of unsound mind take odd likes and dislikes. We must not judge, but I wish this had not happened, for of course all our friends will have their own opinion of the matter."

"So mamma thinks, — she says the sooner Mrs Kemble is off, the better. Stephen was dreadfully annoyed and put out; but the elder brother rattled away and made himself so agreeable to Miss Clavering that she is very much inclined to take his part. I heard her say to papa that she thought we were too ready to blame him."

"She only sees one side of his character," returned the elder girl. "Well, for my part, Lillian is welcome to Mr La Touche, if she can put up with him—and, of course, it would be a good thing for the eldest of all of us to settle comfortably, or uncomfortably, as the case might turn out. The man has got money, and he is fairly well connected. The 'peculiarity' and lunatic tendencies don't come out now, if he have them, and papa has no right to object to what may never happen. Lillian is just the balance for him; in her hands he would never kick the beam."

"I would rather marry an Indian nabob or a Patagonian chief than Percival La Touche!" said Emma, with emphasis. "One would know what the undertaking would be with either of these, and their cruelty would be all on the surface; but as to this luxurious, patronising little snob, — I would rather remain single all my life—I would."

"Oh, if it comes to one of us—I mean, the question of our marrying Percival La Touche," said Etta—" I quite agree with you. He would not do for me, for I should want more sympathy and more money for my poor people than he would let me have. Besides, I don't care for London people——"

"I don't like his style," interrupted Miss Emma; "he thinks a great deal too much of himself."

"And he winked, yes, winked, at the parlour-maid this evening,—so ungentlemanly in a clergyman's house," continued Miss Etta; "and that little grin of his is most offensive."

"And his rubbing his hands together, as if he had got a báll of sand-soap within them, gives me the fidgets," said Emma.

"Altogether, he is out of the question for you or me," returned the elder sister. "Lillian is a different affair altogether; but I do think, if there were not another man in the world, nothing would induce me to marry Percival La Touche."

"Nor I either," returned Emma; "never, as you say, if there were not another man in the whole creation, would *I* marry Mr La Touche."

. . . There was a sliding sound against the wall, as if something had rubbed heavily against its whole length, and a voice in a deep loud tone called out: "Wait,—wait till you are *asked*, young ladies."

Then the dressing-door of the neighbouring room banged heavily, and Etta, as she rushed into bed beside her sister, clung convulsively to that damsel, saying, "Oh, what shall we do? we forgot all about him,—he has heard every word of what we have been saying. I don't care so much for his knowing what we think of him, but it may spoil Lillian's chance."

"And what is worse, mamma's hopes of getting rid of her by a rich marriage; *that* is the worst part of the business."

"Not quite the worst," said Etta; "how on earth am I to face him in the morning? you'll be in the school-room, and so get out of it,—it will be so terribly awkward."

"Never mind," said Emma, who was of a tougher

nature than her elder sister—"never mind; it will be quite as uncomfortable for Mr La Touche. We must all agree that we have had the nightmare. Depend upon it, *he'll* say nothing,—horrid little wretch!"

This was perhaps the best light in which to view the matter. Percival, although he adjudged himself to have retreated with flying colours and all the honours of war, was still in a most perplexed condition of mind when he laid his head upon his pillow.

He now saw, or thought he saw, through Mrs Fanshawe's wiles. The sharp manner which she evinced towards him in the presence of Lillian was merely a blind to lull him into security after all; and, in spite of appearances to the contrary, she was artfully endeavouring to entrap him into a marriage with her eldest daughter—that was evident. The motive, too, was to him so disgraceful. The money was a *sine qua non;* but it was more for the sake of getting rid of an incubus than for even the ostensible pride of establishing Miss Fanshawe, that her mother, and possibly the family collectively,— with the exception of the rector perhaps, and Percival would not vouch for him, in spite of Mrs Kemble's outburst,—would do all in their power to further so desirable an event. The conversation of the young girls convinced Mr La Touche that the subject had been ventilated amongst them, and that without the remotest appreciation of the honour which he firmly believed would accrue to the family by such a stroke of fortune as an alliance with himself would be. And yet he had gone out of his way to seek Miss Fanshawe; and it was only by a wonderful accident of chance that he was not at that very moment congratulating himself upon being the affianced husband of this—he would admit it—distinguished London-looking girl.

The counsel which, it is said, comes with night, now warned him to retreat while it was yet time; but a stronger and more potent reason brought Percival to believe that Providence had at this issue interfered in his behalf in bringing Willina Clavering within his ken.

Those impudent hussies!—he thus apostrophised them—his next-door neighbours, had unwittingly let fall this crumb of consolation in his cup. Miss Clavering had espoused his cause, and had, with intuitive and delicate perception, discovered how well informed and how agreeable in conversation he was. This circumstance, he opined, was letting in the thin end of the wedge in the most satisfactory style. Then tossing his ruminations backwards and forwards, with the refrain of to be or not to be, Mr La Touche fell asleep, and dreamt of well-turned heads, intelligent eyes, and lunatics, in one confused mass, till the early hours found him awakening with a start, and the name of " Willina " on his lips.

CHAPTER IV.

PERCIVAL WAVERS.

EMMA FANSHAWE was right. Mr La Touche entered
the breakfast-room on the following morning with an
air of the blandest tranquillity, stated that he had
slept most comfortably, and neither by word nor sign
did he evince the slightest consciousness of his experiences of the previous night.

His position seemed to be a remarkably happy one;
for Stephen always took his breakfast at the old rectory, and in consequence of the absence of his incipient rival, the elder brother seized the opportunity
to appropriate Miss Clavering and pay her the most
marked attention. This, as it happened, exactly
suited Miss Etta, who was thankful for any person or
thing that would divert Percival's recollection from herself, for she was in momentary terror that some sarcastic observation should be let fall from that gentleman
which might bear upon the conversation in which she
and her hardened younger sister had so lately indulged.

Mr La Touche was, however, either politic or merci-

ful—perhaps he was leavened with a mixture of both
these attributes—and so the young lady, after a few
moments of qualm, continued to preside at the break-
fast-table with her wonted peace of mind.

One thing only caused Percival a tinge of regret ; it
was that he had announced his intention of proceeding
on his business tour on the day following his arrival
at Pinnacles, and his wish to call at Hunter's Lodge
either before or after his departure into a neighbouring
county. Mary Leppell had fixed the time for his visit
to Blythe ; and it was not, as we have seen, till after
these arrangements had been made, that he discovered
that Miss Fanshawe had left home, and was then a
guest of Mrs Leppell. Thus the precaution that he, in
his astuteness, thought he had taken to avert suspicion
as to the motives which prompted him to call at
Pinnacles, now served as a strong barrier to prevent
him remaining even a few hours longer in that abode.

Mrs Fanshawe and Mary Leppell both discerned
the finger of Providence in directing Mr La Touche
to offer his congratulations at Hunter's Lodge at so
auspicious a season ; and though neither of these ladies
gave expression to their hopes or opinion on this head,
they both augured the most satisfactory results from
this happy combination of events.

Strangely enough, the rector, who was supposed to
be no authority on matters flirtatory—to coin a word—
perceived Mr La Touche's attention to Miss Clavering,
and further, he bestowed a few moments' consideration
upon this matter. The outcome of his reflections im-

pelled him to take his wife aside immediately after breakfast, and enjoin her by no means to invite Percival to extend his visit, or to encourage him to remain at Pinnacles. "He cannot," Mr Fanshawe added,—"he dare not go to the old rectory, even for a meal, and I won't have him philandering here: in fact, I shall be very glad to be quit of the whole La Touche family, with the exception of Stephen,—he's the best of the lot."

"Mr La Touche has not the slightest intention of remaining here," said Mrs Fanshawe, in a mollifying tone; "he is going to Yarne by the twelve o'clock train."

"I am glad to hear it," growled Mr Fanshawe; "this man is really dreadful, and now he is actually making love to Miss Clavering. I should like to know what Mr Glascott would think of such a thing!"

Poor Mr Fanshawe! in his solicitude for the stranger within his gates, he was totally ignorant of the fact that there were those of his household who were at that moment rejoicing in the knowledge that this obnoxious visitor would ere long be in company with his own daughter, and that many of his friends were beginning to regard Mr La Touche as a possible suitor for that lady's hand: his wife, too, was ready to expedite Percival's departure with something very like a "God-speed." "Where ignorance is bliss," &c., &c.

Stephen La Touche came up from the old rectory, but merely in time to go through the form of conversing a little with his brother. He also privately concurred in the opinion that Miss Fanshawe was the attraction which led Percival to be so scrupulously polite in the matter of offering his congratulations at Hunter's Lodge; and if his suspicions were correct, it would be as well, that gentleman thought, to look upon the gallantry Percival had displayed towards Miss Clavering as merely an atonement for his disappointment in not finding Miss Fanshawe at home. So he talked with Percival in the manner that was usual with him—carefully, however, impressing upon him the impossibility of his being even seen in the vicinity of the old rectory. It was no longer "Esperanza" for Mr La Touche, for if he ventured within its portals, he would certainly have to leave all hope behind him, Mrs Kemble's intentions being of an avowedly sanguinary nature, and it being reported, moreover, that she was on the watch to execute them.

"I shall write to Dr Williams to-day," Stephen said, continuing the subject of poor Mrs Kemble, "and if he can receive Aunt Arabella on the day after to-morrow, I shall take her to his place at once: the attendant, of course, will go with us."

"And after that duty is accomplished," said Percival, with a nonchalant air, "I suppose you will return to London. You will, I should think, have some accumulation of business to attend to."

"I hope so," replied Stephen, cheerily, and with a lamb-like innocence. "You may as well tell Marcia to expect me in four or five days from this time. I suppose your business will be concluded before I return, as I am to finish my visit here as soon as I have placed our aunt with Dr Williams."

Percival could not say. His business might detain him longer than three days: he would, however, advise his brother not to waste any more time in the country. "After you have given up the old rectory, and settled everything with our friend here"—alluding to Mr Fanshawe, with a backward jerk of his thumb —"you will be home at once. Marcia wants you, for we are going to have one or two dinner-parties. One of them is rather of the shop: some French fellows from Bordeaux, to whom the firm must do the civil. Ta-ta," he continued, with an airy flourish of the redoubtable umbrella, as he wended his way towards the hall door,—"I have faltered my adieux to Mrs Fanshawe and the ladies already: ta-ta, and don't forget to come home as soon as possible. Think of Marcia and the dinner-parties."

His last words were almost lost in the depths of the one-horse fly which was to convey Mr La Touche to the station. Stephen looked after him for a moment, and then burst into a laugh. "Master Percival thinks himself very clever, no doubt," he said to himself, "but I fancy I am a match for him. Still, I hope his present errand may be successful; I can afford to wish him good-luck in that quarter."

Some hours afterwards, Stephen found himself in Mr La Touche's study, making the final arrangements for giving up the old rectory, and providing for his aunt's ultimate removal. The rector had declared,

and with good reason, that it was positively dangerous
to allow Mrs Kemble to remain longer where she was
without some restraint; and it was agreed that it would
be as well to despatch a telegram and summon Dr
Williams without delay. "Mrs Kemble has seen the
doctor, and likes him," Mrs Fanshawe said, "and I
think she would bear her removal better if that gentleman were to come for her himself: it would take off
the appearance of everything being strange."

As the business proceeded, Mr Fanshawe could not
help admiring the humanity and generosity displayed
by the younger man; and it was with the utmost sincerity that he expressed a hope that the removal of
the patient would not terminate the acquaintance
which this short visit had so pleasantly matured into
a friendship betwixt him and the family at Pinnacles.
Stephen was given to understand, with more warmth
of manner than the rector was usually wont to display, that whenever he should want a few days' change,
or should at any time come into Yarneshire on Mrs
Kemble's affairs, there would be always a place and a
welcome for him at Pinnacles Court.

Fortunately, Mrs Kemble had sunk into an apathetic
state when the day arrived for her removal from the
old rectory house. We all of us feel somewhat of
regret when leaving a locality wherein we have passed
a good portion of our time, even if the surroundings
and the experience of life therein have not always
been of the happiest kind; but for this poor soul there
was little of remembrance and less of regret.

She was going, she said, where Stephen wished her to go, and she felt sure that what he wished was the right thing. This confidence caused her to accept all that was proposed for her comfort in a spirit of placid resignation, which, while it materially simplified the necessary business consequent on removal, had, besides, something in its expression peculiarly touching. To the last it was evident that she had no opinion of the attentions which the several members of the Pinnacles household now bestowed upon her. "It was all very well," she remarked to her nephew, as they sat together on the last evening of her tenancy; "but why are these women so wonderfully friendly all of a sudden, and just as I am going away? Miss Clavering has been kind from the very first moment I saw her, and I am very, very sorry to wish *her* good-bye.

"It is only for a time, I know," the old lady continued, after a short pause; "and I won't make any fuss when I leave, for the Pinnacles women might think I am sorry to part with them, and that would never do, for I am not sorry—not a whit, my dear."

Early on the day of her departure, Mrs Kemble was particularly mysterious, and somewhat difficult both to understand and to manage. She nodded her head, shook that member at her nephew, shrugged her shoulders, winked satanically, and went through so many other minor gymnastics, that Stephen feared these must be the precursory symptoms of another outbreak, and so stood upon his guard.

However, when the men who had been employed in packing such of the furniture as belonged to Mr La Touche, previous to its removal to London, had departed, the real meaning of these signals became apparent. "Come here, Stephen," Aunt Arabella said; "I want you to take this, and put it in a safe place. I have been so alarmed lest some one should get it from me when I was not—not—well. But I have managed to keep it out of sight; here it is!" So saying, she pulled a folded paper out of the depths of the lining of her wadded foot-warmer, and desired Stephen to read it forthwith.

Her nephew, on looking through this document, found it to be no less than Mrs Kemble's will, properly written and executed some eight years back. Her own small fortune of three thousand pounds, standing in the consols, was left absolutely and entirely to him, as also everything she might inherit or become possessed of at the time of her death.

The young man remained silent, just pressing his aunt's hand in token of his recognition and gratitude. He was greatly touched, not only at this evidence of her strong affection, but also at the tenacity with which his relative had, in his interests, preserved this will. No one, he felt sure, suspected its existence.

"I knew you would come—in all my queerness I felt you would come and see me. I have never forgotten your visit to us at Heidelberg, and how you defended me, boy as you were, from Kemble—never. Now you see the will is quite regular—made out by a first-rate lawyer. Mr Severne, who always took my part, managed all the business for me. I want you to observe that this will was made before I became nervous and queer ; and to be assured that I have never made any other, and I never intend to make another, so you are quite safe, my dear."

"But, aunt, I can't keep this will in my own possession : it is very generous of you, but——"

"I understand — I know something of business. Let Dr Williams and old Fanshawe, if you like, be witnesses that I have made this will over to you. They may, I should think, advise you to hand it to some respectable solicitor. Mind, my dear, I had the power reserved to me under my settlement to make a will. I have good cause to remember that,—my husband never forgave it ; indeed I owe much of the ill-treatment I received to this cause. But my father was so fearful lest even sixpence should go out of the family. Money and greed — the La Touches have always tried for the good things of the land, and what has come of it ? Lunacy, quarrelling, and every evil work. O Stephen ! whatever you do, never marry a near relation,—it's not natural, and never was intended."

"Three thousand pounds was hardly a sum large enough to demand a clause reserving you the right of making a will," returned Stephen. "Had you, may I ask, any other prospects ? "

"That's just it : our uncle, Mr Squash, was alive when I married, and my father always believed that he would leave his large fortune to be divided between my brothers and sisters and myself. As it happens, Mr Squash chose to make that horrid Percival his heir, and he lived much longer than his friends intended that he should live. Has he got the money?" inquired Mrs Kemble, turning round sharply. Everything that alluded to Mr La Touche, even in the most remote manner, always irritated her.

"Oh yes," replied Stephen; "perhaps it were better so than that the property should be cut up into small portions. Don't let us grudge Percival—he will be none the better nor the happier for it."

"That's a blessing," returned Aunt Arabella warmly. "Percival won't spend it, and perhaps he may die, and then *his* money can be cut up and go among the rest of the family. You see I have no other prospects, and my small jointure will of course go to Mr Kemble's relations at my death. They pray for that event regularly every night, my dear. Here's Miss Clavering; now, do you go away—I want to talk to her alone."

Dr Williams arrived in due course, and after some consultation, it was decided that the will in question should be confided to the care of a firm of solicitors whom he named. Shortly afterwards, Mrs Kemble, with her attendant and Stephen, set out for her new home; and it is satisfactory to know that the poor lady arrived safely at her destination, and took at once pleasantly to all about her. She parted tenderly from her nephew, but very quietly also; assuring him that he had done all for the best, expressing her conviction that she was going to be very happy, and that in a short time she would be perfectly well. So, for a season, Aunt Kemble would probably cease to be a source of anxiety to her relatives, and the family at Pinnacles were well pleased that she had taken her departure in peace.

It was with a light heart that Stephen returned to pay the last part of his visit, which the ruthless demands of business limited to three days. Now that he had leisure to review his position, his spirit was exercised more strongly than ever as to his brother's real reason for appearing in the county, and it was with great sincerity that he hoped Miss Fanshawe was the veritable magnet which had attracted Percival from his own immediate sphere at this time. If his suppositions were really correct, he would beneficently wish the latter the most unbounded good-luck, and was even willing to accord him an unqualified and fraternal benediction.

In despite, however, of this magnanimity, a misgiving would often crop up in Stephen's mind concerning Mr La Touche's ulterior motives. He could not forget how thoroughly this usually cautious and wary individual had thrown off all reserve, and given himself up, so to speak, to an unqualified admiration of Miss Clavering, and that too from the first hour of his acquaintance with the lady. Percival's evident anxiety to get him to return home was also a subject of wonder to the younger brother: it was all very well to cite Marcia's dinner-parties as a *raison d'être,* but then, up to this time, Percival had generally been indifferent as to whether his brethren were present or not at the family state - feeds. There had been occasions, indeed, on which, preferring candour to compliment, Mr La Touche had averred that the absence of Stephen from the festive board was a matter of congratulation to himself and the company ; but it must be conceded that this sentiment was expressed at a season when Stephen emphatically declined to take in to dinner the lady whom Marcia had ordained that he should take in, and when this recalcitrant action was stated to militate decidedly against the order of procession.

Thus, after turning the matter over in his mind, and failing to arrive at any conclusion, Stephen was fain to trust to time, and resolved, like a sensible man, to enjoy as fully as possible the few days that remained to him of his visit to Pinnacles Court.

Percival, meanwhile, sped on his way, and soon stood before the gate of Hunter's Lodge. It struck him as he passed up the drive that the house and all surrounding it appeared to be unusually quiet,—no sounds of whoop and holloa, no signs of boys or babies, and the door-step in front of the principal entrance shining at the same time uncommonly clean.

The lawn was dotted here and there with hearth-rugs and mats of every size and description, and a frousy *soupçon* of the dust which had been recently shaken out of these still pervaded the immediate atmosphere. Almost every window in the house was wide open, and the casements were utterly innocent of either curtain or blind.

A tight-rope apparatus stretched out in the field beyond the lawn seemed at first sight to indicate a preparation for some acrobatic performance; but just as Mr La Touche was wondering what this might portend, a huge substance was thrown across the rope, and two men, furnished with bean-sticks, proceeded to belabour the material until rolls and volumes of dust concealed them from the naked eye.

Then it dawned upon Percival that this performance of carpet-beating was one of the phases of a process at that moment going on in full activity at Hunter's Lodge. It was that feminine vernal saturnalia known in the civilised world as the spring clean— a rite from which all bipeds of the masculine gender usually fly in terror and dismay as from a dangerous epidemic, whilst wives and daughters and female servants bear the brunt of the attending discomforts, and revel and exult (it has been said) in finding themselves in full possession of the field, and in the utter exemption from molestation or interference of any kind whatever.

Percival winced as, on approaching the house, he distinctly recognised the clink of an iron pail-handle, and a dim sound which announced an under-current of scrubbing. "How unfortunate!" he said to himself; "there will be only a scrap-luncheon—boiled-beef and bread, or some horror of the kind. I think I'll turn back; or no, better not—I may be seen from the meadow there. I need not stay long: most likely, too, Mrs Leppell will not be at home. Good gracious! what is that looking out at the window?"

It was only Mrs Dabber the charwoman, who, arrayed in the inevitable coal-scuttle bonnet of the profession, and a canvas apron which enveloped her from head to heel, hearing footsteps, had almost thrown herself out at the hall window in order to intercept or turn back any intruder who might seek admission. A long boiled arm protruded itself at the same time, and the soaked hand at its extremity waved the insignia of the scrubber's calling within a foot of Percival's hat.

"What do ye please to want?" said this apparition, as the visitor, recovering his astonishment, fell back some paces, and replied with the query, "Is Mrs Leppell at home?"

"It's the spring clean, sir, and Mrs Leppell have sent all the children out for a picnic, sir; they have been gone this two hours."

"Is Mrs Leppell at home?" demanded Percival, loftily ignoring the previous information.

"No, sir," returned the scrubber firmly, but mendaciously, nevertheless; "she have gone to the picnic with the last lot of 'em."

Percival hesitated a moment, but true to the spirit of contradiction, which was a component part of his existence, he determined to enter the house, solely because he thought he perceived a strong determination on the part of Mrs Dabber to deny him admittance. He therefore replied, " That is very strange, and Lady Asher so ill ; surely she is not left alone ! "

" Lady Asher is better, and she ain't alone, she have got her maid," responded the scrubber, rising to the emergency. " We are very busy, 'cause the Colonel he have writ to say as how he'll be home to-morrow night."

" I've just come from Pinnacles Court," said Percival, " so I had better see Mrs Prothero, as I have a letter and a parcel from Miss Mary——"

" Oh, if 'e come from Miss Mary, that's different altogether. I was told not to let in any callers on no account. Wait a bit please, sir, and I'll open the front door ; it is kep' shut by reason of them dogs. Most of 'em has gone to the picnic ; but Boxer, _he's_ about, and when a gets in, it's next to impossible to drive un out again, sure."

Mrs Dabber sped to the hall door with some alacrity, for it was quickly opened, and Percival entered. After indicating a roll of matting as a convenient place whereon he might sit, Mrs Dabber left the visitor in possession, and set off on the ostensible errand of seeking Mrs Prothero.

She could not have reached Lady Asher's room, for the quick ears with which nature had supplied Mr La Touche made him aware that to some person in close proximity, although unseen, he was being reported as " a young man with a note from Miss Mary,—a _would_ come in," was added in a deprecatory tone.

" What's he like ? " inquired a voice, which Percival immediately recognised; " it can't be Mr Clavering ? besides, you know him."

" Oh, laws, no, 'em—he ain't Mr Clavering ; but a tidy little gent too—a says a comes from Pinnacles."

There was a slight rustle, and in another moment Miss Fanshawe was shaking hands with Mr La Touche.

" You are rather an unexpected Mercury," said the young lady, her face flushed a little with surprise, and perhaps, it may be added, with some disappointment ; for it was usual for Mr Clavering to call after this manner when Lady Asher's illness demanded frequent inquiry. " We did not know you were in Yarneshire."

" I only arrived yesterday on my way to Bath, and, having a few hours to spare, I went up to Pinnacles to see my aunt before she leaves your neighbourhood," said Mr La Touche, with solemn assurance. " Your parents have a large party in the house, and they were kind enough to invite me to join them and stay all night. Here are my credentials," and he handed the note and a little parcel wrapped in silver-paper to Lillian.

" Thanks ; this is a fan which Mary walked off with the other day. Won't you come in here till I see if Lady Asher's sitting-room is in order ? it is our only harbour of refuge during this turmoil." So saying, she opened the door of the drawing-room and ushered Mr La Touche into that apartment, which was just recovering from an elaborate scrubbing, and redolent of Bristol soap, furniture-polish, and all the other olfactory concomitants inevitable to a spring clean. A pronounced feeling of dampness and discomfort made itself apparent and suitable to the occasion—so much so, that Percival shrank together, and expressed a fear that he should catch cold.

"I won't be long," said Miss Fanshawe; "I will just speak to Mrs Leppell—she was with her mother a few minutes ago: you had better stand in the verandah," and off she went before Mr La Touche could get in a single word.

Mrs Leppell was rather pleased than otherwise when she was told who the visitor was; and in the belief that the visit of Mr La Touche was rendered more on her young friend's account than on her own, she at once decided to receive that gentleman. She also opined that this was a most excellent opportunity to bring these young people together; and though she did not much admire the man, she, like the rest of the world, held his fortune in much esteem. Besides, it must be remembered Lilian was the eldest of a tribe of daughters, and it was her duty to marry a rich man if she could get him, and her (Mrs Leppell's) duty to render her aid in the quest. So with an earnest and sincere desire to forward this event, Mrs Leppell went by way of the garden to the drawing-room verandah, and received Mr La Touche with a cordial smile of welcome.

"You find us in a most uncomfortable state," she said, as she extended her hand to her visitor. "Come into Lady Asher's room, and we can offer you some lunch, such as it is."

Percival replied that he was delighted, and that Colonel Leppell had no doubt evaded the horrors of house-cleaning, adding that it was the first time in his life that he had come in contact with the operation, and that really it was not so bad as he had been led to think.

This was intended for a compliment evidently, and so the ladies bowed in recognition. "It is really Colonel Leppell's fault that we have been obliged to carry the operation through in so uncompromising a manner," continued the lady of the house; "we did not expect my husband home for nearly a week yet, and now he has written to say that he will be at home late to-morrow night."

"And of course he expects everything to be in perfect order and comfort," added Miss Fanshawe, with a laugh.

There was something very taking and graceful about this girl when she allowed her usually cold manner to relax, and perhaps she never appeared to greater advantage than when she was at Hunter's Lodge. The position of being understood and appreciated has, more or less, a beautifying effect on most young people, and it was due to this that Miss Fanshawe always seemed more animated and cheerful when with the Leppells than at any other time.

We can never fully understand the mysterious phases of fate and chance, any more than we can explain the great injustices which are hourly occurring in the world; but it is probable that if Lillian Fanshawe had been the wife of Francis Clavering, she would have been a bright and happy woman to the end of her days, because she knew, and felt that he would have known, that she was thoroughly suited to him, and that in intellect and opinion and thought they were as one.

Now this chance—the union of what Miss Fanshawe believed to be two kindred souls—had passed away for ever; and in the face of an uncongenial if not an unhappy home, the young lady set herself deliberately to win Percival La Touche, or rather, perhaps, to accept him as the Charybdis into which she must cast herself from the Scylla of her unrequited preference for Mr Clavering.

Little dreamed he that at the best he was nothing more than a *pis aller* in this girl's sight, but a *pis aller* to which she must resort because she held no place in her mother's heart, and was virtually without hearth or home.

So, following the lead of her friend, Lillian was unusually charming in her manner towards Mr La Touche, and looked so cool and fresh withal, and bantered with him in such easy graceful style, that, with the strange inconsistency of the human mind, Percival found himself hesitating as to whether or no it would be as well that he should dedicate his allegiance at once to Miss Fanshawe, and forego all further attempts to bewitch Miss Clavering. Everything seemed just then to foster this idea : the luncheon was so good that it wellnigh worked the charm of reaching the man's heart through his stomach ; the kindly unaffected manner in which he had been admitted into the privacy of this household ; the absence of all *gêne*, without descending to the borders even of familiarity, —all combined to press upon Percival the desirability of improving his opportunities without loss of time.

He was further induced to this consideration by the invitation which Mrs Leppell (in the interests of her young friend) had given him to attend her daughter's wedding when that event should take place. " She would send Miss La Touche," Mrs Leppell said, " a proper invitation when matters were arranged, and she hoped that Mr Stephen would be also induced to give them the pleasure of his company on that occasion. Should she write ? or would Mr La Touche undertake to bring his brother ? At any rate, Mary and Mr Clavering, being with him at Pinnacles, would very probably secure Mr Stephen themselves."

Percival inwardly resolved to put a spoke in this wheel, but merely replied that he was quite sure they would all be most happy to wait on Mrs Leppell ; and then, luncheon being over, they strolled into Lady Asher's little garden till the room should be arranged.

They had been there scarcely ten minutes when Mrs Leppell found it convenient to fancy that she heard Prothero's voice calling to her from within, and, without waiting to satisfy herself, she turned and went rapidly into the house. " I'll be back directly," she said, looking over her shoulder to Lillian; "perhaps you could show Mr La Touche Dick's game-fowls: they are really beautiful birds, and are well worth seeing."

To the fowl-yard they sped; and with her nose dug into the netting, Miss Fanshawe searched minutely for Raleigh, reputed to be the gamest of game birds in the whole county.

Mr La Touche approached a little nearer the lady, with the view of being directed where to look for this redoubtable warrior, and had got the length of "Dear Miss Fanshawe," when a tread on the gravel arrested his speech, and he just managed to add as he looked round, "here he is," when an elderly gentleman appeared in sight.

Miss Fanshawe never exactly knew whether the lame conclusion of Percival's opening address applied to the game-fowl or to Mr Glascott, for they both appeared on the scene at the same moment: however, as the latter was outside the netted inclosure, he might, perhaps, be considered as having the advantage, he not being in a state of semi-captivity.

Whatever Percival had intended to disclose was certainly effectually quenched by the advent of the human third party, who, after saluting Miss Fanshawe with the graceful, old-fashioned courtesy, began to announce his errand, as he took her hand.

"Allow me to introduce you," said that lady with the most enviable composure; "Mr Glascott, Mr La Touche." A bow, and a very ill-used-looking visage on the part of Percival: this was entirely lost upon Mr Glascott, who innocently regarded his new acquaintance as a young man possessing a most unfortunate expression of face, and thought how good it was of Miss Fanshawe to entertain him.

So it was rather with the opinion that he was doing a fellow-creature a good turn that Mr Glascott said : "It has occurred to me that you would like a ride this fine afternoon ; suppose we go and meet the picnic-party. We might take a canter round Firely Hill, and then escort the youngsters home in a troop. I have just spoken to Mrs Leppell, and she thinks the idea a good one, should you approve."

Miss Fanshawe agreed, remarking, notwithstanding, that she was supposed to be helping Mrs Leppell in the house, and that it would be rather selfish on her part to ride away and leave her.

Mr Glascott combated this assertion by averring that Mrs Leppell, whom he had just left, aided and strongly promoted this suggestion.

"Would you like to accompany us ? " asked Miss Fanshawe, turning to Mr La Touche with a genial smile.

" Oh dear, no," replied Percival; "very happy to accompany you, of course, but horse exercise——"

" Oh, you don't ride,—I forgot," replied the lady ; " it's very unfortunate. Shall we find you here on our return ? "

Percival understood from this that Miss Fanshawe intended to take the ride, and excused her in his mind upon the plea that she could not very well do otherwise. At the same time, it having dawned upon his perception that the late comer was Miss Clavering's guardian, his manner suddenly softened, and he replied—

"My business matters are urgent, and only left me time to come out here to offer my congratulations to Mrs Leppell on her daughter's approaching marriage. From what I have seen of Mr Clavering, Miss Leppell seems to have been most happy in her choice."

Here Mr Glascott bowed, and relaxed his uncomplimentary opinion concerning the personal appearance of Mr La Touche; and after a few desultory remarks, they returned to the house. Percival took his leave; and Miss Fanshawe and her escort immediately set off for a long afternoon's ride.

Colonel Leppell returned home, according to his announcement, and Mary and Miss Clavering ended their visit at Pinnacles Court. Miss Fanshawe remained at Hunter's Lodge for the ostensible purpose of cultivating a further acquaintance with the latter, and she was present when a messenger from the firm of Dupont brought the diamonds, arranged and set, which were Mr Glascott's wedding-present to Mary Leppell.

They were universally admired; so much so, that Mr Glascott, through the Colonel, sent the same number of stones to be set in precisely similar form to Mr Dupont, intending that *parure* to be a present to Willina Clavering.

Francis Clavering was very much taken with Mary's set; at the same time, he remarked that the colour of the stones did not appear to him to be quite so clear as that of the unset gems.

"The mounting may make a difference," said Miss Fanshawe, who was examining them at the same time.

"Ah, yes, to be sure; you put us all right," said the young man, turning towards Lillian with a smile of genuine approbation.

CHAPTER V.

SCIENCE AND CUPID.

At length all was satisfactorily settled: Colonel Leppell and Mr Glascott had each dined in company at the abode of the other, and Mr Clavering was now a visitor at Hunter's Lodge, the acknowledged and accepted suitor of Miss Leppell.

The usual amount of astonishment, expressed and understood, went the round of the family acquaintance as a matter of course. "'Heavenly Moll' to put up with a simple gentleman, after all Ralph's bluster!" was the ejaculation of old Lord Hieover, after he had twice perused the document which conveyed the intelligence, in curt but respectful terms, to the lady's grandfather. "Ralph is coming to his senses," remarked the Colonel's brother Alick, as he digested the news; "rich noblemen are not so plenty, and the poor ones look out for money. They have shown more sense, the whole lot of them, than I imagined them to possess."

"The whole lot" meant the family at Hunter's Lodge,

severally and collectively, in the summary of this relative. As to the Clavering connection, if that were satisfied, it was well; and if it were not, that was no affair of the Honourable Alexander Leppell, who averred, for his part, that he was truly thankful to learn that a comfortable provision would be secured to his niece by this contemplated marriage. Being thus in a contented frame of mind, this affectionate uncle at once penned a congratulatory epistle to Mary, in which he wished her all manner of life's blessings and good-luck. This being done, he mourned over the fact that he would have to give the girl a decent wedding-present, and eventually turned to smoke for compensation and consolation.

Miss Fanshawe was now the only person to whom this engagement did not give complete satisfaction. True, she had promoted it to the best of her power; but her influence with Mary Leppell had only been exerted after she had discovered that her own chances of securing Mr Clavering's affections were utterly hope-less. The result of this influence had convinced Miss Leppell that she did possess sufficient regard for Mr Clavering to warrant her accepting that gentleman as her suitor. Wise in her generation, and far-seeing beyond her years, Lillian soon discovered that the best method for retaining for herself influence and interest with both these young people, was to act at once *en bonne princesse*, and so earn the gratitude of, at least, one of the benefited parties. That she did not (at that time at least) seriously mean to displace Mary Leppell

in Mr Clavering's affections, is certain; and had such
an idea been presented to Miss Fanshawe in a tangible
shape, no one would have more indignantly disclaimed
such an imputation. True, she was aware, and fully
aware (through that wonderful intuition which seems
to be a sixth sense in the feminine composition), that
whilst Clavering loved Mary with more of the meed of
affection, perhaps, than the ordinary run of men bestow upon the betrothed, who, they know, will become
their wives in the conventional style of matrimony,
it was to her that he turned for companionship in intellect; it was to her alone that his conversation was
directed, whenever his favourite science and its later
discoveries was the theme.

There came, too, with this, a perceptible softening
of manner and an unexpressed confidence in her sympathy, which increased so steadily that it became at
length impossible for her not to be cognisant of the
fact that, had she met Mr Clavering before his introduction to the Leppells, her good offices in urging her
friend to accept that gentleman's suit would have
been superfluous. "It is a great pity," she had once
gone so far as to admit to herself; "he and I are just
suited. It can't be helped now. Let me enjoy his
society for a short time; and when Mary is married,
I will take the first man that asks me. At any rate,
her home will be another place of refuge from Pinnacles." So ran the current of Miss Fanshawe's most
secret thoughts at this time.

Those of Francis Clavering, if put into words, might

probably evolve thus: "Mary is no doubt lovely, and my wife will be the most admired woman of the next London season—Lord Hieover must take us to town —but I do wish Moll had more in her,—more education, more love of science. Perhaps it will come. As it is, she reminds me forcibly of Undine before her soul came to her. Lillian Fanshawe, now, possesses both beauty of mind and person, and is in all things thoroughly practical. Why, why can't a man marry two wives at once ?"

Here he stopped. Was not the breath of such an idea rank treason to Mary? Besides, had she not been won with a wealth of affection and hard money down? Had he not, by unwavering persistence, for love of her brought about a reconciliation between two lifelong foes? Was she not the olive-branch, the tender white dove, the peace-offering and gift given out of the hand of her father, and accepted by his benefactor, who had forgotten insult and wrong to place her honourably in his arms? Was there not something due to Everard Glascott, the noble old man who had done more for him in this matter than had done, or would do, ten thousand of fathers for their own sons? "Stay — Lillian Fanshawe is the friend of the Leppell side of the house, the especial friend of Mary, the school - companion whom she desires that I should admire and cultivate. Let it be so: here is a case where a Platonic friendship is perfectly admissible. Lillian is strong and proud, and a woman is all the firmer friend when one never has been, nor never can be, her lover."

So thinking, Mr Clavering corrected a part of the manuscript of his intended lecture, which, owing to these reflections, was not distinguished for strict geological reasoning. The importance of his subject at this juncture impressed itself on his mind, and for some hours he turned to work with that application which alone can command satisfactory results.

When his task was completed, he carried it to Lillian and requested her opinion on its merits. The young lady was alone in the little drawing-room, seated at the piano; not playing exactly, but with her right hand striking out strange minor harmonies, more mournful than soothing, and looking over a newspaper which she held in her left.

"What! doing two things at the same time!" exclaimed Frank as he entered. "This is not the opportunity to enlist your sympathy, I fear, for I came to inflict a third occupation upon you," and he held out his manuscript as he spoke.

"Don't be too certain of that," replied Miss Fanshawe. "Look; I was reading the review of your pamphlet on the mosaic pavement found at Drumchester. I should much like to see the pamphlet itself; but as that is not within reach, I will take your manuscript, and so run two occupations into one."

"It *is* within reach," replied Mr Clavering decidedly. "I sent Mary a copy of it three weeks ago. Haven't you seen it?"

"No. Besides, no one in this house cares for science, so you must expect that Mary will find all matters appertaining to it a little dry. I daresay the pamphlet can be found—unless, indeed, it has been absorbed into Colonel Leppell's den. In that case——"

"It will have made itself useful for lighting cigars or rubbing the gums of a bull-terrier pup," replied Francis, rushing to conclusions. "I'll go and ask Mary about it at once. Do you know where she is?"

"Just out on the lawn there, mending targets and shooting with the children."

Mr Clavering stepped out through the French window, and looked towards the centre of the lawn. This was bounded by a wire-fence which enclosed the meadow which lay beyond.

A beautiful summer meadow, knee-deep in rich grass, daisies, buttercups, quaking-grass, the rounded crimson clover-flower, the tall bugle full in bloom, powdered by the falling blossoms of the fading hawthorn, showing still fair as it covered the floating feather-grass, — all sweet things, soon to perish beneath the mower's scythe, and leave only their subtle perfume to tell that they once had been.

An enormous elm-tree flourished on the lawn, round the trunk of which a seat had been fixed. Mary Leppell sat like a May-queen beneath the branches superintending the manufacture of a target, which was at the bulging-out period of its formation. Dick sat at her feet, a moving mass of twine, straw, paper, paint, feathers, and all manner of rubbish. The youngest infant was sleeping on a cushion, with the drawing-room's best *couvrette* spread over its face. Its nurse, trusting to Providence, was away flirting with a groom in the stable-yard enclosure; and the penultimate baby was busy trying to stick some honeysuckle into the bull-terrier's ears,—all as happy as happy could be.

"Mary—Moll—here; I want you a moment. I can't come out, I am so busy," called out Mr Clavering, quite in the tone of "the man in possession."

Away went the target, bull-terrier and child were cleared at a bound, Dick was thrown prone to the earth, as this gladsome, winsome thing flew past, and only stopped to throw her arms round her lover's neck. "It was so nice of you to call me like that, Frank," said she. "I like it so much better than if you had thought it proper to come to me. What do you want, dear? What can I do?"

It was seldom that Mary had been so demonstrative. A kind of sweet timidity, combined with the feeling that she was not clever enough for companionship with Mr Clavering, had often caused her to remain within her delicate shell. In these days it frequently occurs that young ladies of all ranks are too ready to come out of their delicate shells to seek admirers—going the whole pace, not meeting admirers half-way even. Herein is the embryo from which the "girl of the period" springs.

"I hope you won't think me troublesome," Frank

said, as he drew the young girl close to him, "but I want that pamphlet about the mosaic pavement I sent you the other day. Can you put your hand upon it?"

"No, that I can't," replied Mary. "I just looked it over after cutting the leaves, and saw it was something about the Romans and their camps. You must not mind—it's my ignorance; but I really could not read ten lines of it together, and I hoped you would not ask anything about it."

"Very well, that's natural, you golden locks," answered he, mollified by the honesty of this speech; "but tell me, where did you put the pamphlet?"

"Let me think: the last time I saw it, it was on the mantel-shelf in the nursery; it may be there still, as there are no fires to light now. But can't you get another copy?"

"Yes; but I wish, dear, you would try and interest yourself in my writings just a little more. However, I will go back to Miss Fanshawe now. I left her reading my last effusions, and she must be tired of them by this time."

They passed through the French window into the room wherein Miss Fanshawe still retained the same place and position. Instead of touching the piano, her fingers were now busily employed in marking, here and there, with various signs, portions of the manuscript concerning which she would presently have her say.

"Oh, here you are!" exclaimed Mary, coming close

to her friend. "Frank has shown his sense in giving you his performances to look over. Is this easier than the pamphlet?" inquired she, as she looked towards Mr Clavering.

"It is quite a different thing," replied that gentleman. "Never mind about the pamphlet—I can do without it."

He had not deemed it necessary to state that this emanation of his brain was required solely for Miss Fanshawe's delectation, and, in order to check further remark or inquiry, he plunged into the subject of his article. Lillian saw, at a glance, that the pamphlet was not forthcoming, and maintained a silence which, to Clavering, was as intelligible as uttered speech. She looked straight into his eyes, and all was said. "You need not have troubled yourself,—I could have told you that the book was either in the fire or in the dust-hole. Depend upon it, you throw away your glory in this direction." All this the mute intelligence of Miss Fanshawe's eyes conveyed to the sense of Francis Clavering.

Mary went back to her brothers, rather thankful to leave these two to their own devices; and these two talked and read, and comported themselves generally, as if some secret understanding existed between them, the nature of which they neither wished nor cared to analyse. So sped on the afternoon of this summer day till evening fell.

And Mary, "heavenly Moll," fresh, true, and innocent, without an *arrière pensée* in the world concerning anybody or anything,—was her spirit disturbed, or did any apprehension agitate her breast, as she saw daily the intercourse between her lover and her friend assuming a more exclusive character, and found also that the nature of their conversation was often such as to preclude her from taking any part in it? Not in the least. Loving Clavering as she did, with calm, honest affection, and reverencing his talents as if he were almost a deity to be worshipped—above all, unconscious of evil, it was almost impossible that the demon of jealousy could invade a heart crystallised in its own purity, and at the same time too proud, perhaps, to entertain a single envious thought.

To have secured the affection of this brilliant man was a special blessing in this young girl's eyes, and the position of becoming his wife was, in a great measure, not only a source of self-congratulation, but somewhat also of wonder and astonishment.

The advanced arts were little known and less appreciated in Miss Leppell's immediate family, and thus it was to her as if one of the wise men of Greece, or Solomon himself, had alighted at her feet when Clavering made his marriage proposals for her to Colonel Leppell. This man, with whose name all the scientific world was ringing, who lectured here and lectured there, whose presence frequent telegrams from all parts of Great Britain were constantly soliciting, and upon whose opinion many members of the scientific world based their conclusions,—this man was indeed unto her the personification of one who had eaten of the apple of Eden, and thus held the knowledge of good and evil—and lived.

No wonder, then, that, cherishing such opinions, Miss Leppell found much satisfaction in the fact that Frank could meet with a congenial mind in the society of her friend, Lillian Fanshawe, and so enjoy a literary symposium which her own humble intellect could neither grasp nor fathom. Had Mary Leppell at that time been capable of feeling and evincing an alarmed jealousy, strange to say, many bitter pangs in after-life would have been spared her. Concerning what she believed to be friendship, arising from love of herself, on the part of Francis and Lillian, no suspicion nor anxious thought ever entered.

There was one person, however, who viewed the march and exclusiveness of this friendship with a surprise which soon turned to apprehension, if not to positive alarm. What can escape a mother's eye? Mrs Leppell had, on more than one occasion, fancied that the deference which Mr Clavering paid to her daughter's friend was rather more tender than is customary in the case of a man who is affianced to a lovely girl—so lovely that she might command any number of admirers, and those, too, of the highest "status" in society. Mrs Leppell, to do her justice, bravely put back her suspicions at the outset, and communed from a common-sense point of view with her perplexed spirit.

"Is this girl not Mary's early friend?" argued she; "and was not Mary so anxious that Lillian should be invited to remain here during Mr Clavering's stay in the neighbourhood? Above all, did not Lillian urge the match when my daughter was wavering, and even reluctant?"

Thus the good woman reasoned her fears away. One problem, however, persistently haunted her, nor could she find any clue towards its solution. If Miss Fanshawe were not so attractive in person as well as learned in mind, would Francis Clavering be at so much trouble in fetching and carrying little lumps of granite, and goodness knows what other lumps besides these, and weighting the pockets of his shooting-coat with knobs of stone, and little hammers wherewith to smash them up, and all for Lillian Fanshawe's opinion thereon? He apparently, also, felt no qualms whatever in striding about the country with a faded green-baize bag over his shoulder, in which Dick Leppell (Clavering's boy-friend in the family) averred that he kept all kinds of wonderments.

One fine morning Mrs Leppell watched the pair, as, with this green bag on the floor, a lump of gneiss and a work on geology in their hands, they sat at a small table in the deep recess of a window, and expatiated upon something unusual or peculiar in the conformation of the specimen which lay before them.

Mrs Leppell was occupied in dusting and arranging the remains of some very valuable and much-cracked and much-mended old china,—a remnant that had survived the successive tornadoes in the Leppell drawing-room, when the Colonel had thought fit to expedite the departure of children or dogs by hurling anything that came to hand in the air, and hurling it regardless of direction. (It was only a year before that old Lady Asher had escaped being brained by throwing herself flat on the hearth-rug, and thus allowing a good-sized musical-box, aimed at Fritz, to pass over her head and crash into an Indian bowl.) Some jars, a few good plates, and a pilgrim's bottle, were now the only sound representatives of what had originally been a fair collection of china.

But it was the cracked little cups, and the mutilated little monsters, and the egg-china of Japan, to which the soul of Mrs Leppell clung. A niche mounted with shelves, and lined with blue velvet, was now the sacred tomb of these relics; and it was with a sort of tremor lest in these she should find evidence of a recent spill, or of coming to pieces in the hand, for which no one but the cat could or would be accountable, that Mrs Leppell proceeded to inspect these relics.

Standing at this shrine, Mrs Leppell thus came in for the full benefit of the geological discussion; and further, for convincing herself that no shadow of suspicion nor anxiety had entered her daughter's mind, for Mary was now in the room, and was making merry at the expense of the two students anent their devotion to geology.

"Oh, that is the little hammer, is it, with which you

go about the country smashing up the stones and breaking rocks to smithereens?" said Miss Leppell, trying to speak with sarcasm. "You might set up for an auctioneer, Frank, and so successfully combine two businesses. What is this? and this?" inquired she, as she dived into the green-baize bag and brought out two or three specimens. "Do enlighten my ignorance. Which is pudding-stone?"

"Not a specimen of it here, dear," replied Frank. "Here is a pretty bit, and the name of it is not difficult—mica."

The mother watched from the plate she was holding up to the light. "Lillian looks as if she did not like the interruption," thought she. "I don't know; she is making room for Mary to be seated. I am wrong after all."

She was right and she was wrong, both at the same moment. Miss Fanshawe had perceived Mrs Leppell's eyes looking over the plate, and she thereupon executed the piece of generalship which had discomfited her hostess. No electric light could have flashed intelligence more thoroughly. Miss Fanshawe, sweet and calm, read as from an open book the meaning of Mrs Leppell's presence there, and very much also what was passing in the mind of that lady. So she put into force that sleight of action which is vulgarly called "throwing dust into people's eyes."

"Now that we have got Mary captive, let us give her a first lesson in geology, Mr Clavering," said she; "or better, do you teach us both. I am only in the primer myself, as you know, and at the stage wherein a return to first principles would be a step in the right direction. You should try and learn a little about the matter, dear," continued Miss Fanshawe, with the air of a matron of forty, "for you will in time, I daresay, have to copy out Mr Clavering's lectures for him; and it would be so much easier for you if you understood a little of the subject. Don't you agree with me?"

"I would get through any quantity of writing or copying or anything else for Frank that I *can* do," was the reply; "but these stones, and their names, and where they come from, I really do not care about, nor never shall. I prefer things which grow *on* the earth, you know, and something that has life,—flowers and fruit, and something that can return one's regard; the pony—my dear doggie,—they are far nicer than a pack of stones."

Francis looked very significantly at Lillian during this peroration. If the look may be interpreted, it meant to say, "Do you hear that? flowers and the dog preferred to my objects of study and interest; only listen to the crass frivolity which these remarks exhibit." The mother caught the look, and from sheer nervousness rattled her plate against the head of a shaky little bonze. Her feeling, this time, was that of indignation against Miss Fanshawe, because she remained as impervious to this look as did the wall behind her. Not a sign made she that she had even observed Mr Clavering, and Frank on his part felt sure that his significant expression had fallen un-heeded into space.

Such telegraphic intimations are seldom repeated, and Mr Clavering turned without remark to the first pages of the work before him and began to point out the illustrations which adorned it, and to pronounce distinctly the names of the substances to which the drawings referred.

Mrs Leppell was further aggravated when Lillian, after looking at the lovers for a moment with an air of approbation, rose from her chair with the utmost deliberation, and walking straight towards the niche, inquired in a sweet cool manner if she could assist her hostess in arranging or dusting the precious china.

Mrs Leppell for a moment felt inclined to refuse the proffered aid, and that somewhat sharply, but a glance at the recess mollified her as she beheld Mary in her legitimate place, leaning on Clavering's shoulder, whilst he twisted a strand of her long bright hair round a piece of malachite stone, and thus held the young lady fast.

So the mother waxed gracious and replied, " I have nearly finished now ; but I would be glad if you can suggest any plan for mending this crack before it becomes a fissure. I am tired of diamond cement, for, to say the truth, I have never been able to make it serviceable."

"When a thing becomes thoroughly cracked and tarnished, I give it up for good," replied Miss Fan-shawe ; "but I am no authority on these matters, as

I infinitely prefer the beautiful china of modern manufacture. After this confession, will you trust this cup to me when I go to town? There is a shop in Regent Street where they mend these things in a professional manner."

Mrs Leppell replied that "of course she would," and her late apprehensions were further quenched as she heard Mary call out, "Come back, Lillian; this wicked fellow, this scientific deceiver, is teaching me all wrong. He is trying to make me call this lump 'Nice' (gneiss), as if I did not know that Nice was in France."

"It ought to be pronounced *nis*," returned Miss Fanshawe, with decision, "as you would pronounce the German word *mein*."

Francis admitted that she was right. "He wanted," he said, "to bring Mary nearer the pronunciation by naming a town which must be familiar to her. At any rate, Miss Leppell had the satisfaction of seeing him discomfited by her friend, and now we will go to work in earnest." He added, "Take this gneiss; here is the illustration, here is the specimen. I want you to learn a little, Mary," he said impressively; "for 'heavenly Moll' will have to grow older, just as other earthly angels have done before her, and I wish my little girl to be a highly educated as well as a pretty woman."

There was just a tinge of reproach in Mr Clavering's tone of voice which exasperated Mrs Leppell. "He is bitten with this education craze for women," thought she ; much good may it do him. Again Lillian threw soothing oil over the changeful chopping waves of Mrs Leppell's soul, as she declared that the very look of scientific names, especially those of geology, were enough to scare the strongest-minded female from approaching that study. "You learned folks," continued Miss Fanshawe, turning towards Mr Clavering, "always expect too much from the mere outsiders of science ; ordinary mortals cannot attain knowledge by intuition. I shall horrify you dreadfully by-and-by, and then Mary will have the laugh at me."

"Let us hasten the fulfilment of that prophecy by all means," returned Mr Clavering. "Just now, I should be more than obliged if you will classify these specimens according to this list, and affix the proper labels upon them. I want them to be ready for my lecture at the School of Science at Birmingham."

"Will you have to go soon ?" inquired Mary. "I do hope you will not be away on Tuesday, for Fritz and I have been planning out a riding picnic to a place which is 'rich in geological formations,' as your scientific books have it, and where you can hammer at the places to your heart's content, as I have it."

"Much obliged ; my lecture is set down for Thursday in next week. I follow Professor Deepdene, who reads a paper on the Pleistocene formation. I shan't leave to hear him, for I don't agree with his views altogether," continued the young man, sententiously, "so it is not likely that Deepdene will add to my knowledge very much, as he is obstinately wedded to his own opinion."

"Professor Deepdene!" exclaimed Mary. "Why, Frank, I have often heard him spoken of as being one of the most scientific men of the age. Yes; he was down here a year ago to speak at a meeting of the Margarine Society, and he stayed with those fussy gossiping Braintrees. I was so sorry for the old gentleman, because that impudent Sarah Braintree never rested till she dragged him all the way up the Cathedral tower stairs, to enjoy the view at five in the morning. How I abhor that girl! and I daresay the Professor did too; but perhaps we do not refer to the same man."

"Yes, we do," returned Clavering, coolly. "Deepdene is just the man to be victimised by an awful girl, because he has not the *savoir faire* to evade unwelcome feminine attentions. I heard of his having been down here when I was in Etrúria, and also that he played Triton amongst the minnows with great success; still he does not progress with the age."

"Progress with the age! do the stones and the gneiss and the malachite progress with the age? Ah!" cried Mary, "it would be good for large families if the pudding-stone were to evolve into good solid pastry, apples and all. How the housekeepers would reverence pudding-stone then! Eh, mother?"

Mrs Leppell was approaching the trio, and Frank, in consequence, restrained an expression of impatience which was hovering on his lips. He was silent for another reason also: it was astonishment to find that Mary was capable of apt and ready repartee.

"You are all apparently going to be busy for this lecture, I see," Mrs Leppell said; "I only come to warn you that if any of you want a horse for the afternoon, you had better secure it now. Colonel Leppell, for some unknown reason, has lent the best horses in all directions; but Mysie, Dick says, has been left, and one of the ponies, which either of you young ladies might ride. What do you say, Mr Clavering?"

"Secure and ride Mysie, by all means. This will be a splendid afternoon in which to go over to Dilke's Folly. What do you say, Moll? I want to examine the crags there, only I am afraid it will bore you. It will be hard on you, so much 'dry work' in one day, so name your own road."

"You never bore me," the girl answered simply; "but I won't pretend to take an interest in what does not please me for its own sake. I won't ride this afternoon, for mother requires my help, and Dilke's Folly is newer to Lillian, and a ride is such a treat to her. Another time I will take you a ride of my own choosing, and in that direction when the gipsies camp there again, and you can have the benefit of having your fortune told into the bargain. I should like to hear a gipsy prophesying smooth things to you, Frank, out of the stones," and she rocked his shoulder gently as she spoke.

"If you were a stone, you would evolve at once into

an angel were a fairy to touch you," replied Francis, as he turned back his head and looked at this charming creature. "We will go gipsying some day, with a vengeance. Now, I would really be glad to examine these crags scientifically, so much will turn on that Birmingham lecture; and as Miss Fanshawe is really interested in the science, I should be grateful for a fel-low-worker. · Will you honour me, Miss Fanshawe?"

"Certainly," replied that lady, in a matter-of-fact tone; "and you make it the more complimentary by accepting me as a substitute for Mary."

"I begin to feel as if I were a rose between two thorns," replied Mr Clavering, laughingly.

"Well, don't prick yourself any longer," exclaimed Miss Leppell; "hear a little domestic fact. Papa and the cook had a difference of opinion this morning, and papa is on the war-path and on the other side of the county by this time, I daresay; so you will be two dear people if you will take yourselves out of the way. Mother and Clara and I must do some domestic work, for, as ill-luck will have it, the Rose Prims are coming to dinner. Mother did not like to mention this; now, do you understand?"

CHAPTER VI.

A COUNTRY WEDDING.

"I UNDERSTAND that the cook has caused a revolution in the establishment," Mr Clavering replied, in answer to the query which Miss Leppell had put, in so searching a manner that he felt his powers of intuition to be decidedly challenged; "but which else is the matter?"

"The Colonel, of course," replied that gentleman's daughter; "he is always 'the matter' in this household. He tramped through the kitchen this morning when the maids were at breakfast without knocking at the door, and desired cook to get some blue-stone for one of the horse's backs, and to look sharp and find it, in his usual peremptory manner, I daresay."

"No doubt of that, I should imagine," remarked Colonel Leppell's intended relative with a laugh.

"Cook," went on Miss Leppell, "stuck to her seat, and informed the Colonel that she was not a black slave, and furthermore, that she was not accustomed to allow people to come into *her* kitchen wearing muddy boots and spurs, and without their first knocking at the door for permission to enter; whereupon papa swore at her——"

"I'll be bound he did," interrupted Mr Clavering.

"Well, cook immediately gave notice of instant departure, adding (and this was the sting in the bee), 'In future, Colonel, I intend to live where my soul is attended to.'"

"That, after family prayers and your father's expoundings, was really too bad," Frank made reply. He had attended one or two of these matutinal assemblages by especial request, and had gone near to quarrel with Colonel Leppell because he held different views from that officer concerning the length of the Mosaical day. As this opinion had furnished a pretext for the Colonel to preach on the first chapter of Genesis, Mr Clavering had, as the effect of that exposition, elected to think and to speak sarcastically of his future father-in-law's theology; so he said—

"I suppose cook has never had the good fortune to be made the object of any special preachment, as I have been, consequently she may think that her soul was lost sight of entirely. But, seriously, cannot you put off the Rose Prims?"

"Why, no," answered Mrs Leppell; "they have only lately become our tenants, and Mr Rose Prim is willing to allow some of that stuff which is good for horses to be sown in the fields on the little farm down near the river. This, of course, is a convenience to us ; but I don't think, socially, that they will be any acquisition."

"Mr Prim grunts when he speaks, and the wife makes one's back ache to look at her," quoth Mary.

"Mrs Rose Prim is an uncomfortably good woman," said Mrs Leppell. "She means well, but she has offended my children by calling this place 'Scamp Covert,' and still more deeply, by forbidding her son to play with our boys."

"That precious young Measley!" exclaimed Dick, who had entered the room unperceived and in time to supply some valuable information.

"What about Measley?" said Frank. "Is he a 'prim' in the uncomfortable sense of the word?"

"Worse," replied Dick; "he is a cowardly little beast. However, I got hold of him last week down at the Swallow's ford, and collared him tight."

"Did you choke the little wretch?" asked Mary.

"No ; but I held his head close to a stone just under water till he kicked again. When he had had enough I whacked him, and made him swear by the bones of our old Ponto that we are the best-behaved family on the face of the earth, and that it is balm in Gilead to hear the governor vociferate in the hunt."

"Dick, for shame!" exclaimed his mother; "had I known that, I should have been very angry with you."

"But you see you didn't, ma ; and, besides, there was nobody there but our two selves. I frightened Measley properly, but I did not really hurt him ; and

I was good enough to tell him that when we asked him to play with us again, he could refuse. The little beggar has been very civil ever since."

"What brings you in here at this time, Dick?" inquired Mary.

"Only to know about Mysie," the lad replied. "It is a whole holiday to-day, so I have nothing particular to do. If any of you want Mysie, I will groom her and take her down to the laundry."

"Take her down to the laundry," repeated Mr Clavering, looking up from his specimens; "what on earth for?"

"Why, you see," exclaimed Master Dick, "the governor may pop back, and he may not. If he returns, the first thing he'll do will be to go at once to the stables: then if his eye falls on a decent-looking beast, he is safe to want it."

"What has that to do with the laundry?" asked Frank.

"The laundry is a sort of old cottage among the laurels there, and it has a coal-place into which a moderate-sized horse will just fit. When we want to secure a beast for ourselves we take it down there, and pop a large clothes-rack full of sheets in front of the opening. Fritz knocked in a ring to tie a creature to; but a vicious mare ate up a lot of washing things one day—didn't she, ma?"

"Yes; and a fine state of annoyance the laundry-maid was in. I am sure the servants are very good-natured, for they put up with so much from you boys, and never complain of you to your father," said Mrs Leppell.

"Oh, they like to be teased—at least the maids do," quoth Dick. "I wish the Colonel had not offended the cook, though, for though she did flare up at times, she always had a bit of tart or something nice to give us : but we will never keep a decent servant as long as the governor lives."

"Will you go and see after Mysie at once?" said Mrs Leppell, with the view of cutting Master Dick's comments short. "I suppose," she continued, "the ponies are left."

"Oh yes ; pa would not condescend to look at them, so they may remain where they are. I may perhaps give them a touch," continued Dick, patronisingly, and then he went off to help the groom.

The morning hours went by ; assistance had been procured from the village, and Mrs Leppell breathed more freely.

The Colonel, happily, did not return ; and after one of those comfortable scrap-luncheons, which, if encountered *impromptu,* form one of the most enjoyable of our repasts, the equestrians went forth.

Looking approvingly at the pair as they rode away, Mary Leppell thanked her stars that her friend had so decided a bent towards geology, and further, that she did not mind riding an unkempt-looking pony, and was never tired of Frank's scientific talks. So she, after standing for a moment in the porch, re-entered the house satisfied and content.

"What a comfort Lillian will be to me in the future," thought she.

So days and hours sped away, and then came the short-lived bustle of wedding preparations, and finally the wedding-day itself. It was a quiet, elegant affair, its great charm being that nothing was overdone, and the absence of all pretension seemed to make everybody happy and at their ease. Old Lord Hieover, at the eleventh hour, elected to be present: this, it was alleged by his son, the Colonel, was in consequence of no pressure having been brought to bear upon the Viscount concerning his opinions or intentions on the matter. "My father will come, or he will stay away, just as it may please him," Ralph had said to his wife; "he has had a respectful invitation, and there's an end of it. But I forbid you or Mary to write again, or make it a matter of the slightest consequence whether the Viscount puts in an appearance or not."

"Mary had a very nice letter from your brother Alick only last night," said Mrs Leppell, "apprising her that a parcel is on the way here containing her wedding-present from him. He seems to be very unwell, and I think he is really sorry he cannot be present at the wedding."

The gift arrived in the shape of a magnificent lace veil, and within the packet was a little fancy purse containing fifty sovereigns. "Now, after this," Willina Clavering had remarked, "never do you call your uncle mean or close-fisted." Mary laughed and sighed, and finally wore the veil with her bridal attire, to the immense delight, as she afterwards was informed, of Uncle Alick, the donor.

The Viscount did come, as has been stated, and brought a handsome silver tea-service in his train for the bride. The old gentleman was greatly delighted at his own perspicacity in being the first of the family to seek the acquaintance of Mr Clavering, and he took care to make Mr Glascott aware of the fact. "Saw from the first, sir," he averred to that gentleman,— "saw from the first what was in Mr Clavering: recognised his talent, and made a point—a special point— of having him at Hieover, sir. A rising man, sir— will make his own way in the world; and, above all, he will bring practical ideas into the family."

And then he turned to lovely Mary, as she came to greet him in affection and duty, before she was led out from her father's house to be made a wife. "O grandpapa!" she exclaimed, "what a pleasant surprise you have given me! I am so glad to see you,—my wedding will now be quite perfect. I am so happy now."

It was a pretty sight, the bride standing on the landing-place in the sheen of satin and the shimmer of pearl, extending her arms to the old man, and the bridesmaids trooping from out the chamber behind her, all clad in innocent white, to which their own fair young beauty lent an additional charm. Lillian Fanshawe, unusually pale, but with a presence that was almost imperial, was looking her very best, and stood in fine relief to Willina Clavering, in whom pleasure and satisfaction showed themselves in the rich red of her smiling lips, and the soft healthy tinge of her cheek. Then the little troop of Leppell sisters, small and large, radiant in the good looks which, the tradition of many years informs us, were bestowed by the beneficent fairies for ever on all the race of the house of Hieover, and to which satin ribbons and muslin dress and sweet blush-roses lent their added charm, contributed a most effective body-guard.

Nor would it be fair to pass over the dogs' part in the family grouping: for at Hunter's Lodge these people—yes, they *are* people—formed a very component item in the establishment. They were there loved for their own sake, just as so many of us like them for sake's sake; and in that home they sympathised in the joys and mourned the sorrows of their owners, just because the opportunity to do so was afforded them, and therefore these persons were to be remembered on Mary's wedding-day.

The redoubtable bull-terrier pup careered in the flower-beds, arrayed in a white satin ruff which had been stitched upon him, and which he was popularly supposed to have devoured half an hour after his toilet had been completed, and when he had received the last finishing-touch from Dick Leppell's hair-brush. The ruff was never seen again; but what did it matter? he was so happy. "He knows all about it," quoth the lad; "he knows it's Mary's wedding-day, bless you!"

Then the Skye-terrier, who also knew all about it,

was outfitted with a white satin bow as big as a pancake, and stood half the day besides on his hind legs, begging for the bridal cake which nauseated him; and the great collie-dog, with her dear soft eyes, was allowed for the first time in her life to walk up-stairs to visit "our heavenly Moll," and to be made lucky for ever from the first pat of a girl in her wedding-dress—when the sun was shining fair.

Very trivial, and very small, these innocent conceits may appear to some of us; but oh, when the sharp rain of disappointment pelts its hail into our cup of life, and when the chilling mists of disillusion breathe their tarnish on the golden bowl, then do these little incidents return to remembrance: and if the wedding-day must be recalled as the first act of a lifelong mistake, be assured that, even amid regrets and tears, these fond conceits will evoke a smile, and go far, perhaps, to soften the bitterness which blighted prospects may have unconsciously called forth.

And, after all, we are mostly very jealous and very tender of those conceits which are purely the emanations of a great love towards ourselves. Mary Leppell never forgot the trouble the boys had taken to get the family pets trimmed up for her wedding-day. Every horse in the stable, too, underwent an extra grooming, and there was general rejoicing inside and outside the gates of Hunter's Lodge; and even poor stricken Lady Asher struggled up from her pillows, and insisted upon being covered with some kind of festive array.

"I am not going to resign my place," said the

Viscount to the Colonel, as he conducted his grand-daughter to the foot of the staircase where Ralph was standing to receive her. "Let me take the child to church," the old man continued, in a beseeching tone; "I have a fancy to do so. Remember it was at Hieover that these young people first met,—I introduced Mr Clavering myself to Mary."

Colonel Leppell hesitated a moment: in his heart of hearts he very much objected to bestow his daughter on Mr Clavering, for he disliked the match, and he disliked the connection fully as much. The whole thing and its manner of coming about was repugnant to him, and he had only yielded, as we know, from force of circumstances.

His hesitation proceeded partly from surprise, partly also from some apprehension as to how this would appear in the eyes of the world, and of Mr Glascott. A moment's reflection, however, decided him on the last point: he would get Adelaide to tell the latter that he could not find it in his heart to refuse an old man, and his own father, a gratification upon which he was resolutely bent.

Mr Glascott would appreciate filial respect—which was true enough; and he would also appreciate the Viscount's offices in giving Miss Leppell to his cousin—which was untrue enough: all that Mr Glascott really cared for was that Francis Clavering should obtain the wife of his choice, by respectable means of course, and in the conventional manner of society in general —that was enough for him.

"Do, papa," said Mary; "and mamma will be so pleased if you will give your arm to her. Then you can walk next after us, and it will be all the same thing."

This was arranged, and the procession set forth, filing through the garden, down the meadow, afoot, for it would have been affectation to have had carriages for so short a distance, and in the glorious weather, moreover, of midsummer-day.

Marcia La Touche's rich dress of pea-green silk, whereon was depicted a lattice-work upon which climbed gorgeous birds of every shape and hue, formed a brilliant contrast to the simple colours and white dresses adopted by the younger ladies, and provided at the same time a curious ornithological study to Mr Glascott, who walked behind her, conveying Mrs Canon Braintree on his arm.

That lady was arrayed in violet silk, and looked well; but she had her troubles in a vain attempt to reduce to order a peculiarly unmanageable feather, which art had placed in her bonnet, but which nature, in an unhandsome freak, would persist in sweeping over her brow and occasionally dipping into her eye.

Mrs Braintree, goaded to desperation, at length bent the ornament in twain, and so it hung at the side of her head, with that unhappy expression which a damaged feather, in whatever form, always manages to present to the gaze of a beholder. However, it did not signify, as no human being living had ever known

Mrs Braintree in a perfect toilet, although her raiment was generally good of its kind, and she spent more money upon it than did many a fashionable woman of her standing and pretensions.

Percival La Touche, carefully excluded, through Miss Clavering's management, from the ranks of bride-men and bride-maids, escorted Miss Braintree, at which arrangement neither of the pair seemed to be particularly well pleased. However, they had the consolation of knowing that this forced propinquity was not for life, and they therefore accepted the situation as their trial pace, previous to a ceremony in which each of them hoped and intended to act as principal performer at no distant date.

The church is at length reached, and Mr Clavering advances with his groomsman to meet the procession. He is perfectly composed and self-possessed, and has given his companion a *mauvais quart-d'heure*, by claiming that gentleman's undivided attention to a plan of warming the church by means of an apparatus of his own invention. The groomsman, who much preferred to scan the pretty village girls who crowded the gallery to see the ceremony, had little inclination to observe where a stove might be placed, or where a hot-air pipe might be run up, and was particularly delighted when the sexton (who had been listening to the propositions) burst out with: "Lord bless 'ee, sir! we should ha' the whole place alight like a brick-kiln. This church ain't going to perish by fire—no, no; a's sinking down gradual in the earth, and Passon Vane says as how a's already three feet below the proper level."

"This is a very old church, is it not?" inquired the groomsman.

"A is, sir; a was built in the reign of Richard the Second, and was dedicated to St Lawrence—the grid-iron saint, sir, as likely you knows. But here they comes. Now then, all on ye stand quiet" (addressing the people in the gallery); "and you, Mr Carter" (addressing the schoolmaster), "please strike up a jyful song of praise as soon as you sees the first on 'em come in."

As Mr Carter was behind the little organ, which was tall and thin in its construction, a small boy was told off to make the necessary investigation, and in another minute the whoop of this young gentleman made it apparent that the time had arrived when the "jyful" strain should peal forth; and it did peal forth with all the "timbre" that the performer could command.

"A thanksgiving for getting a husband," observed one of the girls in the gallery to her friend; "maybe it will bring us luck, for lovers are so scarce. Who knows?"

A slight bustle; a little marshalling and ordering; then deep silence, and Mr Fane, without any extraneous assistance, performed the rite which made these two—Francis Clavering and Mary Leppell—man and wife. It was remarked that during the whole ceremony the Colonel remained mute and almost motionless, and that when it was concluded he made no attempt to salute his daughter. Mrs Leppell, not knowing very well what to do, did not venture to move towards the vestry; and Lillian Fanshawe, usually so self-possessed and so ready to meet every emergency, stood still, looking at the newly married pair, shaking in every limb, and her face drawn in a deadly pallor. At that moment she could not have moved had her life depended on it.

The common-sense of Mrs Braintree here acted most usefully. She advanced towards the bride, and, taking her hand, led her to her mother.

Their embrace was the signal for a universal move, and Ralph, recovering himself, shook hands with Mr Clavering and then with Mr Glascott. After the customary business of signing the register in the vestry, the procession returned to the house, and the wedding-breakfast took place forthwith.

This feast went off with great hilarity. The speeches, as had been stipulated beforehand, were delightfully brief, and the Colonel was charmed when Mr Glascott, in proposing the health of Viscount Hieover and that of all his family, dexterously introduced the name of that absent member, Marmaduke Leppell, to public recognition.

The Viscount responded to the toast, and remarked that as Marmaduke was at that moment paying the penalty for his indiscretion in the matter of his own marriage, by an enforced absence at the bidding of the law, it would be worse than unkind if he and the company then present omitted to offer him their good wishes for the future. "We are none of us perfect," the Viscount continued, benevolently, " and on an occasion like this, we are all, I think, naturally led to palliate the mistakes of the absent, and those of the young more especially."

Thus the health of Mr and Mrs Marmaduke Leppell was drank with all the honours.

Ralph, although agitated by secret annoyance, which the presence of Mr Glascott considerably increased, certainly drew a good augury from this speech. It proved to him that whatever the Viscount might choose to do or say against Marmaduke in private, he was not the man to depreciate his own kith and kin on a public occasion like the present—for public it might be considered, as several acquaintances from Yarne and the neighbourhood, who were not included in the invitation to the marriage ceremony, were present at the breakfast.

As the state of Lady Asher's health precluded the possibility of a dance, it had been settled, at the eleventh hour, that a picnic to the neighbouring castle of Barkholme and its woods would be a capital entertainment wherewith to conclude the programme of the day ; and as the newly married pair were bound for Paris, and the train-service demanded early departure, the travelling-carriage was at the door at one o'clock precisely.

The bride went to see Lady Asher as soon as her travelling-dress was donned, and in the privacy of her grandmother's apartment did Mary take a fond and affectionate leave of her mother, comforting her with the assurance that she was really happy, and bidding her to abstain from all anxiety on her account. "Frank is not very demonstrative, I know," the girl said; "but it is his nature, and perhaps that is better than a great show of affection at first."

Mrs Leppell replied that this was quite true; and after a kiss to grandmamma, the rest of the adieux were made, and the travelling-carriage of Mr and Mrs Clavering disappeared through the gates of Hunter's Lodge.

Now all was hurry and bustle for the picnic, for the remains of the bridal feast were partly to furnish the cold baked meats of the next entertainment. The excitement of getting the carriages in order, and filling them suitably, was an agreeable diversion to Colonel Leppell, and the prospect of driving his coach, and handling the wildest team in the county, raised his spirits considerably. Mrs Leppell was to remain at home and take care of her mother; whilst Prothero, and the nurses, and the babies, should preside at a high tea given in the village to every one who might choose to attend it.

Lord Hieover, on leaving, gave a handsome sum for this purpose, and taking the Colonel aside, he presented him with a cheque for one hundred pounds, expressing himself at the same time highly satisfied with the manner in which everything had been conducted. "No outrageous show, no absurd expense, quite the proper thing for a daughter who is marrying a simple gentleman. I am very much pleased."

So also was his grandson Dick, who received a pat on the head and the gift of a guinea. It was a sight to see Dick in the dog-cart with two other choice spirits, and the stable dogs, Flames and Blazer, careering up and down the highroad, all impatience to take the lead of the picnic procession as soon as the wonderful coach could be proclaimed ready for business.

It took some time, but eventually that risky vehicle was announced to be in starting condition. It certainly seemed to be a foolhardy proceeding on the part of those who occupied it, to venture with such unbroken cattle; but Colonel Leppell's driving was renowned, and by a special providence, apparently, he never had come to grief.

It was therefore to his great delight that the "crack" was filled both inside and out, and all apprehensions as to safety cast to the winds.

Percival La Touche, who had hitherto played a secondary part in the programme of the day, now thought that the time was come when he should assert himself. He and Marcia had engaged a nice carriage with a good pair of chestnuts, which was retained for the picnic, and Mr La Touche was much exercised as to how he should induce Miss Clavering to take a seat in that conveyance.

Mr Glascott's carriage was rapidly being converted into a huge pigeon-pie or sardine-box, by reason of a crowd of very young people having seized it, with the declaration that the owner had offered the use of it to each and every one of them; and a fine noise and good-humoured wrangle was the consequence of this wholesale piece of generosity. This was just what Percival wanted. Miss Clavering surely could not occupy her guardian's carriage with all that crowd! He therefore desired Marcia to offer the vacant seat in their own carriage to Willina, and to be quick about it.

"Miss Fanshawe, you mean?" said Marcia, who, all unconscious of her nephew's latest predilection, fancied that he had inadvertently confused the names.

"No, no!" replied Percival, sharply; "allow me to know my own mind. Go and ask Miss Clavering, and be quick about it, or she will be snapped up by the party in Lord Willows' trap."

Marcia did not venture a second remark, and was preparing to do as she was bid, when Mr Glascott suddenly stood near them. At the same moment a happy thought seized Percival. "Nothing like going to the fountain-head," said he—"nothing like it;" and in a moment, with hat in hand, Percival preferred his request to Mr Glascott. The latter, taken as he was by surprise, could not well decline this civility.

"Oh, certainly, much obliged—that is, if she is not already bespoken," said Mr Glascott, answering for his cousin. "Perhaps you will be good enough to ascertain for yourself, as I must arrange matters a little in my own vehicle. Willina," he continued, as he perceived Miss Clavering, "Mr La Touche is good enough to

offer you a seat in his carriage with his aunt, and a
—a——"

"Harold Fanshawe," cut in Percival, as he remarked
that youth retire in contempt, and disgust from Mr
Glascott's vehicle, and saw that he was seeking more
congenial company.

"Very nice," said Mr Glascott, who was pleased, for
Willina's sake, that she would not be obliged to endure
Mr La Touche wholly without some kind of mas-
culine alloy; so he continued, waxing benevolent—

"Mr La Touche's proposition is really very oppor-
tune, and we are much beholden to him for it. Our
own carriage is certainly in the hands of the Philis-
tines, and I am sure you will enjoy the drive with a
smaller party." So saying, Mr Glascott walked away,
and left his cousin to Percival's escort.

He, meanwhile, had by means of telegraphic signals
brought Harold Fanshawe towards his carriage, and
intimated to that youth that he was to get in, and
place himself opposite Miss La Touche. Harold did
so, nothing loth; and as Willina had no other alterna-
tive but to accept the La Touche politeness with a
good grace, she stepped without demur into the place
allotted to her, and very shortly afterwards the whole
cortège was on the move for the fair woods of Barkholme.

Miss Clavering naturally looked about to see what
had become of Mr Glascott, and was pleased when
she descried him comfortably ensconced in the carriage
of Canon Braintree, under the wing of the wife of that

dignitary, and Miss Fanshawe occupying the fourth seat in their vehicle. Lillian had ceded her place in Lord Willows' waggonette, which was supposed to be especially reserved for the bridesmaids, to Miss Braintree.

On perceiving this substitution, both Marcia and Willina jumped to a conclusion which, as it happened, was utterly erroneous. They elected to believe that this was a manœuvre on the part of Miss Braintree to improve her acquaintance with the noble driver of the waggonette, whereas the contrary was the case, as Miss Fanshawe, having her own reasons for preferring the quiet society occupying Canon Braintree's vehicle, had suggested the exchange, which of course the Canon's daughter was delighted to accept, offering as it did so much more amusement and excitement. Miss Fanshawe alleged a severe headache as the reason for making the request, and thus laid low any surmises that Sarah Braintree may have indulged in as to her having made this proposition at the very last moment.

Mr La Touche also looked into this vehicle, and had Miss Clavering chanced to observe him at the moment, she would have wondered what made him smile in such ironical fashion. The expression was merely momentary; but it left Percival satisfied in his own mind that he had discovered the embryo of a secret, which, when developed, might possibly affect the destiny of more than one life. With the conviction that this day must decide his own fate for wife and dowry, he turned, pleasantly, to the ladies. His deferential manner and sparkling conversation allured Miss Clavering out of the reserve in which she had intended to entrench herself; whilst it delighted his aunt, and caused Harold Fanshawe to open both his mouth and his eyes, and maintain that dead silence which is generally declared to be the normal condition of the stock-fish.

CHAPTER VII.

THE FAIR WOODS OF BARKHOLME.

At length the procession arranged itself and was soon beyond the village of Yarne. It was amid the loveliest scenery of fair England that it made its way,—down mossy lanes, shaded by great trees which bore almost every tint that foliage can acquire, as they stood out grandly in the rich apparel of the leafy month of June.

Here and there a broad expanse of upland, bordered by a dark line of distant forest, which served as an enclosure to the ruddy ripening grain, enabled the party to meet together for a time, and to separate thankfully into the cool glens through which ran tiny streamlets watering the wealth of wild flowers which literally carpeted the ground. All was so fair and so sweet,—the glorious sunshine—the distant hazy veil of blue vapour, deepening in the far horizon to the richest purple—the air pierced as it were with subtle fragrant scent,—that it was no wonder that Dick Leppell should declare that he never in his

life had known so magnificent a midsummer day;
and that Canon Braintree should fall fast asleep,
chanted into the land of forgetfulness by the lazy
murmur of distant brooks and the prolonged coo
of the wood-pigeons and doves, challenged as these
were by the wail of the widow - bird — that *vox
humana* of sorrow—interspersing the monotony of
calm content.

Canon Braintree sleeps, and his wife improves the
shining hour. The situation was advantageous, for
there were occasions in which the lady believed that
she advanced the interests of her calling without the
co-operation of her spouse. He was all very well
in his place, and was no doubt eminently useful as a
referee, but sometimes he spoilt enterprise by asking
untimely questions, and by making uncalled-for remarks. It was in the fine work of ecclesiastical business, Mrs Canon Braintree concluded to think, that her
husband was not quite up to the mark; and so it is
with satisfaction that she hears him snore, and resolves
to ask Mr Glascott for a subscription for the Dorcas
Society of Yarne.

Had the Canon been awake, he would doubtless have
considered it an unfair advantage to invite a man
into his carriage, and having got him there, to open
upon him with a request for money, for any object
however laudable: he would have probably winked
disapprobation, and would have perhaps opined with
King Solomon that there was a time and a place for
all things.

Mrs Braintree held that there was no time like the present time, according to the adage; and acting on this conviction, she at once made her application, toning it down with the assurance to Mr Glascott that she knew how delighted he would be to make a thank-offering for the blessings of the day.

Mr Glascott, who had made offerings enough in one shape or another, did not seem, at first, to meet this proposition with very hearty goodwill. Further discovery, however, convinced that gentleman that Mrs Braintree scrupulously restricted her advocacy to the claims of present and visible British misery, to the utter exclusion of unfeasible plans for African conversion *à la hâte*, or to the habilitation of the Patagonian in the flannel vest of respectability. Two guineas would let him off cheaply, and he therefore promised that amount. It was less than Mrs Braintree had expected, but she wisely concealed her opinion, and registered the sum as a yearly subscription from Mr Glascott of Brydone, Island of Jersey.

It was highly satisfactory to think that the "thank-offering" would thus repeat itself for many years to come.

This business being concluded, Mrs Braintree sets her wits to work in another direction, for the benefit of her order, as she sometimes expressed it: a slight incident had suggested the idea, and she now thinks she must fulfil the Christian duty of turning Miss Fanshawe into a well-endowed county woman. The material was present, and she would utilise the same; no time like the present time,—for the Canon, like most sensible men, was averse to match-making, and still snored.

The incident which attracted Mrs Braintree's attention was this. Just as she had registered Mr Glascott's subscription, the carriage containing the La Touche party came up close to the side of her barouche, and as it did so, she saw Lillian Fanshawe cast a glance at one of its inmates, of such peculiar expression, that the good woman was convinced she had surprised a dart of furious jealousy in full flight.

The face of the young lady, which during the whole day had been unusually pale, was at that moment suffused with a crimson flush; and a steady anger, at the same time, gleamed in her eyes.

Mrs Braintree could not quite satisfy herself as to whether it was towards Miss Clavering or towards Mr La Touche that the look was directed; but she had seen enough to be assured that it was one, or perhaps both, of these individuals who had excited displeasure in her young friend's mind,—a displeasure so deep that the latter, apparently, made no sort of effort to control its outward expression—the habitual composure of her manner having quite deserted her. The girl, in fact, literally trembled.

At that moment an opinion rushed through the mind of the Canon's wife, and it took a very peremptory form. Mr La Touche *must* be secured for Miss Fanshawe; the daughters of clergymen nowadays must marry money; Mr La Touche is the friend of the

Fanshawes; it is through the introduction by that family that he has become acquainted with the Leppells, and is here at all; the gentleman is not, by all accounts, one whom it is desirable to ally with the Church; however, his fortune is large, and with a clergyman's daughter for wife, the manipulation of money would be advantageous to the clerical world.

So thinking, and so determining, Mrs Braintree proceeded to render herself agreeable to the La Touche party; woke up the Canon, with the view of making him back up an invitation to dinner which she gave to Marcia and Percival for the following day, under the impression, real or assumed, that they were not immediately on the return to London.

Here Mrs Braintree's hospitality was of no avail; for although Marcia seemed disposed to accept the courtesy offered, a sharp admonitory touch of the foot by her nephew quickly changed the current of her views, and she stated that both she and Mr La Touche were engaged in town for the evening of the morrow. Percival, for his part, testified his deep regret, but hoped on some happy occasion to see Canon and Mrs Braintree at Hinton Square.

So that device fell through. But the Canon's wife in most respects was a woman of resource, and in consequence she managed by some jugglery to mix the occupants of the two carriages in a general conversation; and Miss Fanshawe, now herself again, talked vigorously with Marcia, and amongst other light in-

quiries, she demanded of Percival, with some signifi-
cance possibly, what had become of his brother Stephen, and how it was that he was not then present, he
being such a favourite with all, and with the bride
especially ?

"Ah, indeed!" exclaimed Mr Glascott, following up
the inquiry. "I thought I missed somebody,—very
gentlemanly, good-looking man your brother, sir. I
have scarcely seen him, but our slight acquaintance
has left a very pleasant remembrance on my part."
This to Percival, by way of compliment to that
gentleman.

Now this was the particular subject which had perplexed the mind of Miss Clavering for many hours ;
and if the truth must be told, the absence of Stephen
La Touche had very much militated against the pleasure of the day, as far as she was personally concerned.
She believed that a formal invitation had been sent
to that gentleman amongst others who were bid to
the marriage-feast, and it was natural that she should
feel some surprise at his non-appearance, and be at a
loss to understand why his absence should not have
been remarked by any of the Leppell family.

Her astonishment was further augmented as she remembered that, when she was in London with Mary
for the purpose of buying bridal finery, and had during
that fortnight seen something of the La Touche family
in the aggregate, it seemed *bien entendu* on all sides
that Mr Stephen La Touche was to be a guest at
Hunter's Lodge on Midsummer-day.

It was therefore with some interest that Miss Clavering listened to the response of Mr La Touche to the direct question which Miss Fanshawe had put.

Percival's reply was curt enough, although he reddened a little, and looked somewhat discomposed as he gave it tongue.

"My brother has had no regular invitation," said he; "besides, he is overwhelmed with business, owing to the long holiday he had taken before."

Here Marcia must needs chime in with the information that her nephew was very busy with the affairs of a rich widow, whom his father was very desirous that he should cultivate. "So you see," continued Marcia, adding more intricacy to this game of cross-purposes, "that Stephen is now combining both business and pleasure in the most happy manner."

The real state of the case was, that Mrs Leppell, by a singular malversion of *les convenances*—very much the vogue with indolent natures—had really not sent Mr Stephen La Touche any invitation whatever. She had, when inviting Percival verbally, expressed a hope that he would induce his brother to accompany him, and had supposed that, when at Pinnacles, Mary would arrange the matter with the latter in person. Percival had suppressed Mrs Leppell's message entirely, and that lady's daughter had supposed that her mother had written to Mr Stephen La Touche; and what between supposition and taking things for granted, the young man remained under the impression that in the bustle of concluding engagements he had been overlooked.

Had Stephen been less in love, or more sure of his ground, perhaps, he would have managed in some way to get the matter thoroughly righted; but that subtle delicate shyness which is one of the symptoms of intense devotion, and which makes a coward of the strongest mind, operated to prevent him even alluding to the subject.

Being totally unsuspicious of Percival's mean trick, it was natural that he should await till the last moment some intimation from either Mrs Leppell or the Colonel: as this was not forthcoming, he saw his aunt and his brother depart in triumph, and made no sign.

One crumb of comfort, however, had fallen into the cup of Stephen La Touche. That fortnight which the young ladies spent in London had proved, beyond doubt, that Percival was making no way in the good graces of Miss Clavering. Marcia had called, and there had been an exchange of dinner-parties; they had gone in a huge company to a ball, whereat the barrister had experienced some pleasure in seeing Mr Percival well snubbed by the lady of his own love; and furthermore, he had derived much solace at her expressing a hope that he would pay them a visit at Brydone at no far-off day.

"You tell me you are going to coach a young man in the lore of the law," she had said, in one of the pauses of a square dance; "and you have mentioned that you would like to go to the Channel Islands for the reading tour. If you are in Jersey, I am sure Mr Glascott will be glad to see you at Brydone."

"You are going there soon?" Stephen had inquired.

"As soon as possible after the wedding is over. My cousin is tired of rambling about, and I wish to see him comfortable and really at home before I visit my brother after his marriage."

Stephen there and then registered a vow to make the reading pupil elect Jersey as the most convenient spot in the British dominions for hard work; and Miss Clavering resolved to impress upon Mr Glascott the desirability of showing attention to this younger son of the house of La Touche, whenever kindly fate should place the opportunity in his way.

They still spoke indirectly of meeting at the wedding, and therefore Willina was somewhat astonished and much disappointed when she heard that Miss La Touche, and her eldest nephew solely, had arrived at the Red Lion at Yarne, in order to be present at the wedding on the following day. She was impelled, from a feeling of reserve, to abstain from making any inquiry regarding this circumstance, and the Leppells *en masse* were far too much taken up with their own affairs to bestow time on mere conjecture. It seemed to be tacitly agreed that Mr Stephen would have come if he could, and that later on they would know the reason of his absence. Dick Leppell and Harold Fanshawe, in a spirit of prophecy, declared that

"Touchey" would drop in upon them at any moment, and then the subject utterly passed out of mind.

Although Percival had replied so confidently to Miss Fanshawe's inquiry, the young lady entertained her doubts about the accuracy of his statements, in so far as the part concerning the invitation was implied; and Miss Clavering entirely discredited what Mr La Touche and his aunt had advanced on the subject.

It seemed clear to both the young ladies that a purpose was to be served in keeping Stephen away,— perhaps jealousy, perhaps envy and all uncharitableness. Whatever the cause, Miss Clavering felt convinced that it was owing to the agency of Mr La Touche that his younger brother was not driving in the woods' of Barkholme on that sunny Midsummer-day.

But now the point is reached at which the company are to alight from their several vehicles, and proceed a little distance on foot to that recess in the woods which the noble owner of the property had caused to be erected for the accommodation of pleasure-seekers, and for artists who came from afar to sketch the ruins of old Barkholme Castle, and the surrounding scenery of wooded vale and hill.

Truly it is a pleasant place; the undulating ground stretching into far vistas of graceful foliage, just affording peeps of sunny corn-fields in the ridges of the hills,—the shelving banks thick with moss, through which the tender wild-flowers push up their heads and bow to the wind. Nor must pass unrecognised the silver water glinting here and there in the far distance,—that runaway child of the homely brook, which babbled in methodical rhythm in its appointed place, just as it babbled in ages gone by, when the pebbles which formed its bed were perhaps a trifle less smooth.

And so down to the rustic gates which enclose the little domain set apart for the convenience of visitors. It is a humble quiet place, consisting of a cottage wherein dwells a retainer of the family now past service. His daughter and a grandchild form the household. They are not ill off, but are glad of any addition which they may gain in attending to the wants of strangers and sightseers.

The child is happy to-day—for has not the man who had been sent forward earlier to make preparations, and announce the coming of the Leppell party, told her in strict secrecy that a lump of wedding-cake for them all is on its way, and a bottle of wine and a wedding-favour, and one or two other nice things besides? So little Jessie waits, looking at the great coach with awe, thinking that the packet must be hid somewhere in its wonderful depths; and then she turns to fly as the Colonel, with his loud haw-haw voice, demands a kiss, and proclaims that ere long she will be the prettiest girl in the whole barony, deny this who can.

The horses and carriages are stowed away, and some of the party walk up and down, and some meander into the open until the meal, which is to be served in a thatched-over barn, is declared ready.

Mrs Braintree does her utmost to bring Mr La Touche in juxtaposition with Miss Fanshawe, but he sticks like a leech to Miss Clavering, who, in self-defence, elects to sit with Marcia and admire the beauties of nature from a rickety bench in a dilapidated summer-house. As there is no room for Mr La Touche, he moves reluctantly away, and Mrs Braintree takes him in tow, walks him up and down, and finally manages to secure the promise of a yearly subscription for the Dorcas Society at Yarne, which Percival paid on the spot.

How Mrs Braintree achieved this miracle, and how Percival consented to be thus mulcted, is one of the mysteries which will never be cleared up in this world.

It was thought by some that he paid his guinea as a sort of entrance-fee into the society of the clerical magnates of the earth; others opined that Mr La Touche had done a good business turn in securing Mrs Braintree's patronage as a customer for some of the wines of Hungary which his firm was just then importing, and that the guinea would eventually return tenfold into his bosom.

Be this as it may, Percival's name was down on a charity subscription-list. Mrs Braintree believed that the dye was coming off this black sheep; and Marcia, when she heard of it, declared emphatically that the heavens would fall.

The interview rather detached Mr La Touche from the younger ladies, and he found himself at the *al fresco* meal seated beside a jolly-looking man who was addressed by the Leppell fry as "Old Clothes." This gentleman, who was barely thirty years of age, and bore the name of John Clowes, was a yeoman of the district, who, being in the neighbourhood, had driven over in his gig to present his congratulations to Colonel Leppell. He was going to Scotland, he said, for some months, and would have no other opportunity of personally wishing all happiness to the young married pair.

Mr Clowes had intended to depart as soon as his mission was fulfilled, but the Leppell fry would hear of nothing of the kind; and so the good yeoman had to be dragged hither and thither to give his opinion, as requested, upon the dogs and horses appertaining to the *cortège*, and to submit to much handling of the beautiful mare which he had driven in his gig.

Percival, as soon as the collation was served, took his seat somewhat sulkily, although it had been impressed upon all that the circumstances admitted of scant ceremony, and that gentlemen and the younger people must find seats how and where they could. Colonel Leppell thought he had made a highly apt and Scriptural allusion as he informed Mrs Braintree that at the loaf-and-fish picnic of Scripture, which was the largest which the world had ever seen, he was sure there was no question of precedence, and it was probable that every one sat upon the ground.

Mrs Braintree promptly suppressed the temptation to preach which the situation suggested, and at once proceeded, like the careful wife she certainly was, to install the Canon where the draught was not likely to touch him, and then cast about to moor Miss Fanshawe by her side.

Mr La Touche was greatly chagrined to perceive Miss Clavering in the opposite angle of the table at which he sat, bounded on her right hand by Lord Willows, and on the left by Harold Fanshawe.

What was it that caused the latter to look so supremely important all of a sudden, and at the same time appear to constitute himself as the picked body-guard of Miss Clavering?

Had Mr La Touche lingered near the rickety summer-house a little longer, he would have discovered the source of this mystery. No sooner had he been walked off out of that vicinity by Mrs Braintree, than Willina, anxious to escape, signalled to Harold Fanshawe, who was walking about very much like a desolate fowl, that he should come to her immediately. On his obeying her summons, she said, "Would you kindly get me my little red shawl out of the carriage, and, dear boy, mind you don't leave me, but sit next to me at the dinner-table. I want a change of companions, after having been so long shut up with the same people. I don't wish to be rude, but we are not obliged to be with the same party all day."

"I should just think not," said Harold; "that Mr La Touche may be a great swell, but at the same

time he is an awful bore, and I am getting tired of
the aunt myself."

"Hush!" interrupted Miss Clavering, indicating
Marcia, who had risen, and who, with her back to
this pair, was so attentively watching her nephew
and his clerical friend, that she had not even remarked
the proximity of the youth,—"hush! can we get away
now?"

"Yes; look to the right, through those laurels,—it
will take us to the shed where they are laying out the
food. It isn't lunch, you know, and it isn't dinner
exactly," continued Master Fanshawe," but there's
lots of it,—quite a jolly blow-out."

So they turned and fled, and it was really a matter
of rejoicing to Willina that she effected her escape so
happily.

It was high time, for the girl could not conceal
from herself the manifest intentions of Mr La Touche.
She had ignored these as persistently as possible during her late stay in London, and had, although against
her better judgment, agreed with Mary Leppell that
Lillian Fanshawe's engagement to Mr La Touche was
only a matter of time.

Yet, put the truth away from her as much as she
would, that instinct, which perhaps is the substitute
for the cell wanting in the brain in the feminine composition, warned her that the time was come wherein
she must listen to a declaration of love from Mr La
Touche, and that, moreover, he was only seeking an
opportunity to make the same on that very day.

Her object now was not to be left alone a single instant; and as Harold Fanshawe was, in her estimation, a boy who could be easily hoodwinked, she, with feminine astuteness, determined to make him her knight for the day, and naturally counted upon the satisfaction which this distinction would afford him for being well guarded without any one being the whit the wiser as to her reason for selecting this particular juvenile as her companion in the after-dinner stroll.

The feast was merry enough except to Percival, who now felt all the pangs of jealousy directed against Lord Willows, simply because he was a lord; and all the irritation of uncongenial propinquity against unconscious Mr Clowes, because he was not a lord but a kindly English yeoman.

Dish after dish was presented to Mr La Touche by this good man, who was under the impression that Percival was a nervous invalid who ought to be seated near his fashionable mother—for such Mr Clowes opined Marcia to be.

Miss Fanshawe, with a kind of grim composure, watched all that was going on, but was quite mistaken in her impression that Willina was trying to pit Lord Willows against Mr La Touche, for the especial benefit of the latter; and Mr Glascott, who was full of admiration for Lillian, thought how charming it was of her to devote herself so beautifully to Canon Braintree, and ensconce herself as a kind of rampart betwixt that dignitary and the wind which blew directly into the end of the thatched shed wherein they fed.

Sarah Braintree flirted with the Colonel, and sincerely lamented that the latter could not combine the functions of military chaplain with his other duties. "He had a rousing style," Sarah informed him, "and had just the voice for Gregorian chants."

The Colonel did not quite appreciate the latter part of Miss Braintree's compliment, as he had a vague idea that a Pope, or Popes, Gregory had been in existence, and that these chants were some of the "marks of the beast," proclaiming themselves in hideous howlings. So the Colonel repudiated the chants, but he thanked Sarah for introducing the subject of music, as he wanted to secure the co-operation of her mother in getting a subscription for a harmonium, which he had, it must be confessed, ordered for the soldiers' barracks at Yarne, without having a shilling to pay for it.

"You must get up a meeting," said Sarah, with promptitude; "it is a nice method for inducing people who like one another to come together."

"Yes; and for those who don't like one another also," the Colonel made answer. "But I will get speech of your mother on the subject; she is just the person I want to help in the matter, as she does her work well, and I find is putting a stop to this stupid county-*versus*-town feeling."

"Ah, you see, we have worked on the broad lines

of a London parish," replied Sarah, perhaps a trifle sententiously.

"All the better.   Just fancy that man Mompesson, now Rector of Rooke-cum-Dawe! he was for years a curate in Yarne, and lived in lodgings in Red Lion Square.   He received the greatest kindness and hospitality from the professional people and others living in Yarne, and now, forsooth, because he is a rector, he finds he cannot visit with any but the county people, and drives into the town on Saturdays with a *haut en bas* expression towards the inhabitants which is positively sickening."

"Ma will soon put an end to all that," quoth Sarah. "The fact is, that the wives of the other canons have rather fostered this sort of thing.   Ma will bring everybody to their bearings."

So Mrs Braintree would and did; but the misfortune of it was, that there was so much of the Canoness in her method of acting, that it roused rather more of resentment than respect in those who did not professionally belong to the English Church. The lawyers, doctors, and retired military were not going to submit to a female cleric; and it was only the good intentions and real sincerity of Mrs Braintree that caused her to make her way with those of her own calling.

Her one redeeming point was that she made no distinctions between the town and the county clergy; and as Colonel Leppell very truly said, she spent the income of the canonry in the town, and did good work.

Thus, after the feast was over, Colonel Leppell veri-
fied his favourable opinion of the Canon's wife. He
had a long conversation with that lady, in which
he laid all his difficulties before her, and admitted
that he had acted rashly in ordering the instrument
alluded to without having the wherewithal to defray
its cost.

Then they had a clear understanding as to how the
funds should be raised for this purpose, and Mrs
Braintree promised on her part to inaugurate a meeting at the town-hall, and work tooth and nail to get
people to attend it, or to contribute help in a pecuni-
ary form.

So far so good. The Colonel was delighted, and
undertook to sound the trumpet in the neighbouring
division of the county, Wurstede. His friend, Colonel
Guyse, who commanded there, was a tower of strength,
and would do his best to help. Then Mrs Braintree
left her host, delighted with her mission, and proceeded to look after Miss Fanshawe and Mr La
Touche.

It is at all times difficult to find persons amongst
ruins, and especially if they happen to be inclined to
seek the shade of thick foliage with which these are
generally interspersed. Dips of undulating ground,
rendered partially invisible by rounded tussocks,
which rise up abruptly at irregular distances, are not
exactly calculated to assist a searcher to discern a
distant object; whilst a layer of flint stones and small
pebbles rather invite attention to the maintenance

of the perpendicular, than supply assistance to speculations concerning the far horizon.

Total ignorance also of the topography of the country generally forms a barrier to satisfactory research, and as Mrs Braintree only succeeded in catching the sound of voices, without being able to form the slightest idea from whence it came, she resolved to turn back and trust to chance for finding a fellow-guest or a guide.

The servants and coachmen, she knew, were all dispersed in different directions, and would only come to the cottage at the hour arranged for departure.

The investigations of the Canon's wife were not, however, totally without result. She had neared a small waterfall, and as she stood admiring it, she espied Miss Fanshawe coming round a narrow path, attended, not by Mr La Touche, but by Mr Glascott. The elderly gentleman guided the young lady up a flight of wet slippery steps to gain some summit which apparently led to nowhere; and so Mrs Braintree concluded that some striking feature in the view was to be descried from that height, and she therefore left them to their enjoyment of the beauties of nature without interruption.

"Nice fatherly man," Mrs Braintree said to herself; "but where can Mr La Touche be?"

She walked on, not encountering a creature until she found herself in front of the little parlour at the side of the cottage, which was especially reserved for visitors, and which was principally used as a dressing-room for the ladies of the several expeditions to Bark-holme.

A nearer approach satisfied Mrs Braintree that she heard the sound of voices issuing from the half-opened window of that room, and she hastened forward and looked within, in order to ascertain who were its present occupants. It was scarcely a feeling of sheer curiosity that prompted her to act in this wise, but rather the determination to secure a companion, even if a stranger, for her intended exploration of the ruins.

A moment's inspection, however, satisfied her that under no plea whatever would her company be desirable ; and the scene which met her view was so ludicrous, that the good lady was fain to retire in order to freely indulge her risible faculties,—for there, perambulating the ground on his knees, was to be seen Mr La Touche, holding on to the hem of Miss Clavering's garment, and gesticulating wildly.

A long light overcoat which Percival had donned, evidently to protect himself from the draught, increased the peculiarity of his appearance, as its ends flapped against his heels in the most undignified fashion, and added greatly to the limp and prostrate spectacle which he then presented.

" Pray, pray, rise, Mr La Touche," Willina said, as her admirer stuck tight, and effectually prevented her from reaching the door. " I am sorry to cause you pain, but I cannot, I never can permit your addresses : do be reasonable, and let this occurrence pass from both our minds as if it had never been."

"I cannot!" gasped poor Percival, who really was thoroughly in earnest. "Give me time, then—do not discard me at once. I will promise anything—do anything."

"It cannot be," insisted Miss Clavering, firmly. "It is only right to say, that under no circumstances whatever could I consent to become your wife : it would be unjust to you—nay, it would be dishonest, for I could never yield you either affection or esteem."

"Then you prefer some one else—that's the real truth," snapped Percival, changing his tone; "that's the true cause."

"You have no right to say that,—no right to infer it," she answered, now really angry. "Loose your hold, sir, and let me go." As she spoke, she suddenly snatched her dress from Percival's grasp, and was out through the door in a moment of time.

As fate would have it, she encountered Miss Fanshawe, who had come to this parlour to get Mr Glascott's walking-stick, which lay in security amid some wraps there. Although the latter was rather hurried, she could not help remarking the peculiar expression of Miss Clavering's face.

"Something has happened," she said, almost involuntarily, as she looked at Willina.

"No—not exactly ; but Mr La Touche is within, quite ill, and upset—something like a fit ; but the attack will pass off. It will be better, perhaps, to leave him alone for a while."

The two young women looked at each other fixedly

as Miss Clavering made this declaration. A cold incredulous smile passed over the features of Miss Fanshawe, as, steadily maintaining her gaze, she pushed open the door and resolutely entered the parlour.

Here, with his head bowed between his hands, sat Percival, rocking with emotion. Bitter disappointment expressed itself in every line of his figure: he was too miserable then to hear or see.

Lillian stood looking at him a moment, and then retired. Had she entertained one spark of regard for this man, she would have commiserated his grief, and even felt honest anger against his fickleness.

As it was, Percival was only a good income and position lost to her. She philosophically accepted the fact; but, woman-like, she vented all her indignation upon her rival woman, and thenceforward she detested Willina Clavering with all the strength of a hard nature,—a nature that rarely forgets or forgives.

Shortly afterwards, through the management of Mrs Braintree, it was whispered that Mr La Touche had been taken ill, and that Mr Clowes had offered the sufferer a seat in his gig and driven him straight to Yarne. There was no reason, however, to alarm Marcia.

CHAPTER VIII.

AN AFTERNOON WITH A HARMONIUM.

MRS BRAINTREE had worked vigorously, and had carried her point also in getting the schoolroom of Saint Jude's Church for the meeting that was to be held for the Harmonium Fund, and in further securing many promises of attendance and support. The rector of Saint Jude's parish was thankful for the two guineas which were allotted to him for the hire of the room for one afternoon, and great was the sweeping and garnishing that went on in that apartment to make it worthy of the occasion. Colonel Leppell handsomely expressed his conviction that Mrs Braintree was not half a bad woman ; wished she would dress a little better, but allowed that under-dress was better than over-dress ; and that Sarah, in the matter of ostrich feathers, would strike terror into the heart of the most hardened Hottentot.

At present there were other matters to be considered than dress, and the Colonel fixed his attention upon what the duties of the chairman should be : in this he was ably assisted by the Canon's wife. It was a great feature in that lady's diplomacy that she had persuaded the Colonel that he could make a speech in public. "I need not remind you," said that astute manager, "that the dignity of the chair would be seriously imperilled were you to say too much, or introduce any remarks irrelevant to the matter."

"All I have got to say, at least at first, is that we have bought a splendid harmonium for the soldiers' church, and we want the audience to pay for it,—in fact, that we depend upon the collection we can squeeze out of them," replied the pupil, with a knowing look which just fell short of a wink.

"Of course you will put that into nice language," returned the lady. "But, you know, part of your business will be to introduce the speakers, and compliment them, and thank them in the name of the public for what they have said, and for the support of their personal attendance."

"And then I have got to sing out 'Hear, hear,' and 'Attention,' at some of the remarks, I know."

"It just requires a little management to time these expressions. You know your own speech will come in at the end, as there will be a vote of thanks to you for taking the chair. The great point is to press the subject of the subscription home; it would be so desirable to wipe off the cost of the harmonium, and have a sum over towards the funds of the establishment. I have thought that the harmonium should be opened by the organist, and the first two or three

pieces be played by him, to do the instrument justice;
but," continued Mrs Braintree, "the organist of the
Cathedral cannot be offered less than a guinea, and
that is rather much for one or two performances."

"He ought to play for nothing, out of respect to the
cause, and send the harmonium a subscription," said
Colonel Leppell decidedly.

"You see, Colonel, a line must be drawn, and if Mr
Westmacott were to play for every charitable purpose,
he would have little else to do : he has been tormented
by people all over the country for gratuitous musical
help, and really it is not without reason that Mr
Westmacott insists upon a fee."

"People are deuced fond of putting their charity
upon other folks," answered Colonel Leppell; "just
look how doctors are often imposed upon, and ladies
are the greatest sinners in that line. A medical man
can't come into a house but what the mistress finds out
that somebody besides the patient must have their eyes,
or their teeth, or their toes examined. But about Westmacott,—I suppose it would not do to offer him five
shillings for an overture ? You see it would be as well
to pay a professional to bring out all the tones well."

"Mr Westmacott cannot be offered less than a
guinea, Colonel."

"Well, it can't be helped. For myself, I hate harmoniums as a rule,—I would much rather have a trumpet and harp; but, of course, can't be had—though
trumpets and shawms *are* more Scriptural. King
David, you know, he always had his psalms well

accompanied. However, we may as well keep it dark that harmoniums are not mentioned in the Bible ; but could not our specimen be introduced under the general head of an instrument of music ? " And here the Colonel looked as if he had scored a very telling point by this suggestion.

Mrs Braintree agreed that this was a good idea. " There is an expression, ' all kinds of music '; but that is not of much consequence," the lady went on to say. " A harmonium is now generally accepted as a small kind of organ, and of course the make will be improved as years pass on."

" Much need," returned her visitor ; " as they now stand they make the most infer—I mean dreadful sounds, unless, perhaps, the noises which people perpetrate in singing what are called Gregorian chants be excepted. However," continued Colonel Leppell, " we must be thankful for small mercies, and my men do like something that rings warlike and strident. By the way, though, one of my fellows does play the harmonium,—I forgot all about it ; by all means let things be done decently and in order, madam," continued the officer, warming with his subject. " Private Bill Crasher in full uniform, presiding at the harmonium, will have a telling effect."

" Yes," replied Mrs Braintree ; " what can he play ? "

" Oh, ' Drops of Brandy,' and ' The British Grenadiers,' and one or two military marches, naturally."

" Anything sacred ? " inquired the lady.

"Well, there's the 'Dead March' in 'Saul.'"

"That, I think, would be scarcely suitable for a joyful and pleasant assembling together," Mrs Braintree replied. "If you have no objection, I think it will be better to have the man here and see what he can do, —and also, some kind of programme would be advisable; don't you think so?"

"Just as you please—perhaps it would be as well. But mind we must have 'See the Conquering Hero Comes,' to strike up when the Bishop enters the room; or perhaps that had better be reserved for the Bishopess,— she represents the Church militant in that direction. As for the Bishop (he's a good little soul), I really should like something special played up to glorify him. The question is, what is the most appropriate musical glorification for prelates, eh?"

"'Ecce Sacerdotus Magnus,'" struck in Sarah Braintree, who was becoming pronounced High Church; "that's a fine tune, and it would suit the harmonium."

"Ecce nonsense," replied the Colonel, who smelt Rome in the Latin words; "that is not the proper march wherewith to usher in a Protestant bishop."

"But the Church of England is really Catholic," persisted Sarah; "we are finding out that the Reformation reformed too much."

"Just you remember, my good young lady, that our Queen is the head of the Church of England, and that she by her coronation oath undertakes to back up and propagate the Protestant faith. If you want another example, remember that King Charles I., before the battle of Edgehill, summoned his army together, and in their presence stated that he accepted the Protestant reformed religion of the Church of England. I am very certain that I read this, because the address to the army drew my attention to it. No, no, don't sail under false colours; you know very well that you would not have been so keen about calling yourself a Catholic in the days of William and Mary, or even under the Georges."

The Colonel was so perfectly correct in all this, that Miss Braintree merely replied, "Then we can't have 'Ecce Sacerdotus Magnus'?"

"Not at any price," returned the Colonel; "for to be consistent, we should have the Bishop marching in vested as a Roman Catholic prelate."

"But he is coming in his everyday clothes," said Sarah.

"I suppose so, therefore there is no need for Ecce —what you call it? even if his lordship were to be arrayed in the black and white uniform,—no, gear, —get-up,—robes, I should say, of an orthodox bishop. You see, they had the sense at the Reformation to make the difference of costume mark the difference of the religion, eh?"

Not caring to be taken further into the depths of the Colonel's theology, Mrs Braintree exclaimed, "What *can* we have played when the Bishop enters? I think the Hundredth Psalm would be rather professional."

"'Praise God from whom all blessings flow'? No; they sing that when they have bagged the collection," said the Colonel, with the utmost *naïveté.* "What do you say to 'Hail, Smiling Morn'?"

"I don't quite see the point," said Mrs Braintree politely, and with difficulty suppressing a smile.

"Well, you see, 'hail' is a Scripture word, and 'smiling morn' might be taken to allude to his lordship's face. Cheerful countenance, you know,—oil-and-wine effects."

"Perhaps that might not quite suit the temperance people," said Mrs Braintree, "if that idea were to occur to any of them. Cannot you suggest something that would be decorous, and at the same time lively and not too solemn?"

"What do you think of the march in the 'Prophète'?" said Colonel Leppell, suddenly. "Fine air, and the word 'Prophète,'—just enough to give a flavour of—of—sanctity to the affair."

"Rather too military, Colonel. The Bishop is a quiet man, and is rather inclined to 'scuttle' in his manner of walking than to march. Suppose we reserve the 'Prophète' for your father, Lord Hieover. He so rarely attends meetings of this kind, that a public recognition of his presence would be very gratifying to the——"

"Harmonium!" interrupted the Colonel. "You are right—the 'Prophète' will do for the Viscount: he's not musical, and he does not know one tune from another, but it is an aristocratic march, and every one likes it."

So the fine masterpiece of Meyerbeer was set down for the glorification of Lord Hieover.

"As regards the Bishop," continued the Colonel, "do you think 'He's a Jolly Good Fellow' would be too light? It's a popular air with soldiers."

"Rather; but that would apply very well to Colonel Guyse, who is, you tell me, to address the meeting."

"True; we'll dedicate that to Guyse when he rises to speak. He *is* a jolly good fellow, and the men of the Wurstede division all like him," returned the officer.

"The Bishop has to be provided for," said Sarah, "and it is to be the first tune."

"*After* 'God save the Queen'—after that. I won't have her Majesty's tune played as a sign to clear the benches and leave the room, as is so often the case; it is not at all the proper thing. 'God save the Queen' first."

This was acceded to, and then the question of the Bishop's musical reception was earnestly ventilated. At length the conclusion was arrived at that the favourite piece, "The Heavens are Telling," would be the thing wherewith his lordship should be received,— sacred, not too personal, takes in everybody, and well adapted to the instrument.

"If Crasher can't play it, we'll ask the organist to lend us one of his apprentices. They always learn on such pieces as 'Hallelujah,' and all that," said the Colonel.

"Pupils, you mean, Colonel, not apprentices," said Mrs Braintree, deprecatingly.

"All the same. I dish up all sucking lawyers, musicians, and so forth as apprentices, and mean 'em no offence. It's an old-fashioned term, and it comes readier to me."

Mrs Braintree having vindicated the dignity of the Precinct, graciously accepted this explanation, and then went thoroughly into the arrangement of the musical programme.

"We must not make it too long, Colonel," the lady insisted with good sense; "we must not tire people."

"No, I was thinking of that," replied Colonel Leppell, who was quite submissive to Mrs Braintree so long as she agreed with him; "but there is one thing,—Basil Sheepshanks must be asked to speak: good man, done lots of good, but he is awful at a speech. We must have him, for he is coming all the way from Wurstede-cum-Woolley to be present at this meeting."

"What does he do?" inquired Mrs Braintree sharply, who had not hitherto enjoyed the privilege of listening to the oratory of this gentleman from Wurstede-cum-Woolley.

"Do!" replied the Colonel viciously; "it's what he does *not* do, ma'am, that is so trying to an audience. He hesitates, stops, loses the thread of his discourse, never tries to raise the interest of the ladies, and when he comes to the end of his speech, one never knows what he has been talking about. It's a thousand pities, for a nicer fellow never breathed, nor a more thoroughbred gentleman; but he *will* speak, or rather bleat, in public, and it drives me wild to listen to him."

"Mr Sheepshanks," said Mrs Braintree thoughtfully, " is he not the gentleman who has done so much good, and built a seminary for poor homeless boys in the neighbouring county ? "

" That's he. Sheepshanks founded ' Scamp College,' as I call it, and his heart and soul is in it; in fact, he spends all the money his wife and her mother and the butler allow him to have of his own patrimony on it. He comes in a good fourth in his own household; but what's the odds ? he is happy, and Scamp College is a success."

" What about his speech ? " said Mrs Braintree, bringing the Colonel back to the point.

" You see, Sheepshanks is apt to make long gaps and sobs between his sentences, and he hesitates a good deal also. I think some air might be played in spasms—gently, which would draw off the attention of the public from my friend's little defects."

" Do you think Mr Sheepshanks would like that ? " inquired Mrs Braintree, with a suspicion of doubt in her tone.

" He ought to like it, and be thankful. Besides, there's an opportunity of showing the unrivalled touches which this instrument is capable of producing. Put it before Sheepshanks that he would act as an advertisement to the cause, and we have him. These little harmonies need not be intrusive, you know," continued the Colonel; "just melodious chords swept with a light hand."

" Mr Crasher would not be equal to that kind of

manipulation, would he?" inquired Sarah, with a grin.

"Perhaps not. I'll rout up some lady; or you might assist in that way yourself, Miss Braintree." This the Colonel said with some emphasis, for he fancied he detected a disposition towards levity in Sarah's suggestion, backed up as it was by the grin.

Some other selections of music were named, and the programme was filled with great care, Mrs Braintree wisely keeping a restraining power upon its length.

"So far, so good. Now for the British army in general all the world over, without which you parsons and traders of all grades would have to sing uncommonly small. We will have 'Rule, Britannia,' for the last, and the 'Girl he left behind him,' or perhaps the 'British Grenadiers,' as the lively movement to follow. That will finish the whole thing up splendidly." And the Colonel, in his enthusiasm, very nearly clapped Mrs Canon Braintree on the back as he spoke.

That lady, meanwhile, accepted "Rule, Britannia," with alacrity; but she made a mental reservation to erase the two last-named *morceaux* from the list as soon as the Colonel's back was turned. "He will never miss these in the excitement," thought she; "and if the worst comes to the worst, Mr Bill Crasher will be accountable. We must get in the Doxology somewhere at the end."

Colonel Leppell soon afterwards took his leave, after arranging that Mr Crasher should come to the

Colonel's office, where the harmonium was in waiting, and display his prowess on that instrument. The soldier did not appear to be particularly elated at this prospect when communicated with by his commanding officer; but there was nothing else for Mr Crasher to do than salute the Colonel, and inquire the time when he should be in attendance.

"To-morrow morning, ten o'clock sharp—just to go over the pieces, you know. Several amateurs will help at the meeting; but I want you to play the greater part of the military selections, and you had better take a turn at them in private. Westmacott opens with an overture and 'God Save the Queen.'"

"Very well, Colonel, I will do my best." And so the man departed, wishing that he were well through with it, and resolving, like the good fellow that he was, to do his utmost to show off the powers of the harmonium in the best style possible.

The practice that followed being, after the usual difficulties that usually attend such endeavours, successfully overcome, the harmonium was conveyed to St Jude's schoolroom, and there displayed to the greatest advantage. Mr Westmacott had turned out "trumps," as Colonel Leppell expressed it, for he had undertaken to play "God Save the Queen" and a short overture, without fee or reward; and, what was more gratifying still, this gentleman had declared that he offered his services out of respect to the military of the town and county of Yarne and Wurstede.

"Just fancy that from the Cathedral organist," said

the staff-officer of pensioners in ecstasy to his friend
and ally, Colonel Guyse, of Wurstede. "Depend upon
it, we shall break up the miserable little cliqueyness
of the conventional cathedral town before long, by a
strong introduction of the military element. I look
upon Westmacott very much in the light of a conversion,—indeed I do. Why, sir, a few years ago, Westmacott would have declared that he proferred his
services out of respect to the Bishop's wife."

"But you have asked the Bishop's wife to be present
at the meeting?" said Colonel Guyse. "I suppose she
would be reckoned as the first lady of the town?"

"I fancy the mayor's wife would claim precedence,
strictly speaking, but I am not sure, and it don't
matter. I have asked the Bishop to bring his wife and
lady friends, just as I have asked Mr Smiles the baker
to bring his wife, who is a fine-looking woman, and
very nicely mannered,—far more of a lady than——"

"Never mind," said Colonel Guyse; "don't be drawing comparisons. Now let us see what I am to do.
How many men am I to bring up from Wurstede?"

"Bring up as many as you can, and let them be the
pick of the lot. That Sergeant Armstrong for one, he
might be Goliath of Gath; and you have a couple of
nice lads among the drums, just of a size,—they would
look well stationed at each side of the entrance-doors,
with plates in their hands, to collect the cash. All
the women like the look of a pretty boy, especially if
he be in uniform."

Colonel Guyse grinned, but wisely held his peace;

and the two fell into ways and means, and parted in much mutual admiration. "Ralph is a queer fellow," thought Colonel Guyse as he walked down the street, "but he is thoroughly in earnest. I believe he would go through fire and water for his men, and I do hope this meeting of his will go off well."

There was every chance of it, for when the day arrived the sun shone gladly; and there was such a muster of military, retired and otherwise, that the streets of Yarne glowed with colour, and the old time-worn houses of its narrow ways seemed to laugh out-right as their brown and venerable faces were flapped by the flags which streamed out from their diamond-paned casements. Carriages from the country, laden with ladies and pretty children and flowers, poured in hourly; and everybody went to lunch with everybody else,—a general feeling of amusement being mixed up with the universal sympathy with Ralph and his cause.

That gallant officer drove in from Blythe, his famous rakish-looking coach being literally crammed inside and outside with handsome young faces of both sexes,—all of them ready to swear that day that, after all, there was no better man than their governor. The four horses went so well, that Dick gravely asserted that their instinct must have impressed the fact upon the whole team that they were going to a special meeting wherein decorum was the pervading element. Lord Hicover actually had come out to Blythe from the hotel whereat he usually put up, in a nice little

carriage drawn by a pair of ponys, in order to fetch
Adelaide, and to convey her in peace and quiet, as the
Viscount said, "to the scene of action." A respectable-
looking groom attended this vehicle, which the old
soldier of eighty years drove himself, and drove
well.

Alick wandered about the town, looked approvingly
on all, and then lunched at the Braintree's hospitable
table. He afterwards went and changed a sovereign
(buying a quire of writing-paper as an excuse), taking
care to have the principal part of the change in
shilling pieces. One crown he put aside carefully,
reserving it for the collection should he be specially
moved to extravagant expenditure; but if a shilling
would pass muster, Alick resolved to bestow that coin
and no more on what he considered to be a whimsy
of his brother Ralph.

As the hands of the town clock veered towards the
hour of two, the little playground which surrounded
St. Jude's schoolroom was filled with an unwonted
company—to wit, a number of the pensioners drawn
up in a square, and their band playing "Hearts of
Oak" with a vigour and *timbre* enough to electrify
a tortoise. Soldiers in different uniforms, amongst
which that of the Yeomanry Cavalry of Yarneshire
predominated, perambulated the streets in all directions, and finally concentrated themselves into the
playground, waiting respectfully till the company
should assemble and file up the staircase which led
to the schoolroom, and which, prettily decorated and

well arranged as to space, was very soon closely packed with a goodly assembly,—the harmonium occupying the floor in front of the platform, and nearly *vis-à-vis* to the first row of seats. Mrs Braintree had taken care that the first chair on the left of this row should be reserved for the occupation of the Bishop's wife. This lady soon arrived, bringing her husband under her wing, and as soon as that gentle and good dignitary ascended the platform, the meeting was opened with the formalities usual at the like gatherings. After a little whispering and polite "asiding," Ralph was moved to the chair, wherein he shone resplendent, and made the Bishop look very much like his own private chaplain.

Then Mr Westmacott, at a sign from the chairman, played "God Save the Queen;" but as the whole audience liberally contributed a hearty vocal *obligato* to this fine air, it cannot be said that the merits of the harmonium could be fairly represented by the first trial. "The Heavens are Telling," which followed, gave, however, the fullest evidence that the harmonium was equal to any fair requirement of its powers; and as this piece had turned into the "overture," which was especially intended for the glorification of the Bishop, his lordship came forward and avowed his conviction that he only expressed the opinion of those present, when he emphatically declared that Colonel Leppell deserved the thanks of the community at large for introducing this noble instrument of music. Nor did he forget to mention the great discrimination which that gallant officer had displayed in the selection of this article—"for," said the Bishop, as he concluded his address, "we all know there are harmoniums and harmoniums."

Then came a speech from Colonel Guyse, which was much applauded, as that favourite officer of the Wurstede Militia expatiated upon the right of the soldiers to have good music in their barrack chapel, and the privilege which it must be to the inhabitants of Yarne and its neighbourhood to be invited to pay for it. During this address Mr Westmacott, having another engagement, went his way, generously leaving a sovereign in the plate as he passed through the door.

It was now Mr Crasher's turn to "preside at the instrument;" and as that good fellow took his seat, the knowledge that he was nearly opposite the Bishop's wife did not tend to raise his self-confidence, knowing, as he did, that the ear and eye of a severe amateur were upon him. He, however, pulled himself together under the benign smile with which Mrs Canon Braintree greeted his appearance; and he played a few chords with the desperate audacity which often electrifies timid people into action when they find themselves in situations from whence escape is impossible. The piece to be now played was the march from the "Prophète;" and as this was intended to compliment Lord Hieover especially, Mrs Braintree, with a view to awakening that nobleman to his responsibilities, poked him on the arm to draw his attention to the performance. The Viscount, who had forgotten all about it, and not having the faintest idea of what the Canon's wife would be at, thought it was required of him to back up Mr Crasher, and so called out, "Very good, ver—ry good; go on, my man!"

This, as it proved, was easier said than done. Crasher had played about four bars of the march, when, to his own amazement as well as to the consternation of the company, the instrument suddenly took matters into its own hands, and precipitated itself into the depths of the Hundredth Psalm without the faintest sign of hesitation or compromise. "Not that now!" called out Colonel Leppell,—"a little later on, please: don't you see that the thing from the 'Prophète' comes on next?" Despite this reminder, the air of the Hundredth Psalm resounded in all its fulness to the very end,—the unfortunate Crasher meanwhile pulling out and driving in sundry stops, in order to reduce the instrument to silence. A suggestion, emanating from Mrs Braintree, ran along the line of the front-row seats, and was whispered to Mr Crasher,—"Take your feet off the sounding-board, and push in all the stops." This the performer, purple in the face from annoyance and discomfiture, immediately proceeded to do, but his efforts were fruitless, and the harmonium was now in full swing for the Austrian Hymn. Every one looked towards "the chair," the occupant of which was speechless from amazement.

Mr Sheepshanks came to the rescue, and assured the audience that this *contretemps* was only the matter

of a few moments ; the instrument would soon run
itself out, &c., &c. Meanwhile he would suggest to
Colonel Leppell that Mr Stokes might be invited to
address the meeting. That gentleman, he believed,
had promised to contribute a paper upon organs from
their invention to the latest time. Here Mr Sheepshanks amiably remarked that now was the fitting
time for Mr Stokes to ventilate the matter, and he
expressed himself convinced that the knowledge
that Mr Stokes possessed of the subject would
eventuate in " a lucid ex — ex — planation of
the peculiar conduct of the instrument before them,
which he would designate as a—a—musical va—
vagary."

Mr Stokes scowled at Mr Sheepshanks, and was
about to reply " that he was not going to lecture in
such a din," when the harmonium changed tune again,
and wailed out the melancholy psalm known as " St
Bride's," the words of the psalm being, " From lowest
depths of woe." This was too much for the audience ;
the whole assemblage literally shouted with laughter,
and nobody seemed to enjoy the fun more than did
the Bishop, who, in a gentle " aside," proposed to
Colonel Guyse to have the instrument removed.
" Just give it another chance," said " the chair," to
whom this suggestion had been conveyed ; " it *can't*
go on for ever—confound it : and Sheepshanks, do say
something to keep things going—a word here and
there. Tell 'em about the effect of music on Sca——
your industrial place ; *do*, there's a good fellow ! "

Mr Sheepshanks, who was a good fellow in every sense of the term, complied; and as the tune then at work was in a low minor key, he succeeded in making himself audible. And whether it was from the stimulus of the excitement, or from the protection of the accompaniment, certain it is that Mr Sheepshanks delivered himself of a capital address, and was never known to hesitate as little in his speech. He received a regular ovation; and as the harmonium had now entered upon the "Portuguese Hymn," he sensibly proposed that the meeting should turn itself into a sacred concert, and that all should stand up and sing, "O come, all ye faithful." The audience heartily concurred, and the proposition was acted upon with the greatest celerity, great fear being exhibited lest the harmonium should get too much ahead, and have it out before the first verse was well through. The air being a popular one, it was twice repeated, and so the "Portuguese Hymn" went with a will. The sweet "Sicilian Mariner's Hymn" followed, and this too the harmonium graciously repeated.

During the singing of this last, Ralph's mind was greatly exercised as to what to do with Mr Stokes. "He *must* read his paper, and in peace," whispered he to Colonel Guyse, who stood near him. "Stokes has come a long way to oblige me. He's a highly scientific man—don't care a rush for psalm-singing. He's looking as black as thunder. What shall we do?"

"Tell off three or four men, and have the thing put

into the playground at once," replied Colonel Guyse, practically.

Then Ralph rose to his feet, and made it known to the assembly that he was not the man to deprive them of the benefit of the able and scientific address which Mr Stokes, of half the literary societies under heaven, was there expressly to deliver—"*the* scientific address of the programme, in fact" (here Mr Stokes bowed, and his stern visage relaxed into a grin). As the harmonium could not be quenched, continued the Colonel, he would request their patience for a few minutes, whilst the offending instrument was conveyed into the playground below.

Three men, at a signal from Colonel Guyse, at once lifted the harmonium away, headed by Mr Crasher, who had been privately enjoined to keep watch and ward over this treasure in the place of its deportation; and then Mr Stokes came forward and delivered an able and very interesting short lecture on "Sounding Instruments," from the first organ on record, unto the apparently unmanageable specimen which even then was testifying its powers beneath the rug which, in order to deaden its sounds, some one had thrown over it. Notwithstanding this precaution, the breeze wafted the subdued strains of the tune on hand through the open window.

Mr Stokes then explained that some harmoniums were constructed with a barrel within, which, being wound up and set for a certain number of tunes, could be used like a chamber-organ, without any touch of the hand whatsoever. "It is possible," he said, "that our friend has been wound up, but the works being new and stiff, they have not got themselves into proper action until the manipulations of the performers, and possibly the drawing out of the various stops, had loosened the machinery, and set the interior mechanism agoing." This, on closer inspection, proved to be the case; and Colonel Leppell discovered, to his great delight, that the instrument, which was the object at once of so much solicitude and annoyance, was really a most valuable acquisition.

As Mr Stokes concluded, the harmonium below struck up the Doxology in its loudest and most strident tones. To step down from the platform, and roar out at the window, "Take off that rug immediately!" was but the work of a moment for Colonel Leppell. "Now let's have the Doxology with the full benefit of the harmonium accompaniment," said he, addressing the meeting. "I am sure our friends will give as heartily as they can sing; and so here goes— 'Praise God, from whom all blessings flow.' The plates will be handed round, ladies and gentlemen; the plan saves a crush at the door, and I believe the collection will benefit by free circulation."

The pretty drummer-boys then handed the plates to every individual present, whilst the Doxology was being sung with stentorian emphasis and expression, —the harmonium graciously going over the tune to the extent of three verses.

The collection was soon gathered, and the plates

containing the money were placed on a little table which stood on the platform immediately in front of the chair. Then a vote of thanks to the chairman was proposed. This passed with all the honours; and then Colonel Leppell rose to his feet and delivered his valedictory speech—a speech so characteristic and so remarkable, that for years afterwards it was remembered as the very pith and salt of the oratory which had been poured forth on the occasion of the Harmonium Fund meeting at Yarne.

"It was impossible," the Colonel said, "to give adequate expression to the feelings of pride and elation which animated his whole being as he looked round and surveyed such an assemblage of beauty, learning, talent, and excellence, which he might say, in the language of King Solomon, encompassed him about on every side. Haw!—yes, it was a good meet, a very good meet, and he had no doubt that a nearer acquaintance with the collection would entirely confirm this happy impression. Whilst referring to this last most important subject, he would ask one of his friends to reckon up the amount in the plates whilst he read out a list of donations which had been sent to him by persons who could not attend the meeting. Here they were: First, Mr and Mrs Summerbell, two guineas. These good farmers, you see, although they are always abusing the times and the weather, can stump up handsomely at a pinch. Secondly, old Mr Kingsford of the Bays, one pound. It might have been more, but he is a worthy good friend. ('Hear, hear,' from

Colonel Guyse, vigorously, who sought to smother the first observation relative to this donation.)

"Now comes a noble gift—ten pounds from the old wo——lady, I mean, at Catalonia, Miss Elmore. She's a trump, that old ca——lady, for she always helps the soldiers; and though she never stirs abroad, her presence is always felt, my dear friends—felt by her good deeds—haw—hum—good deeds—doing good works, and never talking about 'em. People do wrong to run down old maids; they are great helps and blessings in the aggregate. God bless 'em all, both rich and poor. ('Hear, hear,' from the Bishop.) Here, again, is a most generous gift, although the amount is small—ten shillings and sixpence from the Reverend Abbé Rousé, Roman Catholic priest, with thanks to Colonel Leppell for allowing the Catholic soldiers to attend mass so regularly. Now I call this a large-hearted, kind, unsolicited act; and I should just like to hear any one running down the Abbé to me—I'd make it hot for 'em. ('Trust you for that, Colonel,' roared a voice from the door.) Well, here is one pound from the head huntsman of the Y. V. H., who can't be here because he is down with rheumatism—haw. I am sure you will all wish this good Christian many a run over the country yet. Now here come two pounds and sevenpence, collected in pence, and two shillings and sixpence from an individual who signs himself a 'Converted Cobbler.' Wish he had given me his address; we might have all put a little shoe-mending in his way. However, he brings up the rear of the special donations. Now let us see what the collection amounts to."

A slip of paper was handed to the speaker, who, with a face radiant with satisfaction, announced that the munificent sum of eighty-three pounds nine shillings had been contributed by the assemblage there present.

"Whilst expressing my warm thanks to all for this generous help," the Colonel went on to say, "I should be wanting in gratitude—haw—gratitude and common courtesy, did I not specially thank my fellow-worker, Mrs Canon Braintree, for the assistance she has rendered me in this business. This good lady deserves a vote of thanks, for she sticks to her work all round, and keeps residence, and spends the income—or Canon Braintree's income, it's all the same —in the place, a virtue which has not always been practised; but that is neither here nor there. Mrs Braintree has devoted the best part of her life to pious—pious—well, pious begging; and to her honour it may be said that there is no better manager in the way of getting money out of people's pockets—in fact, she has grown grey in the service."

Here no one could repress a smile, for Mrs Braintree wore a coffee-coloured front, which was as often awry as not, and which was certainly innocent of any attempt at imposition; so she naturally swelled with indignation as the Colonel repeated with triumphant elation: "Yes, grown grey in the service; and the inhabitants of Yarne were to be congratulated on such an acquisition. The wife of a Canon of Yarne Cathedral going about among the poor, and doing her duty as any other clergyman's wife, was a refreshing sight, and long might this worthy woman be spared to fill the post she represented so well."

"What about the Canon?" called out a voice from the lower end of the room.

Ralph glared at the spot from whence this irreverent inquiry proceeded, but not being able to discover the offender, he determined to leave personalities alone, and proceeded to conclude his peroration with what he intended to be an overwhelming tribute to the ladies in general.

"I cannot conclude," the Colonel said, "without tendering my warmest thanks to the ladies for their presence here to-day. They have given a warmth and brightness to this meeting, and have made up for any—haw—any disappointment which the harmonium may have occasioned. Without the aid of the ladies, this wonderful instrument could never have been purchased; and I am sure I express the opinion of every man here, when I say that without them life would be without music—haw—and—haw —veal without salt. The women are the working-bees of humanity, adding honey to the wax; they are the flowers in our path of life, and without them— without them—haw—without them, not a man of us would be here!"

Three rattling cheers for the ladies and Colonel Leppell, and one for everybody else, were the spontaneous results of this last speech, and Colonel Leppell descended from the platform covered with glory. The "meeting," meanwhile, poured out of the room and down the staircase, making directly for the harmonium, which, divested of its rug, stood very much like an unrepentant sinner in the middle of the playground.

Orders had been given that this recreant instrument should be conveyed at once in a cart to the barracks; but although it was popularly supposed to be pumped out, it did not allow itself to be lifted into that vehicle without displaying a parting evidence of its vitality. Just as it was being hoisted from the ground, it emitted so hideous a squeak that the men employed to convey it away nearly dropped it from sheer terror. A stop had been inadvertently left out, and the sounding-board being pressed in lifting the instrument towards the cart, these had conjointly caused the noise, which, for the nonce, had seriously startled the bystanders. At length, amid laughter and cheers, it was safely deposited in the cart; some branches of laurel, which had decorated the schoolroom, were thrown over it, and the vehicle was bowled away in great force by two youngsters, who drove at a slashing pace, and finally discharged their cargo at the barracks, with the valedictory parting that they " wished that blessed harmonium would do 'em much good, and never take to squeaking when Colonel Leppell was preaching."

CHAPTER IX.

THE ANGEL OF DEATH.

"ADELAIDE," said Lord Hieover, after the universal greetings and hand-shakings had somewhat subsided, "I don't want to attend this dinner which the officers of Yarne are giving to their brethren of Wurstede, and, what is more, I won't attend it. The fact is, I hate public dinners, and I am feeling my age also. Will you think me very intrusive if I ask you to allow me to return to Hunter's Lodge with you, and remain the night there? I can drive you back, and Alick and Ralph can make my excuses, or perhaps I had better write a note at the hotel. Can you make room for me?"

"Most willingly," answered the Viscount's daughter-in-law, who, it had been universally remarked, had not looked so handsome for years as she then looked. Mrs Leppell was not only becomingly attired, but her cheek was tinged with a faint soft bloom, and an un-wonted animation brightened her features.

"Make room for you? most willingly," she repeated,

in answer to his lordship. "You know that our accommodation is by no means luxurious. Ralph will be as delighted as I am, when he knows that you are staying beneath our roof."

"But about that horrid coach, and the people that came in it," said the old gentleman, in dread that he might be brought in contact with that vehicle, or still worse, with some of it's occupants,—"does it return to Blythe?"

"Ralph arranged with Mr Langton that he should drive the coach back, and deposit the seat-holders at their several homes. I hope you will not object to Clara coming with us in the pony carriage. I don't like her to return among that wild crew without her father."

"You are quite right. Henderson can get a horse from the hotel, and ride after us with my dressing things. Ralph, I take it, makes his toilet at the barracks?"

"Yes; he always does so when he dines in town."

"Well, we will have a quiet little dinner together, which I shall enjoy thoroughly. The crush and heat of that room have made me long to get into your sweet garden again. Allow me to bring some fish; it can easily be put under the seat of the carriage without inconveniencing anybody."

The pleasure conferred by the homeliness of this proposition, together with its being so totally unexpected, imparted a vivacity to Mrs Leppell's manner which of late years had rarely been witnessed. She acquiesced in the arrangement with thanks and her brightest smile; yet the water glistened in her glorious eyes from the intensity of her feelings. Her husband's father, for the first time for a lengthened period, had addressed her by her Christian name, and had proposed to come as a guest under their roof; surely there was going, at the last, to be peace and forgiveness amongst all the members of the house of Hieover. Was not her heart still palpitating at the remembrance of the affectionate nod and smile with which Ralph had greeted her as he descended from the platform, amid the ringing cheers which were excited, perhaps, more as a recognition of his earnest goodwill than as a tribute either to his oratory or to his tact? The combination of these auspicious circumstances certainly caused Mrs Leppell to feel happier and more hopeful than she had done for many a long day; and so she gathered her young daughter and her purchases into the little carriage, called at the confectioner's as a precaution against her cook, and then drove to the hotel, where she picked up the Viscount, and so happily back to her own home.

Shortly after the little dinner had come off, Adelaide found herself walking in the garden with her father-in-law's arm within her own, discoursing of those terrible ways and means, which had been the lions in her path during the whole length of her married life. The Viscount first spoke of Duke; his language was decided but not unkind. "The restraint

Duke was now under was the best thing for him,"
said Lord Hieover; "and after all, the running away
with an heiress was no moral sin. He hoped much
from the young wife; and he declared himself disposed
to think well of her from the way in which she had
worked not only to remain with Duke, but also to give
up her income for his use. "Foolish thing to do, of
course," commented the Viscount, "but still, it shows
that the girl is thoroughly unselfish. I hate your
calculating, worldly wise young people."

Adelaide listened in silence, pondering on the sad-
dest part of Duke's career, hoping, perhaps, that his
moral sins might never be laid bare in the grandfather's sight. She was, however, thankful when the
subject was turned in the direction of her other son
Dick.

"He is a fine lad," the Viscount said,—"a very fine
lad, and it is time he went to another school. Rugby,
I should say; good discipline there, and no nonsense.
Now if you like, I will undertake to keep Dick at
Rugby for three years, paying all expenses. Don't
thank me, consult Ralph; it will do if you let me
know in a week. I feel that my days are numbered,
and it is high time that something should be done
for the younger members of the family. I have left
Ralph an annuity; it is the wiser and the better
course. You know well, though you are too good
to admit it, that if Ralph had ten thousand a-year,
he would spend twenty thousand. It may be a satisfaction to you to be assured that I have made some

provision for him, and also that you and your children have not been forgotten."

She could not reply: she could only press the old man's arm, and inwardly bless the Father of all who had so touched the springs of benevolence in the Viscount's heart. The manner of the bequest was, perhaps, quite as grateful to her as the bequest itself: be that as it may, a load heavy as lead was at one stroke lifted from off her mind. The sigh which she heaved was a sigh of relief, and the tears which she could not quite restrain were tears of happiness,—the drops which the sun of human kindness had turned to dew.

A little after ten o'clock the Viscount retired, saying, as he was about to do so—"What about Ralph? who is waiting up for him?"

"I shall do so this evening," Mrs Leppell answered, "for Ben Rifles has been sent into Yarne to help wait at the dinner. It is seldom that I sit up alone, but I shall do so to-night, as Ralph is sure not to be late: so many of the guests will have to get away by the last mail, that the Colonel must needs return early for lack of company almost."

"After my man has finished with me, he may as well sit up. I don't like to think that you will be waiting alone," Lord Hieover replied.

"Don't trouble about that; it will be only an hour or so at latest, and Ralph has the dog-cart, a fast mare, and Ben Rifles. The latter is a great help," she said with a smile; "he manages Ralph so well, and never lets him stay late at dinners if he can help it. I have several things to do before I go to bed, and so time will not press heavily. Good night, sir; thank you heartily for making this day a red-letter day to me."

"God bless you, my dear daughter," was the reply. "Good night: if Ralph is late, just go to bed and trust to somebody hearing the bell. Good night once more."

Mrs Leppell soon afterwards went to her mother's room, and saw that both invalid and nurse were in their beds, and, as she thought, quietly at rest. Thinking that Lady Asher was asleep, she, after looking at her for some moments, moved softly away; but the old lady called her back, and putting out her hand, drew her daughter towards her. "Kiss me, my dear," she said; "you look so well—so like what you were when you were a girl. God bless you, Adelaide; you are a good dutiful daughter."

Leaving her mother's room with this benison on her head, Mrs Leppell made her way to the rooms where her boys and girls were sleeping,—stooping over them, yearning over them, but through great love not touching them. "Poor darlings!" she murmured; "they are hot and tired, and are so restless that a feather-touch might rouse them. God bless them!" Then she sped to the nursery rooms above, where her little children, fresh and open-mouthed, slept soundly and well. These she covered and kissed tenderly, standing by their cribs, and wondering if the angels in heaven could be fairer and sweeter than they. Then back to the drawing-room, where she stood some minutes before an exquisite crayon portrait of Mary Clavering. "My heavenly Moll! Ah, will your life be happy?" she whispered, "so gentle, so loving as you are. Ah no, I cannot, I will not think that sorrow can touch you: to God's keeping I wholly commit you, my dear, dear Mary." Taking a tea-rose from a vase, and holding it close to her and caressing it as if she folded her daughter in her arms, she sat down in a low chair to think, and from thinking she fell a-dreaming till all things were lost to her remembrance.

Two hours later Lord Hieover's attendant was aroused by hearing Colonel Leppell's voice outside the house, loudly expressing wonder that no one had answered the summons at the bell. Knowing that his father was in the house, the Colonel did not in consequence employ his usual emphatic and per-emptory language, nor stamp about, nor hammer on the door with his whip, as he possibly would have done had Hunter's Lodge held none but its usual inmates. Still the appeals at the bell were vigorous, and as no response came, Mr Henderson, who had been aroused easily, in consequence of sleeping in a strange bed, concluded to think that Mrs Leppell, having been kept up longer than she expected, had retired to her room, and left her husband's admission to chance. Consequently the man hastened to open the front door, begging the Colonel, as he did so, to enter as quietly as possible,—"for his lordship," he said, "if startled out of his first sleep, seldom rested again till daybreak."

"I suppose Mrs Leppell has gone to bed," said the Colonel, under his breath. "No, she must be in the drawing-room, I see a light there,—unless the lamp has been left burning for me." As he spoke, he strode through the hall and entered the room.

His first act was to turn the light of the lamp to its full strength, just looking cursorily about, evidently not expecting to find his wife there. It was her usual custom to leave a light for him in one of the sitting-rooms, on those occasions when her husband would probably return through the stables, or be admitted by an outdoor servant.

Suddenly the bright colour of her evening dress caught his eye, and thus attracted, he exclaimed, "Why, Adelaide, asleep, old woman? Here I am, safe and sound; come, wake up, and let us be off to bed—it's past twelve o'clock!"

The rigidity of her figure and the stony silence alarmed him. "Adelaide," he said, in a low frightened tone, advancing close to her, "are you ill? What's this? Rouse up, I tell you, Adelaide."

His words appeared to drop harshly one by one, for Colonel Leppell was one of the number of those people who become angry in proportion as they become frightened. This lasted but a moment; he looked again, then touched her hand as it lay on her lap with the tea-rose clasped tightly within the fingers. That touch told all the tale,—Ralph knew that his wife was dead.

How he got back into the hall and fell there prone to the earth, he never remembered,—never knew that, ere consciousness left him, a strange wild sobbing cry, a summons for help, burst from his lips, which awoke many of the household in terror, and brought Ben Rifles (who had been outside sitting in the dog-cart awaiting final orders) like lightning into the house, to cast himself down by his side and wrench open the fastenings of his dress. Never had he discerned his old father, more grey than pale, bending over him with horror-stricken gaze, feebly inquiring what all this might mean ; and the old man's faithful attendant gently alluring him away from the place wherein Death was master. Never perceived he that Prothero, with the vigilance and intuition of much experience, had darted from the room of her mistress, in the full conviction that her fears entertained for some time past were now suddenly and most painfully realised, and that something was very wrong with Mrs Leppell. The woman just looked at the Colonel as he lay on the hall-floor, walked straight into the drawing-room, and went up and stood in the presence of the dead.

" Poor darling ! " she said, in a broken voice ; " dear, sweet lady, she has left us. I am not surprised, Mr Henderson, — I have long expected this. Ah yes, disease of the heart has done it."

The terrified Henderson, who had followed Mrs

Prothero into the room, begged her to advise him
how to act. "The Viscount won't leave his son," he
whispered,—" he thinks he is in a dangerous fit. I
dare not tell him Mrs Leppell is dead; and we must
keep him out of this room.

Prothero glanced into the hall, where the Viscount
and Ben Rifles were still engaged, the one tending,
the other watching over, the now motionless form of
Colonel Leppell. She turned the lamp partially down,
and then, with Henderson's assistance, placed the cold
dead body on a sofa and reverently covered the face:
they came out together, and Prothero locked the door.

Going straight to Lord Hieover, she begged him to
return to his room, for she had something to say to
him. "The Colonel will recover soon," she said, "and
Ben must drive into Yarne at once for the doctor: Mr
Henderson, I am sure, will raise the Colonel into a sitting position and attend to him." Then she drew the
poor old Viscount into his room and told him all.

It seemed abrupt, but it was the right thing to do.
Alarmed as Lord Hieover naturally was, the knowledge of the real truth explained of itself the reason
of this sudden seizure; and though he persisted in
returning to watch his son, the vague expression of
alarm and apprehension had vanished from his face.
Further assistance being summoned, Colonel Leppell
was with great difficulty undressed and placed on his
father's bed; the anxiety concerning his state materially assisted in diverting the Viscount's mind from
the terrible calamity which had befallen the family.

Indeed, in fussing about in a half distracted manner, and seriously impeding Mrs Prothero and Henderson in their good offices, the Viscount contracted a fixed idea that his visit at that time to Hunter's Lodge was a special guiding of Providence, and further, was fully persuaded that nothing could be done without his advice and aid.

Pass we over in the silence of sympathy the surprise which fell upon all, both far and near, when the reason for the mourning aspect of Hunter's Lodge was given abroad. The frantic grief of the children, the dumb stricken sorrow of the older folk, the lamentations of the servants, as they wondered how the house was to get on in the future,—it was all so sincere and so sad, that those outside this sorrow felt it kinder, for a while at least, to keep away.

"He giveth his beloved sleep," said good Mr Fane, as he strove to comfort the bereaved shrinking mother; and then he went to the grandfather and reminded him of Mary and Mr Clavering. "Shall I telegraph for them?" he inquired; "it will break the child's heart if she is not in time to see her mother once more. What is their address?"

No one knew. The last letter had announced that they were going into some out-of-the-way place in Styria; none could say what the address was, and all were ignorant of the whereabouts of the letter which contained this information. A conjecture was hazarded that it might be permissible to search the Colonel's den; but even in this misery it was thought better to wait and see if Colonel Leppell would be in a condition to issue his own orders; if this were impossible, then Lord Hieover must act. Uncle Alick had been sent for, but he had gone to Wurstede with Colonel Guyse.

The lapse of a few hours brought return of sense to Colonel Leppell, in so far as the full comprehension of what had occurred, together with the responsibilities which his sudden bereavement had cast upon him, were concerned; but as to any active management or capability of issuing orders, he was as helpless as the youngest child in the nursery above.

He seemed to entertain absolute horror of burying his wife. She was dead, that he knew and understood; but she was in the house still, and near him. To carry her away and hide her in the earth, out of his sight for evermore! it must not be done—it was not to be spoken of. And so, declining all comfort, he turned his face to the wall; and refusing all solace, he mourned bitterly.

Thus two days passed wearily away. Alick Leppell had come post-haste to Hunter's Lodge, and wisely persuaded his father to return to his home,—for the first excitement being over, the old man was beginning to miss his accustomed comforts, and to become querulous and discontented. The manner of the former was so kind towards Clara, that the girl began to think that Uncle Alick had been sadly misrepresented and misunderstood: she, however, could not persuade her father to admit his brother to his presence.

"I will come again the day after to-morrow," said Mr Leppell, in answer to Clara's expressions of regret. "Poor Ralph hardly knows what he is about, I daresay; he will look up in a few hours. Tell him I have persuaded the Viscount to return to Hieover."

The imperative necessities of the situation, however, demanded that Colonel Leppell should exert himself. Mrs Braintree had called and declared that the Colonel must be roused, and even offered to stay at Hunter's Lodge and direct matters till some of the female relatives could arrive. This threat had a very pronounced effect, for as soon as Mrs Braintree's propositions in the guise of a message reached Ralph's ears, he was stimulated into decided and vigorous action.

"I'll have no woman ordering and directing here," said he. "I suppose Mrs Braintree thinks, because I allowed her head in the harmonium business, that she is going to reign supreme in my house. She's a very good person, no doubt, but I don't like your managing clergywomen. My compliments, and say I am much obliged, but my daughter and Mrs Prothero are quite sufficient for my needs, with a lady for whom I am going to send; and mind, don't let in any more visitors." So saying, the widower shot into his den and banged the door of that retreat.

"I am so glad he's cross and put out," said Mrs Prothero, drawing comfort from these symptoms. "When men like your father, Miss Clara, get very meek and mild in their illnesses or in their troubles, it's often all up with them."

"Do you think you could get papa to make some arrangements about—about—you know,—about the funeral?"

"Don't cry, my child," said Prothero, who, good soul, suffered as much as any of them; "don't upset me, there's a dear, or I shall never be able to get through my duties. If I break down, what will you dear children do?"

"Ah, what indeed!" said poor Clara. "You are the only person who is not afraid of papa."

"I am going to him now," returned Prothero, "for I am so anxious to get Mary's address (I *can't* call her Mrs Clavering); and we must see who is to be invited to the funeral: it's dreadful to speak of, I know, but it must be done."

Trembling, and really very nervous, Prothero nevertheless assumed a business-like manner, and set her face as a flint as she knocked at the door of the den. Like a true woman placed in the like circumstances, she did not plunge into her business at once, but approached by zigzags.

"Oh Colonel," said she, "a telegram has arrived from the hotel in Paris where dear Ma——Mrs Clavering was last. Her present address is unknown there, but I have been thinking that Mr Glascott or Miss Clavering ought to have it. Had we not better send to them? besides, he"—alluding to Mr Glascott—"he ought to be asked to attend the—to attend down here, —Miss Clavering is a near connection of the family now."

Colonel Leppell, to the surprise of Prothero, answered her quietly, and even gently. "You are right; send a telegram to Mr Glascott at once,—his bank address will be the safer. And now tell Rifles to take the dog-cart, and drive over to Pinnacles and bring Miss Fanshawe back here. Tell her she must come. She is the very person for me to have in the house. I mean no offence to you, Bothero,—you are invaluable; but Lady Asher keeps your hands full now. I don't want to see Mr Fanshawe—still less his wife; I won't see 'em, so they need not trouble to come with their daughter."

"Miss Clara had a kind letter from Mr Fanshawe this morning, sir; he offers to come here at once if he can be of any service or comfort," replied Prothero.

"He can't be — nobody can but Lillian; we look upon her as one of the family, and she is so like *her*, you know. Ah, so like!"

Prothero did know, and, despite the sorrow and solemnity of the time, a thought flashed into her mind.

"It is not impossible that she may presently become one of us in right good earnest; it would be just like the Colonel to make that girl mistress of his house in a few months' time." As instantaneously, Mrs Prothero chased the thought back to its source, ascribing it on the spot to a prompting of Satan: notwithstanding, it did not occur to her that the lady in question might entertain her own view of the matter, should it ever be submitted to her consideration.

"Well, sir," said the attendant, after a gulp in which she conscientiously repressed Satan and his promptings, "Ben Rifles will be as good as an answer to Mr Fanshawe's note, unless you would like to write a line yourself."

"No; I don't like, and I won't be bothered. Clara can answer the note, and just you send Rifles here at once."

Mrs Prothero lingered a moment in the hope of getting speech regarding some very pressing arrangements, but receiving no encouragement, and further, being desired to look for Mr Glascott's address in the visitor's book, and to send a telegram to that gentleman without delay, she wisely opined to obey her orders, and for all else to trust to Providence without reservation of any kind.

"It's useless my saying anything more to him," mused Prothero; "Miss Fanshawe is sure to come, and it is just as well,—she can manage him, and all the responsibilities will fall upon her. She's never meddlesome, that's one comfort; and if she can induce the Colonel to do as he ought to do, it will be a blessing. There's no other way of getting my poor dear peaceably buried; but oh! I long for Mary to be here."

So Prothero hied to Lady Asher's apartment and wrote out the telegram intended for Mr Glascott. Then with a sore heart she set herself to collect together all the black raiment she could find in the house, with the view of practising the domestic economy of cutting down what was available and turning it into the mourning gear of the younger children, and to carry out the art of "keeping up appearances," which in all impecunious families, on such an occasion, is more or less a matter of much anxiety and forethought.

Happily for us all, perhaps, the most trivial demands of life are strong enough to wean us from overwhelming sorrow, and to keep us in remembrance that grief for the dead must, in externals at least, give way to the requirements of the living. Strong in her duty, this faithful servant did her utmost to lighten the expenses which must now necessarily fall upon Colonel Leppell in reference to mourning and burial. As she contrived and worked, she drew a happy augury from the visit of Mr Alick Leppell the evening before, and from the delicate manner in which he had persuaded Lord Hieover to return home without letting the old man suspect that this was done to relieve the family from the extra trouble which his presence necessarily entailed. The patient manner in which Mr Leppell received his brother's refusal to admit him, and his promise of coming again, all greatly mollified the ill opinion which Prothero had certainly entertained against that gentleman.

Three years had elapsed since Alexander Leppell had put his foot in his younger brother's house: there had never been any positive quarrel between them, but annoyances had occurred, arising from the frequent demands made by both Ralph and his son Marmaduke upon the purse and credit of the Viscount and himself. Thus their intercourse had become gradually less frequent, and was at the time of Miss Leppell's marriage so rare, that it was hardly to be wondered that the majority of their acquaintance lent themselves to the opinion that a serious estrangement was in force betwixt the denizens of Hieover Grange and Hunter's Lodge.

Lord Hieover's late attentions to his daughter-in-law were at this time gratefully remembered by poor Ralph, and perhaps his chief comfort lay in the knowledge that Adelaide, on the last day of her life, had been treated with marked respect by his father; and the recollection of her happy handsome face, as he last saw it, brought with it a world of solace and relief.

The time was not yet when the conscience of Colonel Leppell would reproach him for the many times he had treated her carelessly, if not unkindly. At this juncture he was far beyond recognising aught else than that she was lying dead,—strong and beautiful in her gracious middle age; whilst her mother, afflicted and pallid, lay moaning on her sick couch, weary of life and longing for release.

Then he bethought him of Lillian Fanshawe—the girl who, more than any one of his own children, so strongly resembled *her;* and with the conviction that it was a duty he owed to his dead wife's memory that this young friend, whom they had both so lately made the recipient of their confidences, should be invited to act as the most intimate female friend of the deceased, and share the privileges of a *bonâ fide* daughter of the house, Colonel Leppell decided to send for Miss Fanshawe. The widower was, of course, too much absorbed in his own trouble to consult Lady Asher or his eldest unmarried daughter as to the desirability of this arrangement.

Prothero, meanwhile, was most anxious about Mary. "It will kill the poor child, all coming so suddenly upon her, and perhaps not to be able to arrive in time;" of this last the good woman was very doubtful. "He's,"—she remarked to the nurse, in allusion to Mr Clavering,—"he's taken up with a lot of foreigneering stocks and stones, and goodness knows down what pit or under what cairn they may be by this time!" The hours went by, but there was no return telegram from Mrs Clavering.

Towards the close of the day, Miss Fanshawe arrived in the dog-cart, and was received by all at Hunter's Lodge as the machine which would cause everything to work. The Colonel hastened out to help her to alight; and Alick Leppell, who had been a few moments in the house, and had got over the meeting with his brother most satisfactorily, stood on the hall steps, thinking how very handsome Lillian Fanshawe had become.

It occurred to him, however, that Miss Fanshawe did not exhibit very much affliction at the loss of one who had been in every way so kind to her; but then, mused Alick, perhaps she had her cry out when the news first reached her—people are so different in their ways. "By George!" he went on to himself, after a puff at his cigar, "it would not be a bad thing if Ralph were to marry her—in due time, of course,—he's safe to do something of the kind." Then recollecting himself, "I won't think of such a thing now; it's indecent, it's brutal. Good gracious! what could have put such an idea into my head?"

One thing in regard to this arrangement did not enter into the Honourable Alexander Leppell's brain— it was the trifling circumstance that the lady in question might possibly not view the alliance in a favourable light; for Lillian was certainly not a person to overlook the slightest disadvantage in any one who might aspire to the honour of her hand.

Her presence at Hunter's Lodge brought all the alleviation upon which that household had reckoned, and it was certainly due to Miss Fanshawe's influence that Colonel Leppell roused himself to transact the most important business with regard to his wife's interment. Miss Clavering and Mr Glascott arrived at the Red Lion as speedily as travelling would permit; and the former drove to Hunter's Lodge almost immediately upon her entrance into Yarne, hoping to find her brother and sister-in-law under Colonel Leppell's roof. The young lady's disappointment was indeed great at being greeted by Miss Fanshawe, and to be further informed that no news had been received from the travellers since they left Paris ten days ago. Mrs Clavering's last letter from the Hôtel de Nice had merely announced that they were just starting to some place in Styria—a place where Frank had been before, and which is one of the paradises of the geological student.

All this Miss Fanshawe related with a coldness of manner which was hard and business-like. She expressed neither regret nor surprise at the non-arrival of the Claverings, nor did one word of sympathy for Mary escape her lips; indeed the equanimity with which she imparted the information that, despite Viscount Hieover's influence, the Court of Chancery would not permit Duke to attend his mother's funeral, thoroughly exasperated Willina, whose generous heart was full of sympathy for the bereaved family. "And that girl," she said to herself, "is Mary's early friend! What a misnomer. Let me do Miss Fanshawe justice. I can see that she does not like me; perhaps it is on that account that she is so reticent and so cold."

Miss Clavering was, however, not alone in her astonishment at Lillian's conduct. The air of *locum tenens* which pervaded that lady had not only excited the amazement, but it had also aroused the indignation, of the Honourable Alexander. The latter had come over to remain at Hunter's Lodge for the two days previous to the funeral, and did not feel particularly complimented when he found that it was owing to Miss Fanshawe's influence that the Colonel had been prevailed upon to allow his brother the control of some of the business relative to the interment. Then Miss Lillian had thought proper to treat Mr Leppell as a black sheep, who was only in his brother's house

on sufferance. Yet she was always polite and atten-
tive, and listened patiently to his remarks in the
conferences they held together concerning the inevitable duties which the position had thrown upon them.

Notwithstanding that he was not a lady's man, in
the general acceptation of the term, Mr Leppell was
delighted to find that Miss Clavering came daily to
Hunter's Lodge and remained a great portion of the
day there. It was a relief to him, after the harness in
which Miss Fanshawe constantly kept him, to be able
to speak unreservedly to one so full of the milk of
human kindness, and who was so sisterly in all that
she said about his niece Mary. Together they lamented her absence, and contrived every means in
their power to communicate with her; and it was to
Miss Clavering that Alick spoke of his regret that
there was as yet no renewal of acquaintance between
him and Mr Glascott.

"I am afraid Mr Glascott is keeping away because
I am here," said Mr Leppell, boldly putting the
question.

Miss Clavering did not assent to this fully, so she
replied, "My cousin is at present dreadfully cut up
at Mrs Leppell's death; she was an early and very
dear friend of his. Mr Glascott is to attend the
funeral, and I am sure, if only for her sake, you will
shake hands then. I will, if you like, speak to
him this evening, and tell him what you say. At
this time it is no question for calling, as you must be
aware."

Mr Leppell was delighted at being assisted so opportunely in what was certainly a serious dilemma, and he thanked Willina with great heartiness for her good offices.

"Somehow," said he, bluntly, "I feel much more at ease with you than I do with Miss Fanshawe, although I have known her from a child. I had thought of asking her to set matters right, as she is so intimate here, but I could not do it. She is very handsome and clever, no doubt; but she has become such a very gentlemanly young lady — if I may be permitted the expression, — that I am half afraid of her."

"Opinions differ," replied Willina, with a quiet smile. "Mr Glascott thinks Miss Fanshawe the most perfect girl he has ever seen."

"Does he!" exclaimed Alick, opening his eyes in astonishment. "Well, you know, her likeness to my late sister may account for that. Poor Adelaide! or rather poor Ralph!"

They waited till the uttermost moment, and then all that was mortal of Adelaide Leppell was consigned to rest in the country churchyard of Blythe. The absence of both Duke and Mary naturally added indignation to the grief of the widower. He, however, acted as chief mourner with becoming decorum, and when the ceremony was over they led his little children to him, and left them with him to do the work of consolation.

At this same time Mr Glascott and Mr Leppell

joined hands, and buried their enmity over the scarcely closed grave. "O Lord, forgive us our trespasses, as we forgive them that trespass against us!" The glow of the evening light streamed on the turf hallowed by this vesper prayer.

CHAPTER X.

A FOE'S GIFT IS NO GIFT, AND BRINGS NO PROFIT.

IT was not till five days had elapsed that the Claverings at length arrived at Hunter's Lodge. They had returned to Paris with the intention of spending some little time in that city, as Mr Clavering had scientific friends to meet there.

The telegrams which they received at the Hôtel de Nice, however, caused them to travel forward without an hour's delay. Frank felt convinced that by this time it was quite useless to hurry, but his arguments only increased the nervous agitation of his wife; consequently, he could not do otherwise than expedite the travelling arrangements, although this premature return interfered seriously with his own plans.

Mary's grief on arriving at home was dreadful to witness, but it had the effect of rousing the Colonel into some approach to action; and it gave Miss Clavering the opportunity of lavishing the most tender sympathy on her sister-in-law. This was fortunate for the sufferer, as Miss Fanshawe's kind offices were greatly increased by the presence of Mr Clavering. "It was very hard upon him, poor man," Miss Lillian remarked; "he could not be expected to enter into the feelings of the family to any great extent. Of course he was very shocked, and all that; but he must not be moped to death." And so they walked, and read, and geologised as of yore, and Mary was thankful to her friend for entertaining her husband so pleasantly; indeed she felt convinced that were it not for Lillian's companionship and literary aid, Francis would not have consented so readily to remain quietly at Hunter's Lodge during its first season of heavy grief.

Mr Glascott and Miss Clavering also thought it to be their duty to extend their stay at Yarne; the latter from real sympathy with her sister-in-law,—the former, ostensibly, because he always was ready to meet the plans of other people.

The Colonel grieved now for the absence of his eldest son. It is scarcely an exaggeration to say that the news of his mother's death fell like a thunderbolt on Marmaduke Leppell.

Had he been at home, or so circumstanced that he could at least share the sorrow of his family, and be as one of them, however short the time, his grief would probably, after its first ebullition, have evaporated in such active exertion as might conduce to drown his thoughts and modify his self-reproach.

But in the stillness of a close imprisonment, albeit not rigorous, wherein no distraction was procurable,

Duke was perforce driven into himself; and in the communing of his spirit, conscience asserted her part, and set before him in stern array his numerous offences towards the gentle being whose face he could never see again, whose loving tender voice was mute for evermore.

"Dead! dead! without word or message to me!" Duke at length exclaimed, as he rose out of that dull stony stupor which is worse than a swoon; for in this —whatever some may allege to the contrary—the sense of pain is acute to agony. "Dead! my mother dead, and I know nothing of her last hours; and I have helped to kill her! I see how it has been: she has thought and thought over what I have done, and she has put off writing to me, for fear of expressing her displeasure too strongly. Yes; I see it now. Then grandma's illness, and Moll going away, and the governor's botherings,—it has all been too much for her, and she has mourned silently over us all, and—died. Oh, mother! Yes; you are dead—the sweetest woman in all the world—and I not even near you! God knows, I would suffer years of pain for only one touch of your dear hand! but it is all useless, all vain now!"

He took up the letter which conveyed the mournful intelligence to him, in the hope that another perusal would throw some light upon the fact, and at least inform him if Mrs Leppell had been able to speak with even one of her family before she breathed her last. It was written by Lillian Fanshawe, short and concise as a lawyer's communication, merely giving the bare facts of the case, and ending with very sparse condolence. The modicum of this last was expressed in such terms as rather to exasperate Duke against the writer than otherwise.

"Confound her impudence!" he burst out, whilst the great tears rolled down his face; "she hopes the trial will be blessed to me, does she? takes a tone of superior virtue, as if she knew all about my—my gravest — misdoings. Clara might have written,—I do think she might."

After a pause, in which Marmaduke broke down utterly, not only at the news of his loss, but also from the conviction that he was now kept out of the pale of his family, a light broke in upon him.

"I daresay the governor has got Lillian to undertake all the correspondence for him—that's it; but I think Miss Lillian might have expressed a little more sympathy for me. She must know that I should feel rather differently from herself on losing a mother. Mrs Fanshawe's death would not trouble her eldest daughter much, I fancy."

He tried to steel himself with this sarcasm, but it would not do. Stamping his foot on the ground, as if he would trample and rend to pieces the faintest knowledge of the truth, the lad again bowed his head, and wept the bitterest tears he had ever shed in his life; all his hardness, all his undoubted pluck, were melted at once in the seething furnace of a merited affliction,—an affliction that struck home.

It could scarcely be otherwise. Was he not in trouble and disgrace? and never could he, let life be long or short—never throw his arms around her, and hide his face on that forgiving heart, and acknowledge that he had sinned in Heaven's sight, against Heaven, and against her.

Ah no; the time for that had passed away for ever.

But he could, he thought, pay her the last respect. He would attend her burial; he would stand with his father's arm within his own, and support him in the sorrow which he felt would bow his parent to the earth. Yes, at her coffin-head they would stand together, and resolve there to be better men for her dear sake: for after all, there is no purer remembrance upon this earth than that of loyal, true womanhood. God and woman should be mankind's watchword—his battle-cry in strife, his golden crown in peace.

Then rushed across his mind the doubt as to whether he would be allowed to leave his place of detention even for one day, to fulfil a duty so sacred. He resolved to make a direct application to the proper quarter, and he felt certain that his father (and possibly also his grandfather) would exert himself to get his release, if only for a few hours. His knowledge of the ways of the law was very misty; but he held a confused idea that he would be placed on " parole," and that this indulgence would be based on military lines. In that case, Marmaduke felt that he would know what he was about. Of course he should keep his " parole," and return cheerfully to his prison.

Those about him, however, did not foster this opinion; but kindness and respect for the lad's sincere grief caused them to keep silence on the subject, only reminding Marmaduke that the Chancellor was out of Britain, and it might be a question as to whether the Vice - Chancellor could or would undertake the responsibility of letting him go to Blythe, even if attended by an officer of the Court of Chancery.

That day was one of long suspense. It was not to be expected that an immediate answer could be returned to the application which Duke eventually made in respectful language and very fair grammar; and it so happened that a couple of days elapsed before any notice was accorded to his petition.

It was curt and decided enough. The missive ran that it was utterly impossible that Mr Leppell should leave the Queen's Prison, Holloway, for a single hour.

Marmaduke bore this like steel,—turned over some other letters which were handed to him at the time, and pounced upon one bearing Peggy's handwriting on the envelope. It was an epistle of condolence, and ran as follows :—

"MY DEAREST OLD BOY,—I have been thinking of you night and day, knowing how troubled you will be, not only at your dear mother's death (I am so glad now that I never saw her), but also about this dreadful Court which won't let you out, even for the funeral.

It is enough to make us all hold it in contempt for the rest of our lives.

"My 'dragon' is turning out quite amiable. She agreed with me that I ought to put on deep mourning, for the Court can't prevent me being a daughter-in-law to poor Mrs Leppell. She has helped me so kindly, that I feel it would be mean to go on being disagreeable, so I have turned civil, and 'dragon' says that I have the makings of a fine character. Fancy that!

"Well, dear boy, I am having several black dresses made; one of them, covered with crape, for the evening, has a crape tail, just like a comet in black (I should like to catch the Chancellor treading on that). I tell you this because I know you would wish me to show respect to the memory of your mother.

"Clara has written me a nice letter, giving me a few particulars. She says that Miss Clavering, who is staying now at Yarne, counselled her to write, for she thought that we must both feel being cut off from the family at such a time, and that it would be proper to send a few lines to me especially. Clara mentions that your old friend, Miss Fanshawe, is staying at Hunter's Lodge, and that she wrote fully to you by your father's desire, who is too cut up to do anything. As you know all about it, I will not harrow your feelings, dear Duke, by saying more on this subject. I only hope you won't dislike me for being the cause of your imprisonment: at any rate, you must be very down-hearted.

"My 'dragon' tells me that these Chancellors really

cannot help themselves; they must carry out the law, but in the main they are no worse hearted than their neighbours. The Vice-Chancellor, it appears, could not let you out in the absence of his superior, who is kicking up his heels on the Continent just now. It seems it would be as much as the Vice's place is worth to do so, because the orders are that you are to be kept strictly, on account of your contumacy before we surrendered.

" You know it is only because I howled so desperately that we are allowed to correspond without restraint; so it will be as well to 'grin and bear it.' I am saving all the money I can, in order that we may enjoy ourselves when you are set free. Be sure I will make it all up to you, dear, and be a kind and loving wife. I know you will get steady in time.

" It is just as well that you can't rejoin the Gold-spinners. I have thought that we might take a farm in Ireland, where there's safe to be a little fighting if you look out for it. Keep up your spirits for the present, and believe me,—Your loving, dutiful, affectionate wife,   MARGARET LEPPELL."

Marmaduke read and re-read this epistle with mingled feelings of affection and respect. The candid freshness, the unselfishness of the writer, struck him very forcibly, and the conviction dawned upon him that he never could repay the warm-hearted girl who, through his act, was at that moment in a measure circumscribed in liberty, if not in actual honourable captivity.

What had he done to merit a dutiful wife? Did he deserve that this young creature should resign all the enjoyments of early womanhood in order to live with him on a remote farm?—To resign all the pleasures to which her large fortune entitled her, for the purpose of keeping him steady, and inducing him to lay the foundation of a permanent home?

Here she was, saving her allowance in order to spare him the pressure of money embarrassments when he should be free. The whole tone of her letter assured him that, if need be, she was ready to sacrifice every penny, nay, even dear life, for his sake; and was he worthy of all this?

The answer he made to himself was perhaps the turning-point of his whole future life: he honestly, and without seeking to evade the mental query, avowed that he in no respect was worthy.

This admitted, came resolution; and the first-fruits of this resolution were evinced in schooling himself to patience, and in writing to his wife a letter in which, without making many promises, he undertook to be guided by her wishes in his future career. "Only," he wrote, "be always with me: the presence of my wife and the dear memory of my mother will be like the guardianship of two angels to keep me in the right path."

Marmaduke then wrote to his sister Mary, and to his father; but to Miss Lillian's letter he never vouchsafed, either directly or indirectly, the slightest notice. It is possible that the lady never remarked this omission; she was at this time entirely taken up with Mr Clavering's geological researches.

The rest of the family had also their anxieties and duties; for Lady Asher had suffered a relapse, and it was as much as Prothero and her two eldest grand-daughters could do, to bestow all the attention which the infirmities of the old lady demanded.

Thus it was that Mr Glascott lingered at the Red Lion Hotel, and the departure for Brydone remained in abeyance for a while.

The frequent visits of Mr Glascott to Hunter's Lodge had scarcely the effect of adding to the comfort of the master of that abode. True he was glad, and sincerely glad, that a friendship had been cemented by himself and his brother Alexander with Everard Glascott; and that the wings of the Angel of Death contributed to cover all former animosities and the remembrance of early injuries.

To say truth, the forgiveness was much more hearty on the part of Mr Glascott than it was on that of Colonel Leppell. The latter could not forget that he had not been his wife's first love; and he was restless and impatient that their son's deliverance from disgrace was entirely due to the man to whom, of all others, he would the least choose to be indebted. His conscience told him that for the sake of Adelaide Mr Glascott had foregone all the comforts of married life; and his pride was galled because, on reviewing his position, he could not see his way to requite his benefactor, or by any means discharge the debt of obligation which he conceived was due to that gentleman. A trifling incident, however, suddenly changed the current of the Colonel's thoughts. He was sitting at the window of his den, listlessly turning over a file of unpaid bills, and according to custom selecting those that were the most pressing, and upon which a sum "on account" would be likely to be accepted by the creditors.

The sound of voices diverted him from his occupation—they were those of Miss Fanshawe and Mr Glascott. There was nothing to distract him in this, but he happened at the same moment to look up, and his eyes fell directly on Mr Glascott's face.

Ralph was not naturally astute, but that moment would have revealed to one even more dense than he the innermost workings of Everard Glascott's soul. The radiant face, that peculiar luminous light in the eye which is never seen but in those who love, all told their tale,—all told of the deep strong love of the elderly man, which, forgetting time and space, believeth all things, hopeth all things; and is ever more loyal than the fleeting passion of early youth, because in the majority of cases it endureth all things—and endureth to the end.

Then the Colonel's gaze travelled to the face of Lillian Fanshawe. Had his dead wife stood there in the first blush of her girlish beauty, he would scarcely have been surprised. That remarkable likeness which

Miss Fanshawe had always borne to the deceased lady
seemed at this moment to be increased and rarefied,
as it were, by the soft expression which was so rarely
seen on the young girl's face. She was looking upwards, listening with a pleased smile to what her
companion was saying. Ralph could only catch a
word here and there, but he thought he could make
out that Mr Glascott was pressing Miss Fanshawe
to come and make a stay at his house at Brydone.

Some expressions which fell from the lady informed
the listener that Miss Fanshawe had so far confided
in Mr Glascott, as to make that gentleman aware that
she was not quite happy in her father's house. Lillian,
the Colonel thought, was too proud to enter into
family grievances with one who was so lately a
stranger; "but then," thought that officer, "I have no
business to sit in judgment upon a few stray words:
moreover, I rather think I have no business to be
looking out here at all." So thinking, Ralph moved
away from the window; but he had taken a resolve,
and set himself to think how best he could act
upon it.

The result of his cogitations was, that he now saw
his way to returning some of Mr Glascott's good offices
towards himself.

What should prevent him from using his influence
to promote a match between Mr Glascott and Lillian
Fanshawe?

Difference of age! Nonsense; the man was fifty-
eight and the girl nineteen, but what did that signify

when the man was so handsome and debonair? It might injure young Clavering's prospects somewhat, but that was no matter; and with so much already given, Francis could afford to be liberal and grateful.

Then there was another and most important point to be considered in the possible arrangement of this project, and that was the greater security it would supply for the preservation of the secret of Marmaduke's disgrace.

Colonel Leppell had never been quite satisfied that he and his late wife had acted wisely in bestowing their whole confidence on Miss Fanshawe; but the risk attending this, if any, would be quite neutralised should Lillian eventually become Mr Glascott's wife. In that case the secret would not go beyond those who already possessed it; indeed the wife would naturally second her husband's wish that all concerning the affair should be buried in oblivion: in this a most trying anxiety would be quenched utterly.

Would Mrs Leppell have liked the idea of her quondam lover, in his ripe middle age, marrying a stranger, whose chief recommendation to his regard was the extraordinary resemblance she bore to herself in her palmy early days?

Most assuredly she would have accorded her approval, was Ralph's answer to this question, mentally put.

Mrs Leppell would only have been too happy to further this alliance, and so contribute her quota in wiping off the debt of gratitude which they owed to

Mr Glascott. It was possible, also, that Adelaide might have regarded the event as a direct testimony to the potency of her own charms.

This last reflection caused the Colonel to work himself into the belief that it was due to the memory of his late wife that he should do all in his power to promote this marriage; and then he bestowed a little attention upon Miss Fanshawe's part in the programme.

The opportunity for her, Colonel Leppell regarded as most providential and most fortunate. Her family might object?—not they. Did not everybody know that Mrs Fanshawe no more cared for her eldest daughter than if she had been the child of the Begum of Bhopal; and that the rector showed his affection for her by doing his best to keep her in other people's houses and out of his own? Hunter's Lodge was more a home to Lillian Fanshawe than that of her parents; and she entertained as much affection for the people of that home as it was in her nature to bestow.

"Yes," Ralph determined, "the thing shall be done: it will repay the wife I have taken from Everard Glascott; it will give me the satisfaction of making reparation in my lifetime for the wrongdoing of my youth. Let me but have the matter in my own hands, and nobly will I reward this man for what he has done for me and mine. Here at last we shall be quits!"

So mused, and so honestly thought, Colonel Leppell; but a deeper reason was the dominant influence which impelled him to assist Mr Glascott in obtaining his heart's desire—that lingering, undefinable dislike to the relations in which he stood with regard to that gentleman. His pride was so mortified, that to discharge his obligation he would have lent himself to any scheme, however eccentric or even outrageous, if he could have by such means made Mr Glascott in any manner his debtor.

Now the opportunity had arrived, and it should not be the fault of Ralph Leppell if all were not carried out to the desired end.

It was a bold stroke, thus building upon a chance expression of face, perhaps, or an unusual warmth of manner and utterance. The Colonel, however, had the courage of his convictions, and he very shortly afterwards had occasion to verify them entirely to his own satisfaction. Then he went to the fountainhead — or, to put it more plainly, he attacked Mr Glascott.

That gentleman fenced and parried his host's downright questions, as persons similarly situated generally do: at length, after rather a brisk game of mental cutand-thrust, Mr Glascott acknowledged the truth of Colonel Leppell's surmises, and, to the great delight of the officer, concluded by asking his opinion of his chances of success.

"You have no reason as yet for supposing that you have won Miss Fanshawe's affections?" Ralph inquired, with an air of the deepest wisdom.

"Oh no; it is on this point that I am so very dubious. I am not blind to the fact of the immense

difference in our ages: that, I feel sure, is greatly
to my disadvantage, and it might weigh as a serious
objection with the parents."

"Not a bit of it," replied the Colonel, reassuring
his friend—"they would be only too proud of the connection; and the difference in age is your affair, and
that of the lady, I rather think."

Mr Glascott agreed so far; still he could not but
feel very diffident as to the advisability of the affair.
"Yet," continued the poor gentleman, "Miss Fanshawe is so like what poor Adelaide was at her age,
—and my meeting her under your roof, all concur to
interest me most deeply in this young lady,—she is so
superior to most other girls——"

"That's it," broke in the Colonel. "Lillian has got
the head of a woman of thirty on her shoulders; and
she has more knowledge of the world than poor Adelaide ever had. Sharp mother too; has had to keep
up appearances, and has had always too much to do
to be flirting and philandering with youths who mean
nothing,—nothing, I mean, in the way of business."

"You do not know if there be any possible rival in
the way?" inquired the elder man, almost timidly.

"I am sure there is not," the Colonel volunteered,
with all the hardihood of thorough conviction. "It is
not every man who would suit Miss Fanshawe—you
can see that yourself. See how she devotes herself
to my family, and what a companion she is to Clavering, now Mary is so much with Lady Asher."

"I have remarked that with very much pleasure,"

returned Mr Glascott; "for it is but right that I should study closely the character of the lady whom I should wish to make my wife. I have never ventured to make my sentiments known to Miss Fanshawe; indeed, my great difficulty is to discover whether she would really respond to them."

" Well, that is difficult, certainly. Lillian is naturally reticent. The way her mother has treated the girl has caused her from an early age to keep her thoughts and opinions under very great reserve. Do not be in a hurry; take time and stay here. You will manage much better by keeping quite clear of Pinnacles Court. To tell you the truth, poor Adelaide said once or twice lately, how thankful she would be could Lillian make a nice match, and get out of Yarneshire."

So Mrs Leppell had said; but her remark was prompted by the strong desire she entertained to see Miss Fanshawe safely married and out of Mr Clavering's way. Had she imagined that Mr Glascott would be the bridegroom, it is highly probable that she would have been delighted to know that the fixed home of that gentleman was over the sea, and that they would stay at the London house but once a-year.

The Colonel being only cognisant of the fact that such were his late wife's hopes, and being at the same time profoundly ignorant of the reasons which prompted them, he pressed this very much on Mr Glascott's attention; for he knew well enough that nothing would act as a greater incentive to that gentleman's aspirations than the knowledge that they would have been fostered by Mrs Leppell had she been in life. Mr Glascott said little more, after he had averred that he would do nothing precipitate; and that little referred to an apprehension that the proposed match might not seem good in the eyes of Francis and Willina Clavering.

The Colonel, however, disposed of this qualm of conscience in a very summary method. "It's no business of theirs; Francis is married, and his sister will marry. Look to yourself, my friend, and provide for the comforts of your old age: don't sacrifice too much for people in your lifetime,—you will get no thanks for it."

"Willina has reckoned so much on making Jersey our home, it seems rather hard to dethrone her before she has been actually the mistress of the house," said Mr Glascott, pensively.

"All the better; there will not be the custom of years to resign. Besides, you give Miss Clavering great advantages when you make Miss Fanshawe the mistress of your house—haw!"

Mr Glascott jumped at this suggestion, which had not occurred to him before, and therefore he replied, "Certainly, *most* certainly,—a very great advantage."

Then said the Colonel, "You know well, Glascott, that I wronged you very much in the matter of my marriage with Adelaide Asher. I am heartily sorry for the way in which I behaved to you, and so is my brother, for aiding and abetting me in my evil doing. You have repaid this wrong with noble kindness, and there is nothing I would not do to help you, or assist you in your plans—haw!—hum! I think so well of Miss Fanshawe, that were I unmarried,—I mean, if I could give my late wife a successor,—she is the only person I would choose. But, no; I will never marry again. Let me, then, use all my influence in your favour: the girl has confidence in me, and is almost like one of my own children—indeed at this moment I feel as if she were my daughter. Let us suppose it; and let me say that I give her to you as a trusting father would give her. She will be a glorious atonement for what I have made you suffer in the past; only take time, and leave all to me."

Mr Glascott acquiesced, but was too much absorbed to wonder how it was that Ralph spoke so glibly, and seemed to be quite confident of bringing this matter to a happy conclusion. He was, in fact, so enamoured of the prospect in view, that he could think of nought besides it. No man, either old or young, was more thoroughly heart-smitten than he.

Then the gentlemen parted, agreeing on both sides to act cautiously, and to keep silence.

The family at Hinton Square had been duly informed of the trouble which had suddenly thrown its shadow over the inmates of Hunter's Lodge; but it so happened that the La Touche family had received news of the death of a near relative, which, if it did not cause any grief, certainly tended to upset their plans, and possibly bring an unwelcome kinsman into closer contact with them than they quite liked.

An unexpected and a somewhat uncomfortable letter had conveyed to Mr La Touche the intelligence of the death of his eldest sister, Mrs MacTaggart, the widow of a Presbyterian divine of some repute. The writer, being the eldest son of the deceased lady, further informed him that, after settling his younger brothers and sisters with some relatives of their father, he, Colin MacTaggart, intended to come at once to London in order to seek employment for himself.

He was glad to say that the firm of MacTaggart & MacTaggart, the well-known Writers to the Signet of Macnahanish Street, Glasgow, had taken his brother Donald into their office, and that his two sisters were to be the guests of a cousin of his father for a year.

He therefore ventured to hope that his mother's family would endeavour to assist him, and thought it possible that his uncle might have a vacancy in his office in the city which he could fill. Colin concluded this epistle by stating that he would be in London on the evening of the 18th,—that he felt sure of a warm welcome from his uncle and cousins,—and hoped that his aunt Marcia would secure him a lodging near Hinton Square.

It was explained in a postscript that Mrs MacTaggart had died suddenly in a remote part of the Highlands, where she had been on a visit, and where the communication with Glasgow was irregular. On this account it was impossible that Mr La Touche could have arrived in time for the burial.

"Well, you have been saved the expense of attending the funeral," said Marcia to her brother, after she had read the letter; "but if he comes here—Colin, I mean—we shall have to be in some kind of mourning."

"Why, yes," returned Mr La Touche, slowly, "the proper thing must be done—mourning, of course. I have got the suit which I keep for attending funerals, and so has Percival, I believe."

"Oh, you men can do well enough," cried Marcia; "but what about the girls and myself?"

"Furbish up your black silk dresses with crape," interposed Percival, amongst whose many littlenesses a capacity for man-millinery shone out conspicuously. "Get some cheap bonnets, and a few black crape flowers for yourself and some white ones for the girls, and the thing is done."

Marcia did not quite relish this prompt adaptation to circumstances, and persisted bravely in making objections, hoping thereby to extract a cheque from her brother; so she continued—

"There must be other things supplied, more substantial than flowers. We can't live in one dress for three months at a time—the thing is absurd. We ought to have new black cachmére dresses, black mantles, and a number of little items besides, which you know nothing about."

"Stick a black lining under your black lace shawl," answered Percival, "and put some bugle trimming about it. Colin will only be here for a few days, and you can return to gay raiment as soon as he is gone."

" I am not so sure of that," replied the aunt. " Colin evidently intends my brother to get him some employment, and he will be here off and on till something is procured for him. However that may be, it is only right and proper that we should have decent mourning, and that we should wear it for more than a few days. I am sure I am only asking what is just and right."

CHAPTER XI.

DOMESTIC ECONOMY.

As no response was made by the elder gentleman to Marcia's appeal, Stephen, who was present at the family conclave, and had been a silent listener, now spoke.

"I will give you a black cachmére, or whatever you call it—mourning dress, Aunt Marcia: you at least ought to put on decent mourning for your own sister. As for the girls, I do hope my father and Percival will do something towards helping them out."

Mr La Touche looked at his son, but he said nothing. Percival sarcastically hoped that briefs were becoming plentiful; whilst Marcia, thinking it advisable to strike whilst the iron was hot, proposed that now that Stephen had done his part—the one who could the least afford it, she added with emphasis—the other two gentlemen should present the girls with the *de quoi* wherewith to furnish the decency of aspect required for mourning for their father's sister.

"It must be done," continued Marcia, valiantly. "If

we have no clothes I won't preside at the dinner-party which we are to have next week. I won't be present," she reiterated, "unless we have all proper clothes."

"Dress, I presume you mean," said Percival, with an aggravating grin. "Whatever happens, that dinner cannot be put off. I am going to the country almost immediately afterwards. Besides, the *ménu* is the best we have had this season."

"This feast is arranged for Thursday next, is it not?" inquired Stephen of his aunt.

"Yes; there are twelve people coming, and a few of the girls' friends afterwards. We had hoped to get up a little dance."

"But you see," said Stephen, deprecatingly, "this will be the very evening that Colin MacTaggart arrives in town: it will be most unseemly to be entertaining company at the moment he enters the house."

"What does that signify?" asked Percival roughly; "we can't help people dying. They always do expire at the most inconvenient seasons for their friends. It is a well ascertained fact."

"But remember the feelings of the son—our first cousin," persisted Stephen. "The Scotch are so particular on this point; and the MacTaggart family would look upon our entertaining company on the evening of Colin's arrival as a dreadful insult."

"He comes at his own time and by his own invitation," said Percival; "the party can't be put off for him: he had better go to a hotel."

"Could you not meet him at the station," said Marcia to her nephew Stephen, "and take him to the Zoological Gardens? No, they would be shut up; Cremorne would be better. There he could be as quiet as he likes, walking in the alleys among the trees out of the crowd. He need not look at the dancing, or at any of the fast people, you know."

Stephen did not at all relish this proposal, and declined it positively, saying that it was not his habit to frequent Cremorne. He had his own reasons for wishing to be present at this dinner-party, for the reading pupil was to be one of the guests, and Stephen had already determined to settle with that youth that their reading-tour ought by all manner of means to take the direction of the Channel Islands.

"Why not write," suggested Stephen, "and ask MacTaggart to defer his arrival for a day, and offer him a bed in the house at once? This would not only be kind to him, but it will show the MacTaggart Clan that the La Touches are quite as ready to give countenance to these orphans as they are."

This was a grand stroke of diplomacy on the part of Stephen.

The old gentleman shook up his feathers, metaphorically speaking, and looked the prosperous British merchant every inch, and as if he were capable of protecting a whole wing of the British army at a stroke.

The expression, "countenance the orphans," had the effect also of dulcifying the vinegar of Percival's temperament. The offer of a bed in the house was so easy a piece of hospitality, that no objection could be raised to the introduction of Colin as a guest.

"He can have the little room at the top of the house, and nobody will see him," said Marcia, pursuing the advantages.

"And you can be dressed like Christians for the dinner-party," added Percival; "and as I am very anxious that this should come off well, Marcia, and you may have some trouble, I don't mind giving a five-pound note between you and the girls for black gloves and ribbons and all that."

"Just one pound for each of us!" answered Marcia ungratefully, but to the point. "Really, Percival, you might give another ten pounds for your own sisters; with your wealth, you ought to be a more generous brother. Do give ten pounds to divide between the two elder ones; they could get a handsome dress apiece."

But Percival was obdurate. "Five pounds among the lot," he replied, coarsely, "for gloves and ribbons; I don't undertake to do more than that."

"You had better hand the sum to Aunt Marcia at once," said Stephen, who took a quiet delight in teasing his elder brother. "Amid your varied distractions, this little trifle might be overlooked."

"So it might," said Marcia. "Hand me a five-pound note, Percival, if you please. Here are two witnesses to testify that you have fulfilled your promise."

"But I do wish," she continued more earnestly, "that you could make up your mind, at least once in a way, to be generous to your sisters, and give them a decent present now and then. You are always ready to find fault if their dress is not exactly *comme il faut*, and yet you never give them any aid in helping them with their wardrobe."

Mr La Touche was either struck with the justice of this remark, or perhaps with admiration for the persistency with which Marcia always advocated his daughters' claim upon their rich brother, for he said, "Never mind, Marcia; I will see what I can do for the girls without straitening their allowance. I may also manage something for yourself. You certainly are a good aunt."

Mr La Touche said no more than the truth when he made this last assertion.

Whatever Marcia's failings might be in the matter of self-indulgence and worldliness, she never forgot her duty towards her brother's children. More than once she had suffered hard rebuffs in her attempts to obtain some advantages for them, either in lessons from professors or in some additional amusement or article of dress: in these cases no benefit to herself could possibly accrue.

If Marcia excelled in one thing more than in another as to the manipulation of chaperone life, it was in the making of hay whilst the sun shone. The vicissitudes which she had witnessed in mercantile circles, especially, urged her to take advantage of present opportunities small and large; and her object now was to get her nieces safely married in the lifetime of their father.

Full well knew she that nothing was to be expected from Percival; and she was haunted, in addition, by a strong misgiving that Mr La Touche lived almost up to the greatest extent of his income. True, there was a little to divide, but what was that amongst so many?

The girls must marry, and so long as the La Touche family kept open house, and gave *recherché* dinners, men, and men of mark and substance, moreover, would diligently frequent it.

Miss La Touche also deserved great credit for the perfect good-feeling and harmony which existed betwixt herself and her nieces: little jealousies and distrusts were unknown amongst them. Few ladies, and those maiden aunts, could possess more genuine admirers than did Aunt Marcia in the persons of these young girls. They believed her to be the handsomest and the best of relatives; not one of them would admit that their father's sister could be possibly at fault in anything that she might say or do.

The bond of fellowship was perhaps unconsciously strengthened from the fact that the gentlemen of the family were looked upon as the common prey of these, their near females relatives, in all matters monetary; and Miss La Touche, notwithstanding her preference for her eldest nephew, always judiciously utilised his flower-show and concert tickets, his "bones" for the opera-stalls, and his "bones" for the Zoo, to the advantage of her young charges.

The proclivities of the elder Mr La Touche towards missionary meetings, and taking the chair at evening lectures, &c., were also most dexterously managed. These engagements kept the master of the house out of the way; and if these absences fell during the time that Percival happened to be travelling or visiting from home, the triumph of the evening delectations was assured and complete.

It sometimes happened that Marcia wanted a quiet earlier dinner, whereto she could safely invite some pet male friend of the ladies of the family, who, though perfectly irreproachable, was not *au mieux* with the old gentleman or with Percival: then the meetings and the lectures came in most opportunely. Stephen or Andrew was ready enough to represent the head of the house on these select occasions: they were sensible young men, who volunteered no remarks on the morrow concerning the guest or guests of the previous evening. The servants, too, thoroughly appreciated these little arrangements; the courses were fewer, the attendance less elaborate; and some one of the establishment below stairs secured a long evening out, and usually recuperated his or her forces at the theatre.

But to the kitchen-maid these were truly halcyon periods; for the cook-housekeeper had a penchant for the meetings over which Mr La Touche presided, and usually followed her master thereunto in an omnibus, as close upon the cab which contained the chairman of the meeting then convened as the loco-motive powers of the pursuing vehicle would allow. Then Betty had it all her own way in the culinary art. She worked her best, and had her reward in the company of Private Tucker of the "Cavaltree," who on these occasions contrived to drop in to supper and drain a comfortable cup.

It was on the whole a difficult family to manage; and a woman of more acute feeling, and even, it must be confessed, of a more delicate sense of honour, than was Marcia, would certainly have steered less ably, and have possibly come more frequently into direct collision with one or other of its members.

As it was, she accepted her position, and deluded herself into the belief that she was doing her duty to the rest of the family by winking at Percival's immoral life, and by pandering to his luxurious tastes. It was like making bricks without straw—she received neither gratitude nor consideration; but she truly ob-served, "If my brother makes no objection, how can I interfere? Besides, if Percival behaves respectably when in the house, what business have we with what he chooses to do out of it?"

"Very questionable morality," replied Stephen, to whom this remark had been addressed, with the view of quenching some uncomfortable inquiries which he had propounded on the matter—"very questionable. If all goes smoothly on the surface, no matter what corruption infects beneath it! I am no prophet, but I venture to predict that if this laxity obtains, the difference betwixt right and wrong will be a very unknown quantity in the country in a few years to come."

"Well, I can't help it," returned Marcia, snappishly.

"I think you can, a little, Aunt Marcia," replied the nephew gently.

"How? in what way?" asked Miss La Touche.

"In order to answer you, I must speak plainly. Did you not ask Percival this morning—aside, it is true—if you were to expect him to be at home, or if he was going to his country house to find metal more attractive there?"

Marcia could not deny this indiscretion, but declared that nobody else could have overheard what was said.

"Pardon me—Fanny did; and moreover, she observed the little knowing glance which was interchanged between you and my brother. It almost seemed as if you aided and abetted him in this scandal. Now, if you will allow me to advise you, never permit Percival to approach the subject with you by sign or hint; and by all means never allude to it yourself, for if you do he will naturally think that you regard his conduct with no very great disfavour."

Marcia was silent for a moment, then she said suddenly, "You are angry with Percival just now, because he is urging you to make up to Madame Rudolph Heine—that German drysalter's widow, I mean."

"Yes, I am angry at his impertinence in meddling with my private affairs," returned Stephen hotly. "It will be a dreadful nuisance if I am supposed to make love to every lady with money who puts her business into my hands. Madame Heine is my client, and as my client only do I regard her."

"But she has lots of money, and your father would be so delighted if you could make a match of it," persisted Marcia. "You know, I suppose, that she is invited to the dinner-party here on Thursday? My brother made me send her an invitation, principally on your account."

"Did he? he's very good. But just understand this, Marcia, that I am not going to be disposed of in matrimony against my will. I am quite satisfied to remain as I am, until I can make enough to be independent of fortune with a wife. And I may just as well tell you, that if I am to be meddled with by Percival, I shall at once go and live entirely in chambers."

Marcia washed her hands of Percival, but insisted that it was his father's wish that he, Stephen, should marry Madame Heine.

"I have told him that I will not, and there's an end of it, as far as I am concerned," quoth Stephen. "If the lady is looked upon as such a valuable acquisition to the family, he had better try his luck himself in that quarter."

"Nonsense, my dear," answered the aunt, very briskly; "mind you don't put such a thing into your father's head. I suffer great anxiety on this account as it is; don't augment it, pray."

"Why, what do you mean?"

"Well, I cannot exactly define my meaning, for I have no evidence to go upon; but I cannot help thinking that these meetings, and charitable conferences, and refuges, at which your father is always acting as chairman, are only a blind for a little quiet flirtation—in the pious way, you know. The number of tickets for various charities, and the letters addressed in female handwriting to him, are positively alarming. He will be bringing a serious wife home some fine day. I have told you all so before, but of course none of you will take any precautions till it is too late."

"But, Marcia, what are we to do? Besides, he can't marry all the serious ladies. Take comfort,—there's safety in a multitude, as the saying goes."

"Do!" replied the aunt. "You ought to go to these meetings with your father, and look after him, and see that these women don't have it all their own way. I am sure I don't know how he will get on when the dark weather comes. Have you not observed that your father is very shaky on his legs now?"

Stephen answered that he had remarked this; but he reminded his aunt that Martha—the cook-housekeeper—was fond of attending these serious meetings. "Depend upon it," the young man continued, "if there was anything going on, Martha would let you know."

"Yes; but her attendance is very irregular," answered Miss La Touche; "and she never goes or returns in the same conveyance, so a great deal might happen which she never sees. I think, when the evenings are longer, I shall advise my brother to let Martha see him home, on dark nights especially."

"I don't think my father would relish that," said Stephen, laughing.

"Of course, I should put it on the shakiness of his legs, and the fear of his falling," said Marcia. "At any rate, it will put a stop to his staying to little comfortable suppers after these meetings; and if their returning together in a cab is objected to, an omnibus would do just as well. Martha is a nice respectable-looking woman, and she has been with us so long that there would be nothing remarkable in her attending on him on these occasions. I know it is quite useless to ask any of you young men to accompany your father to these meetings."

"Oh, quite," replied the nephew, in a tone meant to imply that such a thing was not to be thought of. "I am much too busy in the day, and besides, I fancy my father undertakes these duties under the idea that his doing so is necessary for his commercial interests among a certain set."

"He is a nice-looking old man, and the women flatter him," returned Miss La Touche; "but I think it is time that he should leave these matters to younger people."

"Exactly; that is my feeling. Still, if it is an interest to him to speak in public, I hope he may long

be spared to do so. Could you not once in a way go
with your brother to some of the gatherings you allude
to yourself ? He is a nice-looking old man, as you say,
and has all the air of a benevolent bishop."

" Impossible, my dear," replied Miss La Touche, in
a tone of great decision—" my duties keep me at home ;
and now little Anna is an additional anxiety. Oh dear,
no ! Fancy me at a meeting, and at night too !   Quite
absurd."

Stephen held his peace. He could have inquired
how it was that his aunt was always equal to dinner-
parties, theatres, concerts, and such like distractions,
at any and at all hours of the night ; but as his object
was to secure his father being properly attended, he
avoided any remark that might be regarded as litigious,
and so allowing the actual subject to drop, he turned
to another bearing of it.

" Don't you think my father is breaking in health a
little, Aunt Marcia ? " said Stephen.   " He is now and
then so abrupt and peculiar, that I fancy something
is wrong with his health."

" Percival says that he is very difficult to manage in
the office at times," answered Miss La Touche.   " It
would be better, it seems, if he would not be so per-
sistent in going there every day ; it is too much for
him, and he often makes mistakes with the correspondence."

" I think he is beginning to be aware that he must
stay a day at home now and then," replied Stephen.
" In that case you will sometimes find it difficult to

occupy him, and you may find him a little trying. It has occurred to me that Colin MacTaggart would be a nice cheerful companion, and that it is perhaps a fortunate thing that he is coming up to London."

"Um! I don't know," answered Miss La Touche. "Colin is not a society man, by all accounts. Percival has seen all the family, and he can't bear them."

"That is of no consequence," returned Stephen loftily. "I don't want Colin to be constantly here, but in the event of my father requiring a companion now and then, I think you might do a worse thing than encourage his own nephew to take him about, and show him some little attention. Colin is great at meetings and charitable clubs, I believe, and he would be a far better attendant than Martha, don't you think?"

"In some ways he would be, in others he would not," answered Marcia. "He could not keep off any of the women who might make up to your father at the meetings, and so forth, because he would never suspect what they were up to. Still, it might be convenient to have him here sometimes."

"MacTaggart is not a youth to be treated in a patronising fashion," Stephen replied. "He is a good, sturdy, straightforward lad, and I wish to bespeak your kind offices for him, Aunt Marcia. I fancy he wants employment in London, and I hope you will stand his friend."

"Oh, he cannot expect to be employed in the London office of our house," replied Marcia—"it would never answer. Percival would never hear of such a thing; but I will try what I can do."

"There's another matter to which I want to direct your attention, Aunt Marcia, and that is the way in which you keep the house accounts. My father, if he remains more at home, will be looking closely into them as an occupation."

"How come you to know anything about the house accounts?" inquired Miss La Touche, reddening.

"My father gave me the house-book this morning, and asked me to sum up the total before he wrote the cheque," replied Stephen. "Fortunately, I could aver that was quite right; but on looking over some of the items, I confess I was rather amazed at their peculiarity. For instance, what a sum we pay for faggots—quite enough to illuminate half the city of London."

"Not faggots, you stupid boy," cried Marcia; "you should read 'forgets'—things I don't remember."

"That's it!—you spell the word in more than one way; but the forgets amount to a large sum in the aggregate."

"You see I have so much to manage to make all expenses meet," replied Marcia. "Now that Percival pays a good board, your father will not allow the slightest margin. I have to go through a great deal to keep the house up to the mark, with these expensive dinners, to say nothing of the girls' dress and my own. As for dress, Percival would as soon think of giving the elephant in the Zoological Gardens a gold collar and badge, as he would give one of us an ornament of any kind, and yet he won't be seen with us if we are not dressed in the height of the fashion."

"The height of the fashion!" exclaimed Stephen; "that I take it is only the province of carriage people. As we are generally walking people, I should say the heels of the fashion would be near enough for the ladies of this house."

"There it is," said Marcia. "Percival and many other men are never weary of declaiming against the extravagance of women and their love of dress, and yet they censure their female relatives unmercifully if these do not appear to advantage, or if their toilets are not strictly in fashion, and, above all, fresh. It was only the other day that Percival declined to take Fanny to the Botanic, because her hat was not of the fashionable shape. It was very good, and she looked quite pretty in it; and this, after he had urged my brother to give the girls a smaller allowance than the sum which I had suggested."

"Too bad—much too bad," answered Stephen.

"Yes; and he preached about the folly of giving young girls an ample allowance, urging that it led to vanity and waste. Now I know the very contrary to be the case. A small allowance compels a woman to think of her clothes, and cutting and contriving, and moreover to be imposing on the public by trying to make old clothes look like new."

"Many ladies have to do that," said Stephen.

"Then," continued Marcia, "the annoyance of having

to borrow the pattern of your well-dressed friend's raiment, and the humiliation of being caught in the act of taking a bird's-eye view of the cut of another woman's sleeve, and the wearing imitation lace, and other cheap horrors, and after all this, the insult—yes, it is an insult—of being censured for not looking in the fashion. Bah! the men want everything in the first style, and they object to pay for it, where women are concerned; but they never grudge themselves their cigars and *recherché* dinners—not they."

There was so much truth in what Marcia had advanced, that Stephen contented himself with an exculpation, in so far as he was himself interested; so he said—

"I do not care to see any woman very expensively or fashionably dressed,—all I look for is good fit, taste as simple as you please for girls; but all must be bright and fresh—freshness is the first thing in any toilet. Good boots and gloves."

"The most expensive toilet of all is this one of freshness, at least in London," said Marcia. "The bill of the laundress would scare you into convulsions, if you go in for Arcadian simplicity and washing dresses. As to fit, the dressmakers charge quite as much for making a print dress as they do for making an expensive silk; and good boots and gloves cost simplicity quite as much as does a more pretentious toilet."

"At any rate," responded Stephen, still preserving the thread of his original caution, "don't you put down 'forgets' and 'faggots,' meaning bonnets; only think what a hold this would give Percival over you, should my father make any investigations concerning these items."

This was, perhaps, the most forcible argument which could be brought to bear on the subject, and Marcia, without committing herself to any promise, thought it, nevertheless, well to agree with her nephew that it would be advisable to let the house-book, in future, represent its own legitimate expenses. Besides, if her brother remained much at home, it would not be safe to juggle with the house accounts,—she fully admitted this also. Then they turned to other talk, and it transpired that a missive from Hunter's Lodge had informed Marcia that the Claverings were going direct to Brydone, there to finish the rest of Frank's holiday. Miss Clavering and Mr Glascott had taken their departure already, and Miss Fanshawe was coming at once to London for a week, to transact some business, and would be the guest of Lady Hautenbas.

Stephen smiled, but said nothing. He, however, re-solved to let the advantages of the Channel Islands, and those of Jersey especially, be placed before his pupil in the strongest light, and at once have the time arranged for departure on their reading-tour irremediably fixed.

There was a great contention afterwards over Colin MacTaggart. Percival declared that he should not be employed in the La Touche office, either at home or abroad. The old gentleman declared that he ought to be; and the whole family, with the exception of Stephen, opined that it would be the best thing for that youth if he could go out of the country at once. The crime of poverty suggests the punishment of immediate expatriation — especially that phase of poverty which is termed genteel. This is the worst phase, because it demands recognition from the equals of the criminal. "Go abroad," say they, not so much for the benefit of the sufferer as to relieve themselves of the incubus of a poor relation—the "incubus" of whose *presence* is oftener more oppressive than the duty of affording him help, either monetary or by personal influence. The poor relation, unless his or her state be redeemed by a patrician appearance, should in all cases be felt, but never be seen.

When the family *Vehmgericht* was concluded, Marcia inquired *who* was to counsel Mr MacTaggart, and put all the resolutions before him.

"Oh, you certainly," replied two or three in chorus; "women always manage these things well."

"That means," replied Marcia, "that when there is anything very disagreeable to be said or done, the lady of the house is always supposed to be equal to the occasion. However, I will manage this."

Colin arrived in due course, and it was very satisfactory to his cousin Stephen to perceive that the young Scotch gentleman was perfectly able to bear the brunt of the whole of the house of La Touche.

CHAPTER XII.

IT IS THE UNEXPECTED THAT ALWAYS HAPPENS.

"Now, Colin," said Marcia, a few days after his arrival, as she plumped herself down on the spring sofa, trying to look business-like, which was a complete failure, and really looking like a comfortable matron,—"I want to speak to you about your future prospects, as if I were your mother, you know."

"Weel, just for the time being," replied Colin, cautiously. "Ye never troubled much about my mother when she was in life, and ye are no ma-an's wife yet, ma good auntie; still, for the time being, I will listen to ye as if ye really were my mother."

Marcia bridled up a little at this answer, which was delivered in rather a broader Scotch accent than usual—for Colin was nervous, and in consequence he cast the load on his soul into his speech; and although he neither stammered nor hesitated, he emphasised his words most painfully. He might certainly have kicked, or wrung his hands, or even plucked at some near object, and thus come within the range of his aunt's reprobation. As it was, she merely said: "You must get rid of that accent, my dear; you are very bad to-day,—perhaps you have it at intervals." Marcia spoke as if she were treating of a case of ague or intermittent fever; but as her object was to conciliate this rough diamond, and to get him to go quietly when opportunity should present itself, she confined her attention to the matter in hand, and spoke with a little air of authority which was far from unbecoming. Leaving the accent to take care of itself until a more convenient season, she said—

"My good lad, I have had the experience of a dozen women in bringing up such a family of nephews and nieces as I have here; and by this time I know pretty well what occupation is best suited, not only for them, but for most other young people in whom I may become interested. Of course, as your aunt, I have been thinking how best to get you provided for; and I am truly pleased to find that you are ready to work, and to set about it at once."

Colin merely inclined his head, but stuck himself tighter into the wicker-basket chair in which he had seated himself, making it creak at every movement.

"Oh, you must never sit in that chair!" cried Marcia, hastily; "get up directly. That is Fanny's chair—my little dog; it is her own property—dear little faithful thing! She bit you, you remember, the night you came."

"I remember the little brute," quoth Colin,—"a cross-grained character, I should say. Be assured I

do not care to sit in her chair.   Chair! what an un-
natural life for a dog!"

"That I should live to hear my Fanny called a
brute!" returned Marcia, indignantly.   "However,
never mind,—we are talking business now.   About
your occupation,—I think you would not do well
in the same office as my brother, eh?"

As no time was left for a reply, Marcia went on:
"Relations never do agree in the same house of business, even if they are in widely different departments.
You would not be available for the foreign branch of
the house, would you?"

"At present I speak and write no language but my
own," Colin made answer; "but I could easy learn
any other,—I don't mind work and study.   I think
also," he added, with a quiet pride that was quite en-
nobling, "there would be little to find fault with in
my accounts."

"There is no vacancy in the foreign branch just
now," continued Marcia, without seeming to heed her
nephew's remark.   "Mr Percival told me yesterday
that there was no occupation for another clerk there."
(Marcia always spoke of the La Touche nephews as
Mister So-and-so, thereby drawing a distinction between
these and the inferior members of the family, as she
termed the MacTaggarts and some worthy cousins of
the name of Fulton: these last were trying relatives,
who always contrived to call at Hinton Square at the
seasons when Marcia was in full blow, and did not look
for the advent of country cousins.)

"I'm not particular," Colin replied; "my great wish is to get a situation wherein to earn a decent living."

"Very proper,—very proper indeed!" continued Marcia, giving her hair a pat, as she stole a look at the mirror which was on one side of her. "Very sensible, too, to see that you would not do in the same office with my brother: on this point you quite agree with me."

Colin had said nothing of the kind; but now he replied, with the most comprehensive and delightful candour, "I should not like to work with any of the family here."

"Exactly so," answered Miss La Touche, quite relieved to find that her nephew had no aspirations towards entering the office; "you see there would be so many masters, and incompatibility of—what is it?—and all that. I know them all so well, and have to go through so much myself daily with all their whims and fantigues,—to say nothing of the dinners, which really are knocking nails into my coffin. But I have not forgotten you, and that is why I wanted to talk with you this morning. I had a conversation yesterday with Mr Whyfly, who——"

"Mister wha?" interruped Colin, startled into his broadest accent at the sound of this extraordinary surname.

"Whyfly!—no, I think it is Highflyer,—yes, Mr Highflyer, the missionary somewhere out in Africa. He came back last month with a dreadful colour,

from being obliged to eat all his food half mixed with
mud or something.   However that may be, his complexion is gone, my dear,—I know it to my cost, for
he put my *Eau de Nil* satin dress quite in the back-
ground when he came near me, the evening he dined
here.   Well, he called yesterday, and I took the opportunity of speaking about you.   Mr Whyfly thinks that
if you would like to go and convert some of the tribes
on the Congo, and try and release the slaves there,—
or was it on Cape Comorin ? all the same thing,—he
could find you some work, and that you might be an
ornament to the cause—that is, if you are not eaten ;
but you can't afford to be nice, and must take your
chance of that."

"I'm not going to the Congo,—that's in Africa,
Aunt Marcia,—and Cape Comorin is on the south
of Hindustan," returned the youth with a grin, in-
cited by the shakiness of his aunt's geography ; " ma
wish and purpose is to get some occupation in or near
London.   I would not object to go to one of the Continental towns or ports ; but out of Europe I cannot
go, at least at present.   However, I would much prefer
to remain in London."

" Why ? " asked Marcia, quickly.

" Just because I have the beginning, at any rate, of
something to do.   The Scots minister who has that
Presbyterian Church near the British Museum has
already secured me three pupils to learn book-keeping
in the evenings.   I'm pretty fair at book-keeping and
shorthand writing, so I hope in time to get up an

evening class; but I want occupation in the day. Your friend, perhaps, might know of something I could do as a city missionary; I am sure there is scope enough for that, without going farther afield. Many good men have worked in the home mission before going abroad. Noble David Livingstone did so."

"David? Not the one that played the harp? I ought to have an interest in King David, for I play the harp myself. Really there is so much to remember nowadays, that one gets confused. There is, or was, a David who composed an opera,—or painted the 'Slaughter of the Innocents,' or something: his name was Félicien, I am sure of that."

Colin very nearly groaned. The heathenism of the moneyed classes was exercising his mind, and no wonder. He refrained, however, from making remarks on his aunt's mixed information, and contented himself with simply stating that he would like to work as a missionary in London.

"Why not go to foreign parts at once," said Marcia, "if you can get a chance of doing so? The Church Missionary Society would send you free. I am sure it *ought* to do something for a relative of this family, seeing what lots of sermons and collections we have had to endure for it. There would be the passage for nothing, you see, and they allow a sum for outfit, which you could keep, for I don't fancy they dress much on the Congo; and I could rake up enough for the voyage, —the lads here have lots of old clothes."

"I'm much obliged to you," returned Colin, stoutly; "but I told you before, Aunt Marcia, that I do not intend to go out of Europe at present."

Marcia was proceeding to administer a searching inquiry with regard to this decision, when she was frustrated in her intention by the door being gently opened. The cause of the interruption was the quiet entry of Lillian Fanshawe.

Mr MacTaggart, who had been sitting opposite the door and very close to it, stumbled against Fanny's chair as he backed himself out of the visitor's way, and so set a little velvet footstool, shaped like a pound-cake, and beaded on its surface with the La Touche arms, spinning over the room. The impetus caused it to rush full tilt against a Chippendale table, upon which a *bijou* service of Dresden china was set out in great state.

This had been a gift to one of Marcia's nieces a year or two ago; but that good lady, feeling that the presentee was not of an age to appreciate the value of it, had quietly appropriated the whole concern, satisfying her conscience that she would leave it to Eva in her will.

The cannon of the footstool against the table very nearly brought the Dresden china to a premature end: indeed nothing could have saved it had not Miss Fanshawe, with quiet adroitness, seized the edge of the table as it quivered from the collision, and held it firmly before it could rock forwards. "There are only a few things displaced—nothing broken," she said, in her measured tones, reassuring both aunt and nephew. "I ought not to have come in so abruptly; but I did not want to bring a servant all the way up-stairs. It is all my fault," she added, bowing graciously to Colin.

"Oh, what an escape! When I heard that dreadful chink, I thought all was over with that precious china," cried Marcia, as soon as she had recovered her breath. "My good lad," she continued, addressing Colin, "you should always be careful where china is concerned. You cannot tell how much I value that set, the gift of an old admirer, now——"

"No more," cut in Colin, in a tone which was intended to be at once sympathetic and conciliatory.

"No, no, not quite no more," returned Marcia, hurriedly; "you should let people conclude their own sentences, my dear. The gentleman I allude to has no business to be no more—at least, not at present. He owes the firm a lot of money. I meant to say that he is now in Japan, or in some of those American places."

"Asiatic, ye mean," corrected Colin, in a rasping tone. "I—all I can say is, that I am very sorry that I have startled you, ladies; but as the gimcrackery is safe, I hope I may say that no harm has been done, Aunt Marcia."

The epithet "gimcrackery" applied to this precious china was quite enough to send Miss La Touche into such a transport of indignation as to render her totally unfit for the ordinary purposes of society, for

an hour at least. Now, as it was Miss Fanshawe's
purpose to secure the attention of Marcia on an important subject, for which reason she had called early
to consult her, that young lady employed all the re-
sources of her genius to at once quench Miss La
Touche, and at the same time to get rid of Mr
MacTaggart.

A telegraphic signal, managed with great adroitness
of eye and expression, apprised Marcia that she would
do well to reserve her philippics for a more convenient
season. The hint was taken with magnetic celerity,
and the two ladies simultaneously joined issue to expedite the departure of Colin MacTaggart.

"You are just in time, Miss Fanshawe," said
Marcia, "for I am rather hurried, and you will be
able to give us some information upon the subject
we are now discussing. Do you know anybody who
wants a missionary, or to send one to the lower parts
of the City? Mr MacTaggart—Miss Fanshawe. I
ought to have introduced you, but the china—well,
as you are a clergyman's daughter, you will be able to
tell us how to set about all that sort of thing,—the
heathen, you know, and the roughs, which abound
somewhere at the East End."

"I have not the faintest knowledge of the subject,"
replied Miss Lillian, with consummate coolness. "In
fact, I make a point of ignoring all religious societies,
for I don't see why the *rôle* of clergyman's daughter
should be made so professional as it often is. But
really, I don't know anything more about the Mis-

sionary Society except that papa preaches a sermon annually for it, and sends the money up to London."

"I don't mean to trouble you," answered Marcia, "but perhaps you know of somebody to whom we could apply, and who could put us in the way of sending out this gentleman. He has a mission in life for converting people; and I believe it leads to some good things if people go at it in the right way."

Miss Fanshawe could hardly restrain a smile: however, as her policy just now was to stand well with Marcia, she replied graciously, "The Church Missionary Society, my dear Miss La Touche, would be the most proper source whereat to apply for information. Is your friend interested in the matter?" she inquired, looking at Colin, and feeling quite sure that Colin was the individual concerned.

Mr MacTaggart assented, and added that it was imperative that he should be employed at once; he would prefer working in the city.

"Waifs and strays and all that kind of thing," interpolated Marcia,—"look up the parents, and preach against the dev—I mean the old gentleman. I think, too, there would be some reading required. Yes; I am sure there's reading among the duties."

"Would that not fall under the head of a Scripture-reader's work?" said Miss Fanshawe.

"Exactly—the very thing!" replied Marcia, who knew as much about the matter as a cat. "Do you know of a place vacant for a Scripture-reader?"

Miss Fanshawe did not, but she would give Mr MacTaggart the address of a friend of her father, a Mr Carbery, who lived in Charterhouse Square, and who, she said, went in for that kind of thing. "And a very good thing it is," continued Miss Fanshawe, turning up her eyes piously, and beaming on Colin as they settled to his focus.

"Very well," said MacTaggart, seeing that an answer was expected of him; "the thing is, how am I to become a Scripture-reader? I am not sure that I understand all the duties required by such an appointment."

"Oh," said Marcia, "you will have to read the Bible, and explain it according to your own ideas, and if the people hold a different opinion, you can let them have it—that's the comfort of Protestantism. And you can look up the low places, and find out where fever really is, and where decent servants are to be found, and——"

"Pick up a choice bit of old china here and there," interrupted Miss Fanshawe, with just a suspicion of sarcasm in her tone.

"Quite so," returned Marcia, *en grand sérieux*. "You must keep your eyes open, Colin, and the chances are that you may fall in with a bit of Worcester or Crown Derby worth pounds for a shilling or two."

"I'm not a connoisseur," declared Colin, when he could get a word in. "A cup and saucer is to me a cup and saucer, and nothing more."

"But you should, in compliment to science," said

Marcia, "endeavour to know something about old china; you must go with the age, my dear. You will be doing a service to your fellow-creatures should you rescue some fine old piece from oblivion. Of course you must make yourself acquainted with some of the marks by which antique porcelain is recognised. I will give you a lesson on the subject some other time. I can only detain you a few minutes, as I want to go out before luncheon."

Here Miss Fanshawe bestowed an approving nod on her friend, as much as to say, "Shorten your advice, and let him go."

"What I want to impress upon you as to your future career," said Marcia, sententiously, "is drawn from Mr Whyfly's experience. You know—or rather you don't know—that Mr Highflyer—I never can remember that good man's name—did up the people in the low part of the City before he was sent out to Tamik-el-Hashid, or Wady something, a place with a *soupçon* of cotton-wool in the sound,—it does not matter. Well, he found the greatest comfort and benefit from having a partner in the work—a female."

"A female partner!" cried Colin, aghast; and even Miss Fanshawe opened her eyes wide and laughed.

"Yes," said Marcia—"a partner and a female; but she must have a *purse*, my dear. You will be tormented to death to feed this one and clothe that one, and attend to the spiritual schooling (which means pay) of a whole back-court. Now, there are plenty of good women—widows—left well off, who like a little pious excitement, and to have their say, and be looked up to; and Mr Why—Highfly—flier—got hold of one of these, the relict of a rich drysalter, and she worked with him, and he made her——"

"His wife," suggested Miss Fanshawe, in the hope of cutting Miss La Touche short.

"His wife! no, indeed; once married and his prestige would have been gone. It's like that with curates: the church is crowded as long as the curate is unmarried, but a great change takes place when he becomes a Benedict; so with the Scripture-reader, when he is young. A wife is a positive bar to his success; Mr Highfly knew better."

"Did he make the drysalter woman——?" Colin was beginning in the interests of strict morality and truth.

"My dear, he made her his almoner," interrupted Marcia.

"That's right," replied Colin, much relieved. "I did not know that such an office was attached to a city missionary or Scripture-reader."

"It's purely optional and honorary: you may not always find a suitable person," answered Marcia. "Of course it must be a woman with money, and one willing to be in subjection."

"The almoner, in this instance," said Miss Fanshawe, turning to Colin, "dispenses her *own* money, and applies it to the cases recommended by the Scripture-reader. Mr Whyfly was in luck; such an experience, I fancy, does not occur to many."

"Much better not," replied Colin, vigorously. "Thank you for your advice, Aunt Marcia. But no female partnership for me! I shall hope to raise a little money by general subscription, should I be fortunate enough to get the occupation I want; and if you will allow me to associate you in any work of mercy, I shall only be too proud to reckon upon the assistance of ma kinswoman."

So saying, Colin rose, and taking from Miss Fanshawe the card upon which she had written Mr Carbery's address, he took leave of the ladies, and went forth in his honest single-heartedness, very much as one who had come off victorious over the world and the flesh. Aunt Marcia, at any rate, respected him as being one upon whom the good things of the world were utterly thrown away, for she remarked as he closed the door—

"He is of the old-fashioned stuff,—nothing will turn him, if he believes a thing to be right: he would go through fire and water for a principle."

"Ay," said Miss Fanshawe, half sadly; "the great thing in this world is to be sure that one is right. Indeed it is a great puzzle to define the right thing: society goes one way, moral and religious teaching often go directly the other. I suppose the height of perfection is reached when we manage to mix all together, so as to stand well with the world."

"Money always binds the most conflicting positions and opinions together," moralised Marcia. "I don't mean to say that it always brings happiness," she continued, looking very wise.

"I don't know," said Lillian, slowly; "money certainly smoothes the way to happiness in many cases. Just look at our family at home: we are striving every nerve to keep up appearances, and only those who are situated in like circumstances can understand the amount of self-denial we all have to go through in order to keep up our position before the world; and yet the world in general must know that the effort is great, and perhaps wonders why we make it."

"I certainly think," said Marcia, with the want of tact which was perhaps the strongest point in her character—"I certainly think you would have been better off had you lived at the rectory, and let Pinnacles Court."

"Then," returned Lillian, "we should have been but parish clergy; now, at the Court we are county gentry."

"Just so," returned Marcia; "then you have your reward for the sacrifices you make: you are the Fanshawes of Pinnacles Court, and if you tell the world that the first Fanshawe came over with the Conqueror and Queen Matilda as the Court tanner, the world will respect you accordingly. My dear, we must go with the times. The maxim of the day is self-glorification; some take it out in money, some in the boast of ancient family."

"Yes; and in the next generation, my father thinks, the boast will be that of the best-crammed young person, male or female, under a given standard of age. Women, he says, will step into the place of men, and we are to have an age of preaching females, medical females, and lawyer females, and, of course, their counterpart also—semi-feminised men."

"How dreadful!" exclaimed Marcia. "What's to become of the babies?"

"That subject my father did not touch upon; but both my parents seem to think there are too many children in the world. My mother is always grumbling at there being so many of us—as if we could help it! However, I, as the eldest, see it to be my duty to relieve them of my maintenance as speedily as possible; but before I make a final decision, I have come to consult you."

"What!" exclaimed Marcia in great delight,—"has Percival come forward in the proper form? I was afraid that he had rather cooled on the matter. He has been, I suppose, to see you at your aunt's house,—quite the proper thing——"

"You are quite mistaken in your inferences, Miss La Touche," replied the young lady, as soon as she could get a word in. "Your nephew is no suitor of mine; I have not set eyes on him since I came to London."

"Of course I only assumed this," said Marcia, wondering. "We heard you were on a visit to Lady Hautenbas, before I got your note last week telling me you were in town on business for Mr Fanshawe. Percival is so close when he likes, and never tells me

more than he can help, that I thought it possible he
might have availed himself of the opportunity of
calling upon you, and following up this privilege. I
know he always admired you very much; and I am
very sorry that I am not to claim you as a relative."

As Marcia spoke she pressed the girl's hand with
real sincerity; for of all the young ladies who had
been admitted as " possible " for Percival, his aunt
most undoubtedly preferred Miss Fanshawe. Not
only would that young lady have done credit to the
taste of Mr La Touche, but as his wife she would
have added dignity to the alliance, and would, above
all things, have kept Percival straight. This certainly
was a great chance missed; but the die was cast, and
Miss La Touche, curious to know who the real suitor
of Miss Fanshawe might be, proceeded to ascertain
that fact by means of a leading question.

" I suppose some one of the eligibles who have the
entrée of the house of Lady Hautenbas has fallen a
victim to your charms ? " said Marcia, smiling.

" No," returned her friend, without any circumlocu-
tion ; " the victim lives mostly in the country, and he
is an elderly man——"

" Colonel Leppell ! " Marcia almost screamed with
astonishment. " Why, the man has only been a
widower a few weeks ! and he has such a host of
children ; and he has no money—not a rap beyond
his pay ; and he must be forty-eight if he is a day."

" You are quite wrong," returned Miss Fanshawe,
who sat enjoying Marcia's ejaculations. " I mean you

are wrong as to the individual, but you are right as to the sum of Colonel Leppell's age; he is past forty-eight years. My victim is turned fifty-eight years. Now, cannot you guess who the victim is?"

Marcia opened her eyes, turned very pink, and then gasped, "It is never, never—Mr Glascott—Mr Glascott of Brydone!"

"The same; and why not?" returned Miss Fanshawe, the marble hue of her skin now flushing with. a lovely colour. As her eyes dilated, Marcia could not help noticing how much the girl resembled the late Mrs Leppell,—never had she been more struck by the likeness.

"Why not?" reiterated Lillian. "Mr Glascott is a handsome, healthy man, very destitute of whims and freaks. His fortune is large; and in my opinion the alliance has only one drawback—not the drawback of disparity of age,—that's nobody's business but our own, — but the drawback of the cousin — ward, as she is called — Miss Clavering. I have come to consult you on this point, for you have had so much experience with girls."

"Do you mean that you anticipate any difficulty as to Miss Clavering's residence at Brydone, in the event of your marrying her guardian?" Marcia inquired.

"That is just the point," returned Miss Fanshawe; "and it is so important that I have refrained from giving Mr Glascott a decided answer till I can see my way to arrange this. There cannot be two mistresses at Brydone—that is quite clear."

"No; but Miss Clavering would cede to her guardian's wife, I should think, without any demur," said Marcia. "You might propose," continued the lady, "that Miss Clavering should live half the year with her brother and his wife."

"Mr Glascott feels inclined to propose that; but he does not seem to be very hearty on the matter. He cannot see why we cannot live amicably together."

"Nor do I," replied Marcia. "A little consideration is due, I think, to Miss Clavering. She has gone to Brydone with the idea that she is to be sole mistress there; all the furnishing and arrangements, I believe, depend upon her. She will hardly have time to get the place in order and assume the duties when she will find herself displaced. You must allow it will be very hard on her; neither you nor I would like it, were we in her place."

"That is quite true," Lillian answered; "but the fact is that I don't like Miss Clavering. I never liked her from the first moment I beheld her."

Lillian confidently expected that Miss La Touche would join issue with her at this assertion. She was not aware that Marcia, so far from resenting Percival's rejection, was in total ignorance that he had made proposals to Miss Clavering.

His leaving the picnic party in Barkholme woods so suddenly was universally believed to have been the effect of a severe attack of dyspepsia, accompanied by fainting; and as he had suffered some time before from a like seizure, Marcia had taken the whole *en grand sérieux*, and highly approved of her nephew's adroit management in getting himself conveyed so opportunely to Yarne in the conveyance of Mr Clowes.

On his arrival there Mr La Touche had, to save appearances, consulted a doctor, and when Marcia returned to the Red Lion Hotel she found Percival in bed, vowing he had taken a chill, and abjuring picnics for evermore.

Thus it was that Miss La Touche was in profound ignorance of Percival's wooing. She had thought him very indifferent that day towards Miss Fanshawe, but she ascribed that circumstance to a proclivity which this nephew had of playing *garçon volage*, and as Percival made no sign, the subject passed from her mind.

Miss Fanshawe at once perceived this, and thought it unadvisable to enlighten her hostess: it would hardly be wise to let Marcia imagine that her dislike to Miss Clavering should have arisen from Percival's attentions. These attentions had at one time been prominently directed towards herself,—so much so, that there was some ground for this inference had Miss La Touche known more, or had she been malevolently inclined.

So Miss Fanshawe kept to general topics, attributing her objection to Miss Clavering as an inmate to the desire she had always had of being sole mistress of a house of her own.

" You know," she said, in support of this declaration,

"how little I have had of real comfort at home: my position as the eldest daughter is completely ignored, or, at least, it is only recognised when I can do what none of the rest can or will do. My presence in London is a case in point. Some family affairs require law business and some interviewing of different persons. My father can't leave home just now, and my mother is only recovering from another baby, so I have been sent, principally, I believe, because I am supposed to be able to manage Lady Hautenbas, who is rather idiotic where business and writing business letters are concerned."

"But you have your reward," Marcia replied. "Mr Glascott, I take it, is in town."

"Yes; he came up from Brydone to be out of the way of the furnishing and so forth, and to make some purchases. He called two days ago, and we settled almost everything but this affair of Miss Clavering's home. All will be finally decided in a week; but I do wish that girl could make her home with her brother."

"Why not?" said Miss La Touche; "I am sure Mrs Clavering would be delighted with such an arrangement."

"Yes; but I doubt if Mr Clavering would appreciate it. The brother and sister are very unlike; and Mr Glascott admits that Willina's outspoken ways and her independence of manner rather irritate Mr Clavering."

"She will most likely marry soon, and well," said Marcia.

"If she would do that, I should not mind her re-siding for a time at Brydone. I think she intends to. marry; but, if I am not very much mistaken, she will neither marry soon nor well—for *well*, of course, means money, or money's worth in position and connection. She will have to wait long before that is achieved."

"Then there is an admirer in the case?" inquired the elder lady.

"I believe so; but I am sure Mr Glascott would not consent to the match,—there are objections to the family of the gentleman."

Now, as Miss Fanshawe was alluding to Mr Stephen La Touche, she could not in common propriety say more; and as Marcia had seriously believed that her younger nephew had been much inclined towards Lillian, she had no idea that Stephen had the remotest idea of aspiring to Miss Clavering, and so she took in this history very readily. She, however, enjoined her friend to accept the present state of things, sweeten-ing the pill by the assurance that Willina would be much from home paying visits. After the first dis-appointment, Miss Clavering would naturally leave home more readily when she knew that Mr Glascott had some one to look after him and make his house comfortable.

Miss Fanshawe conceded that she had not viewed the subject in that light, and she therefore drew com-fort from the suggestions of her friend: yes, she would finally accept Mr Glascott, and leave Miss Clavering to chance. "I believe she dislikes me as much as I dislike her," Miss Lillian averred. "It is just as well, as she will do her best to be as much away from Brydone as possible."

"Of course, she as yet knows nothing of Mr Glascott's plans?—she will be greatly astonished," quoth Marcia.

"I think she suspects something, and I daresay she lays it to my wiles," replied Miss Fanshawe. "Women are fond of indulging in these ideas where an elderly man and a young girl are concerned. But, to tell you the truth, Colonel Leppell has been the main instrument in bringing this about."

"I should not have thought that he was much of a matchmaker," Miss La Touche remarked.

"Nor is he; but Mr Glascott was struck at first by the remarkable likeness which I bear to the late Mrs Leppell when she was young: the Colonel thought he would do us both a good turn, and so he prompted Mr Glascott to pay his addresses to me. For my part, I really like Mr Glascott, and a marriage with him will be a most fortunate method of escaping from home."

"And he never thought of the difference this would make to Miss Clavering?" returned Marcia.

"I suppose not. The Colonel is my friend, and he, knowing how I am situated at home, and that I am penniless, sought to do me a kindness. Miss Clavering has a little money of her own, and I daresay she will be provided for in addition, if she marry to the satisfaction of her brother and her guardian."

"Um! and what will your parents say to your engagement?" inquired Miss La Touche.

"I am sure they ought to be very much gratified," the young lady replied, with the utmost coolness. "My mother gets rid of me without trouble. It is possible that my father will object to the disparity of age; but he will remember his large family of daughters and be thankful, and they will both combine to make my marriage useful as a means of getting off my sisters."

"Very natural," observed Maria.

"But I do not intend anything of the kind," replied the young lady; "and that is one advantage of Brydone being over the sea. Mr Glascott shall never feel that he has married a family, nor shall my mother make a convenience of me in any way."

This was conducting matters with a vengeance, Marcia thought; but she merely said, "I suppose, when all is arranged, your wedding will follow immediately?"

"I think so; but Mr Glascott is going to have a large house-warming, and he wishes Miss Clavering to do the honours. The Claverings are to stay there, and some other friends. The engagement will be announced after that, but of course I shall inform my father. At present, please consider what I have told you as a secret."

Marcia promised; and as Miss Fanshawe had taken her advice, she parted on very good terms with that lady, notwithstanding that she scarcely approved of the manner in which Lillian had mentioned her

mother. " I suppose Mrs Fanshawe has herself to
thank," mused Miss La Touche; "she *is* a hard
worldly woman. At the same time, I don't admire
Lillian for being so ready to impart that fact to
every one she sees. Mr Glascott is a kindly, nice
man; but I think he would have done better to
eschew Miss Fanshawe and stick to his cousin."

Thus Marcia, who, after eating her luncheon in
solitude—for Miss Fanshawe, apprehensive of meeting Percival, who often came home to that meal, had
refused the invitation to remain—proceeded to join
her nieces, who were all out on a shopping expedition.

Lillian Fanshawe returned to her aunt's house, and
wrote to Mr Glascott at his hotel. It was such a note
as to bring that gentleman, glowing with rapture, to
Lady Hautenbas' abode. Miss Fanshawe's aunt had
gone for an airing, and had been advised by her niece
to take the opportunity of returning some visits in the
country, the day being fine, and the roads in good condition. Lillian, therefore, had the field to herself; and
at the end of an hour's conference everything was
discussed and settled between Mr Glascott and his
betrothed wife.

" To think, my dear," said he, " that after these long
years of unwedded life, I should meet my fate with
one who is the exact counterpart of the woman who
was the love of my early days. It is wonderfully
strange! When I look upon you, all my youth, all
my first fresh feelings, return in redoubled force.

Happiness has come to me whilst I have been sleeping."

"I hope so," she answered; "may it ever remain with you. It will be my utmost endeavour to make your home happy,—to prove myself in every way worthy of the choice you have made."

Mr Glascott pressed her hands within his own, and then, bending low, imprinted a kiss on her head. This, in his devotion and timid respect, was all he ventured to do.

"I dread one thing," he said, after a pause; "your parents will take exception to my age."

"No," she said; "I am years older than my own age, and they both know that. Better too for you that it is so. It is a mistake to measure the portion of life by the stiff hard measure of the number of moons that have passed over us. I feel sure that my proper position in this world is that of the wife of an elderly man."

Was she sincere in what she then said?—was it not rather that her wifehood would screen her from the passion for Francis Clavering, which was burnt into every fibre of her being?

Did she not bestow herself upon the man before her from the conviction that, by so doing, she was securing more opportunity and more freedom for intercourse with this dangerous friend than she could with any propriety achieve did she remain single? and would not Mr Clavering, on his part, gladly assent to her marriage with his cousin as the best method of cementing family affection, and adding social status to the head of the house?

Ah, yes; Brydone, by her means, should be the happy harbour of refuge—the place whereto Francis should repair when, perchance, he might be over-wrought in brain, and be glad of intellectual help.

She included Mary in a second-hand kind of way in these ruminations; of Willina she never even thought.

But Mr Glascott had not, in spite of his happiness, been thus forgetful; and the difference which his un-expectedly entering into matrimony might make to Miss Clavering certainly caused him some anxiety, and, if the truth must be told, some reproach also.

He had all his life shown a great preference for Francis. The young man's talent, his ambition, and the fixed intention which he expressed to make a name in the world, took his guardian by storm, as it were; and thus, undesignedly, Mr Glascott came to regard him as the one to whom all must be ceded, and to whom every consideration must be allowed. He loved Willina, but it was in a totally different manner. In the brother he felt pride; with the sister, he could not forget that she was of the sex that had deceived him, and laid his life desolate.

As years passed on this feeling somewhat changed. When Willina emerged from the Brussels convent at which she had been educated—beautiful, frank, and as truthful as the light of day—Everard Glascott began to wonder why he had not more greatly ap-preciated his charming cousin; and on giving this

matter serious consideration, he had resolved, after
providing for Francis, to make her mistress of his
house, and further, to dower her handsomely when
the time should come for her to leave him for a
husband's home.

At the same time, it never occurred to him to think
that she would do other than make a good marriage;
still less could he imagine that he himself would ever
seek to be taken in the toils of matrimony. Strange,
too, that finding himself, late in life, in the position of
a wooer, he should be told that the only objection to
his suit lay in the presence of Willina Clavering as
an inmate of his house!

This objection being now cleared away, and the
reason of its existence being alleged by Miss Fanshawe
to have greatly arisen from a feeling of delicacy in
ousting Mr Glascott's ward from her position, together
with some fear of that young lady's resentment, all,
it was to be hoped, would go on propitiously for the
future.

Mr Glascott undertook to answer for Miss Clavering's ready acquiescence in his marriage scheme. She
was so generous, so keenly sensible to all in which his
happiness was concerned, that opposition on her part
was scarcely possible. Thus he spoke.

The betrothed soon parted. Their adieux were cordial, but neither of them evinced any great demonstra-
tion of affection. This arose on Mr Glascott's part
from a nervous fear of being prompted to act as a
younger man would have acted, and by so doing lose

in dignity in the eyes of his betrothed. In spite of his enchantment, he maintained some regard for the fitness of things.

Lillian looked magnificent, as her wooer kissed her hand and uttered his thanks. "How fortunate I am!" said she to herself. "Mr Clavering will now find in reality a second home at Brydone. Write to my father," she said aloud; "you must ask his consent, but it's only a matter of form."

CHAPTER XIII.

BRYDONE.

AT length Mr Glascott, after much locomotion and sundry delays, convened his guests, and found himself installed in a permanent home under the roof of a habitation which had been more or less tenanted by successive generations of his family. It was here that he had intended, in the first blush of his youthful hopes, to bring his bride, rejoicing, if the truth must be told, that the intervening ocean would be a most successful element in separating her from her mother, and would, at all events, secure that retirement which, to some persons, is indispensable to the comfort of newly married life.

We know that these hopes were frustrated; but if all things come to those who wait, Everard Glascott, with the prospects now opening before him, believed perhaps that fortune had favoured him with the kindliest sympathy; for was not the bride who was coming to adorn that home a perfect resemblance of his first fair love, and had she not been given to him out of the hand of the man who at one time had been his successful rival, nay, his foe?

It was strange, passing strange; but does not history repeat itself in the small ring as surely as in the large circle? What is there new beneath the sun?

It was a peculiar-looking place this seaside home of Brydone—unpicturesque in itself, but largely indebted to its surroundings for many features of interest, which seemed to increase in fascination as the eye dwelt upon them. The reason of this may be, that the whole region was so utterly different from the conventional style of watering-place—combining as it did the wild beauty of the Claddagh with the barren appearance of the ancient Norman farm - dwelling, with its bare stones, unclothed by ivy or trailing brier, its cottars' homes, little else than stone hovels, comfortless and cold. The redeeming points in this part of the scene were the bright slate-blue hydrangeas, which everywhere grew in great perfection, together with the orange-umber tints which dotted portions of the undulating ground. These imparted a glow of warmth, and were in highly artistic keeping with the blue colour of the flowering-shrubs.

The house belonging to Mr Glascott had no particular history: it had served as a refuge in far-away times to the fallen fortunes of a family long extinct, the members of which had fought for Charles I. with stanch fidelity, and had met with—the usual reward when that monarch's son came to his own. How it afterwards came into the possession of those bearing his name, Mr Glascott was utterly ignorant, nor did he apparently seek information on the matter. That it had descended honestly from father to son, or from uncle to nephew, he was thoroughly convinced. He liked the place, and his easy fortune would make it available as a comfortable home for his declining years.

The peculiarity of the building lent it some charm. White stone or red brick would have been somehow out of place, or positively glaring, in juxtaposition with other points of colour; hence its composition of grey small stones did credit to the taste of the builder, or perhaps to the circumstance that no other material was at hand at the time of its erection.

These stones were cemented with a composition of sea-shell lime, coarse gravel, and a proportion of the *Melobesia polymorpha*, a coralline which grows profusely on the submarine rocks about the whole of the Channel Islands.

St Columba knew the value of this coralline. It is said that he caused the cement of which it forms a large component part to be employed in welding together the stones of the Abbey of Iona.

Even under these conditions of its early erection, Brydone could not pretend to approach the appearance of an abbey, nor even to that of a manor-house. It probably had been a yeoman's dwelling at the outset; subsequently, and at various periods, enlarged and added to, according to the taste or convenience of the inhabitants of the time. It was remarkably long and wide in construction, and possibly its only virtue consisted in the thickness of its walls, and the deep embrasures which gave an ancient picturesque appearance to the diamond-paned windows which were set within them. A handsome terrace (an addition of modern times) ran round three sides of the house, and the ground beyond undulated downwards till it joined the rocks and the sea.

Willina Clavering was delighted ; there was so much to be done in addition to what had already been done, so much of that life which a woman only can bring into any dwelling, to diffuse in every form, to permeate, and make the presence of that life to be felt. It was the acme of the young girl's hope—her guardian with a settled home of his own, and she the mistress, dispensing his hospitality, his charity, and all the incidental kindnesses which flow from a good man's heart, and which become doubly blessed when there is a true, good woman to guide their course.

Francis Clavering and his bride came alone. It was thought the kinder thing on the part of their hosts that, under the burden of her sorrow, Mary's visit should be at first as private as possible, and unfettered by the presence of other guests. This suited admirably. The two young ladies were daily drawn together, becoming steadily affectionate from the appreciation of each other's worth ; and the occupation which each day, in some shape or other, demanded, prevented time from lying heavily on their hands.

Much to the surprise of his wife, Frank, who really knew very little of this residence of Brydone—nothing beyond the sea-bathing trips of his holiday times, in fact — began to express himself delighted with the place, and to avow that, as a geological hunting-ground, the island of Jersey had hitherto met with scant justice at the hands of *savans*, and the scientific world in general.

"Have you made any great discovery, Frank?" said Miss Clavering, as her brother promulgated this opinion.

"I can scarcely say that I have hitherto made a great discovery. I have known all along that this island contains no fossils; but my rambles of late convince me that Jersey possesses an abundance of a class of rock known as Old Rhyolites."

"Old who!" exclaimed both the girls in a breath.

"Old Rhyolites," repeated Frank, in a tone which bordered on exasperation. "It is the name of a species of rock which is rare, very rare, in other parts of the globe. Well, if I had been asked six months ago, I could not have stated positively that I had ever met with more than a mere sample specimen of this variety of rock; now, two miles hence, the geological wealth of this peculiar variety is simply amazing. I wonder it has escaped observation so long."

"I think you told me that Jersey rocks belong to the Primary Formation," said Mrs Clavering, looking highly scientific.

"Quite right," replied the husband and master, with

an air of patronage. "You know, of course, what Primary Formation means?"

"Hum!—the first rock or land safe to sit upon after the flood, I suppose," answered Madam Mary.

"Not exactly. The first dry land which was ever created is the Primary Formation," corrected Mr Clavering. "Now it is probable that Jersey had emerged out of the primeval waters long before England and France were known."

"Why, where were they?"

"Still buried beneath the deep. They belong to the Secondary and Tertiary periods," said Mr Clavering.

"Fancy England being secondary in any way! Are there any more rocks with queer names about these parts?"

"If I were to say that, classified scientifically, there would be nearly a hundred varieties, I should not be beyond the mark; but I suppose neither of you could discern the difference betwixt one variety and another."

"I don't know," said Willina, slowly. "Yes, I think I could, if the difference were very striking. Could you classify, Mary?" She turned to her sister, but Mrs Clavering had walked to the other end of the terrace, to exchange greetings with Willina's magnificent collie dog.

"I do wish one of you could help me a little, Willina, whilst I am here; but I know this branch of science has no charms for either of you. Now, Miss Fanshawe——"

"Oh, for goodness' sake, don't mention Miss Fan-

shawe!" replied Miss Clavering, indiscreetly. "We
have had quite enough of her at Hunter's Lodge, with
her airs of superiority. You have quite spoiled her,
Frank."

"How—in what way?" inquired Mr Clavering, a
bright spot on his cheek and a spasm in his voice.

"Why, by always deferring to her opinion, and
asking her advice, and giving her your classification
work. She looks down upon Mary and me as two
females, and nothing more. Oh, I am so thankful she
is not here!"

Francis hesitated a moment, and then expressed his
surprise that Miss Fanshawe did not seem to be invited
amongst the guests who were coming later on.

"Cousin Everard did say something about it; but I
proposed that Clara Leppell should be asked instead.
Poor girl, she has had a great shock, and really wants
a change."

"Um! I take leave to say that it looks rather
marked to omit Miss Fanshawe, my wife's early
friend," replied Mr Clavering, lowering at his sister.

"So it may," replied Willina; "but the fact is,
Frank, I don't admire Miss Fanshawe, with her cold
reticent ways, so unlike a young girl. Besides, Cousin
Everard has promised that I shall invite whom I
please, and that all the honours of the house-warming
are to be mine."

"And you exclude my wife's particular friend, as a
method of evincing your talent for hospitality," returned Frank, with something very like a sneer.

" You can put it that way if you choose," returned Miss Clavering ; " but I will only just remark that in my opinion the lady in question cares far less for your wife than your wife cares for her. Mary is worth a hundred of her ! "

Although Frank longed to contradict his sister, he could not well champion Miss Fanshawe at the expense of his own wife, and so he contented himself by saying, " Just like you women—you are all the same. If any one of your sex happens to combine brains with beauty, there's no end to the detraction she meets with. I thought you had more sense, Willina."

"I do not wish to detract from any merits Miss Fanshawe may possess," replied Miss Clavering. "She is handsome, and she is clever ; but I do not like her. And I will go further, and say that my dislike is much of the nature of that avowed by the individual who failed to appreciate the late Dr Fell. I won't inflict the quotation upon you — it is as proverbial as a household word."

" I know that," returned Francis, sharply. " In its way, the quotation is as inane a confession of idiocy as can well be imagined. I don't wonder that you spare both yourself and me on this point. Let me advise you, my dear girl ; if you really dislike any person, or even any thing, be logical enough to hold some reason, or, being a woman, some show of reason, for that dislike."

Aggravated by the *haut en bas* air of her brother, Willina retorted, more frankly perhaps than wisely,

"I *have* a very strong reason for disliking Miss Fan-shawe—and, moreover, it grows and grows. If I can help it, she shall never set foot here."

"That is strong language," Mr Clavering replied, and then he fixed a searching look on his sister.

What could she mean? Had she divined that his own relations with Miss Fanshawe were somewhat exclusive, and his attentions to that lady rather marked, especially in his position as a newly married man? Could it be—and Francis hoped it could be—merely that unreasoning, undefinable antipathy which, like a marsh fog, obliterates all sense of discernment, or at best presents all objects, foul or fair, in an utterly distorted focus both from the mental and the physical point of view?

Francis knew well enough that Willina's nature was too proud for jealousy—that is, for jealousy of one who was nothing other than a woman, and a woman, moreover, who did not come between herself and any object of affection.

So he dismissed this fancy; and not trusting to make more direct inquiry, he intensified his look, and stood as if in expectation of a ready answer.

Now was Willina's turn for vacillation. She had her strong reason, verily; it emanated from a source to which she was indebted solely to her feminine sagacity for discovery, but she stood alone, as yet, with her reason.

The time was not come when she could venture to say to her brother, "Our guardian is desperately enamoured of Lillian Fanshawe; for that cause I cannot brook her presence here."

But she gave him a reply which was neither doubtful nor ambiguous. "Were I to speak frankly," she said, " I should only render you very uncomfortable, and perhaps very angry also. I am not going to make any further explanation, so rest content with the assurance that Miss Fanshawe dislikes me even more heartily than I dislike her. She has very good cause to do so; and if you question this statement, she will, if she choose—although a woman—furnish you with a very excellent reason for her state of mind."

Mr Clavering stood aghast. However, his sister's concluding piece of information was, on the whole, consolatory. It was evident that something personal, and not his own Platonic attentions to Miss Fanshawe, was the active agent which influenced Willina's determination to exclude that young lady from the hospitalities of Brydone.

However, when standing on ticklish ground it is prudent to be quiescent, and so Francis contented himself by remarking that he would trust to time for revealing this mystery: in the interim, he felt sure that his guardian would know what was the proper thing to do.

Full well Miss Clavering knew this also. Was it not on account of the delicate relations which subsisted between Miss Fanshawe and Cousin Everard that the latter had so readily fallen in with the suggestion that it would be more advisable to invite Clara .

Leppell to Brydone than Lillian Fanshawe!   "If there be any understanding between them," Miss Clavering argued to herself, "it certainly would not be the thing to invite Miss Fanshawe here.   Cousin Everard is a great stickler for the proprieties, I know."

"You spoke of Clara coming here shortly," said Frank; "how on earth is she to travel?   She surely cannot make so long a journey by herself?"

"That, I think, is nearly arranged," returned Willina.   "Mr Glascott, as you know, was in London for three days last week—is it not fortunate that he never suffers from the sea?—well, he fell in with Mr or Mrs Braintree.   It seems they are thinking of coming to Jersey for a sea change, and so Cousin Everard proposed that they should communicate with the Leppells, and bring Clara with them here."

"They are never going to stay here,—the Braintrees?   They are very well in their way, but I don't fancy them as inmates."

"Don't be alarmed; Mrs Braintree has secured rooms at that hotel near Bowley Bay.   They will be here, of course, now and then as visitors," returned Miss Clavering.   "If Mrs Braintree would only not carry such an atmosphere of Canon's wife about with her, I should like her better; but still she is far superior to the average run of the dignified clergy-woman, inasmuch as she is perfectly free from their airs and nonsense."

"True.   What other people have you—to stay in the house, I mean?"

"Some old Guernsey friends—the De Saumarez and a Mr De Brett,—you must remember the families,—and, by the way, one of the La Touches."

"Not that dreadful little cad that was with his aunt at our wedding?" exclaimed Francis, in horror.

"No, the brother—the one you met at Pinnacles."

"Oh, he's a nice fellow—that's all right. He ought to have been at our wedding, I believe; but there was some bungle about his invitation, Mary heard—in fact, nobody seemed to know whether he had been written to or not."

"Poor Mrs Leppell fancied she had written to Mr Stephen La Touche; but it appears she omitted to do so. The Colonel and Cousin Everard put it all right, and Mr Glascott gave him a general invitation to come here whenever it might please him to do so," answered Miss Clavering.

"I am glad he will be here; it will be somebody with whom I can converse," avowed Mr Clavering. "Stephen La Touche knows a little about geology, and he will, I daresay, be glad of a scientific companion in his walks about the island."

"Do not reckon upon him too surely," replied Miss Clavering, piqued, in spite of herself, at her brother's cool proposition of making a convenience of Mr La Touche. "I don't think Mr La Touche will be a visitor in the house, although Cousin Everard has invited him to stay here during his vacation."

"Why does La Touche not come, then?"

" Because he has a reading pupil with whom he is engaged to make a short tour, and——"

" Who's the pupil ?" inquired Mr Clavering.

" A son of General Willoughby. This young man's reading has been arrested on account of ill-health. The Channel Islands have been recommended to him for their climate. Under these circumstances, you see, Mr La Touche could not make any arrangements, as Mr Willoughby might elect to reside at Guernsey or Sark."

" But they are coming here, you say ?"

" Cousin Everard believes that they will try Jersey first, and from here make excursions to the neighbouring islands," said Willina.

" Oh ! I should think they will stay at Bowley Bay. There's plenty of accommodation about that part, and I daresay this young Willoughby will be pleased to come here with La Touche for a few days," replied Mr Clavering.

" Very likely. Cousin Everard thought he had better see what Mr Willoughby was like before sending him an invitation to stay with us."

" Quite right ; an invalid would be an awful nuisance, and sick lads are worse than women," Francis declared. " Well, so as I can get hold of La Touche for some long walks and some exploration work, I shall be quite content."

" I daresay the pupil will turn out to be a very great acquisition to us all," said Miss Clavering, decidedly. She was exasperated by the cool selfish-

ness of her brother, and had no other way of relieving her feelings but by direct contradiction.

"Let us hope so," returned Mr Clavering, without
noticing his sister's tone; "in that case he can accompany us in our expeditions, and obtain some further
information on geology. Where on earth has Mary
got to? Holloa! Moll, just leave off philandering
with that dog a moment; I want you."

Miss Clavering here seized the opportunity to take
herself out of the way; the collie dog was disgusted
because his term of petting had come to an end.
Frank Clavering did not like dogs, and, what was
worse, no dog ever seemed to care to approach him.
Sir Walter Scott was not far wrong when he promulgated the caution, "Beware of the man or woman
whom a dog thoroughly distrusts. At the best, it is a
bad sign of the individual."

During the following week Mr Glascott's guests
arrived by twos and threes. Mrs Braintree brought
her husband and Clara Leppell, and had taken very
good care of both of them. Sarah Braintree was not
with her parents, being then on a visit in one of the
northern counties.

Mr La Touche and his pupil also arrived in due
course; and it is satisfactory to state that Mr Clavering was agreeably disappointed in Mr Willoughby,
the latter turning out to be a fine gentlemanly lad,
fond of boating and of roving over land, and possessing a highly developed proclivity towards geological
research. He had a cough, and he had somewhat

overgrown his strength; but, to use his own expression, "he was safe to be all right jolly soon now; and what a thing it was to get some wrinkles in geology from that scientific swell, Mr Clavering!"

The two gentlemen put up at the same hotel as the Braintrees, and on the day following their arrival the hotel party went together to lunch at Brydone. The general conversation naturally turned upon the experiences of the sea.

"I think nothing of the crossing between Southampton and the islands," Mr Glascott had averred. "It may be a little rough near the 'Caskets'; but, dear me! that is soon over. I cannot understand people being so afflicted by sea-sickness as so many are."

"If you only knew what agony it is, Cousin Everard," said Miss Clavering, "you would not require much explanation. What do you say, Mr Willoughby?"

"Rather; and I must add my opinion that the crowning aggravation of a night of suffering culminates in the landing at this island."

"I quite agree with you," interposed Mrs Braintree; "the landing was nearly the death of the Canon—the pier such a height, and the ascending steps so narrow and slippery."

"Yes," confirmed Stephen La Touche, "and the whole population seems to think it its duty to fringe the summit, and gloat over the woe-begone aspect of the unhappy victims compelled to mount the precipice. Twelve o'clock in the day, moreover, the time for this exhibition, and no one looking their best under the circumstances."

"Two human fiends," said Mr Willoughby, "seemed to appreciate the situation most completely, and were, in consequence, good enough to remark unfavourably upon my complexion as I arrived on the brink. I believe I am indebted for preserving my equilibrium to a harpist who was immediately behind me in the file of passengers, and who was good enough to prod the feet of his instrument into the small of my back."

"That was adding insult to injury," laughed Willina. "The man saw how powerless you were, and so made you bear part of his burden without the ceremony of asking leave. Still, I do wonder that nobody has ever been blown off the cliff in ascending to the pier."

"So do I: my own manner of progression, though not pleasant, certainly steadied the ascent," said Mr Willoughby.

The days that came and went at that time were very pleasant, and Mr Willoughby proved to be one of the most accommodating of pupils, inasmuch as he constantly left his own legitimate bear-leader (as he styled Mr La Touche) to take long walks, and go about tapping and hammering the rocks in the sole company of Mr Clavering.

The latter was delighted with his new recruit. "As to La Touche," he said, "never was a fellow so changed; doesn't seem to care to improve his opportunities,—

seems to prefer dawdling among the rocks with my wife and my sister; sea-air certainly contributes to make some people very lazy."

" I fancy they are making a collection of sea-weeds," Mr Willoughby replied,. in answer to Mr Clavering's observations. " They brought in some splendid specimens yesterday; Mr De Brett knows where all the rare kinds are to be found."

Certainly few places exist in the wide world which borders the ocean where algologists can more fully satisfy their craving for the rare and the lovely in sea - weeds and marine botany than the Channel Islands.

In the immediate neighbourhood of Brydone was to be found the jagged Rhodymenia, lifting its crimson head heavy with the wash of the deep sea—for it is rarely to be found within tide-mark—together with the elegant Cladophora, the tufts of which are delicately dyed with the glaucous hue ·peculiar to the British Isles. Nor must be forgotten that wandering star of the sea—that peculiar sea-weed which floats from afar, and which bears the sweet wild name of Dasya.

Whence does it come? whither does it go? No one can tell; but in the vast dominion of the ocean, in the most unexpected places, and at the most unexpected seasons, the Dasya silently floats along, an alien from its species, but bearing an unmistakable individuality of its own.

It is a beautiful fancy among the natives of Spanish

Honduras that the Dasya was a sea-nymph, who, for always quarrelling with her companions, had, as a punishment, been changed into sea-weed and banished from her kind, and compelled to wander on the surface of the deep, ever fresh and ever young, until that time when the sea shall be no more. Thus it is that the Dasya may be met with in almost all known latitudes, according to this old legend of the mariners of the Spanish main.

Among other enjoyments of the party assembled at Brydone were frequent picnics, and the bright lovely weather enabled them to go long distances, and, in some cases, to remain two or three nights from home. Thus they introduced themselves to the beautiful island of Sark, a little nook all ups and downs, with its hedges covered with honeysuckle, and its face illuminated with a perpetual sunshiny smile, as if in derision at the possibility of a railroad being introduced within its bounds.

They quartered themselves also upon the hospitable owner of the island of Herm, the bay of which is famous for its beach, milk-white with the millions of shells, infinitesimal in size, which time has pounded into a thick mass, forming a solid and by no means unpleasant footway at low tide, and presenting a beautiful line of contrasting colour when viewed from the sea.

" But we must not forget an expedition nearer home," said Mr Glascott, one morning, when the routine of the day was under discussion. " Suppose we walk over to St Oswin's and see the lovely old ruined church there. We can lunch early and return comfortably to dinner."

"I should think Canon Braintree could manage that," said young Willoughby, who had strolled up to Brydone from the hotel. "He is a nice old gentleman, and I'll give him an arm. Do you know, I did not like Mrs Braintree at first; but now I see more of her, I am inclined to change my opinion. She is rather managing in manner, but I feel sure she is very kind-hearted."

Some few assented to this, but Willina Clavering was silent. Had she not overheard Mrs Braintree praising up Miss Fanshawe in the most emphatic manner to Mr Glascott only the evening before?

"These parsons' wives are as worldly as their neigh-bours," Willina said to herself, in her haste. "Mrs Braintree wants to serve her cloth, and I daresay she thinks it a Christian duty to provide for a clergyman's daughter. Perhaps it is; but I hope she will carry her charity further, and refrain from turning me out of Brydone till I have a home of my own."

Miss Clavering was partly right and partly wrong in this reflection. Mrs Braintree certainly wished to serve Miss Fanshawe, but she was equally anxious to further Miss Clavering's prospects, and for this reason the Canon's wife "played gooseberry," and enacted "deaf adder" in the interests of her hostess and Mr Stephen La Touche with the most persevering as-siduity. Mrs Braintree had made her own discoveries;

but, like a sensible woman, she did not spoil sport by making indiscreet remarks, or by appearing to see and know what she was not intended to see and know.

It would be well for the comfort of society at large if Mrs Braintree were more universally imitated in this particular. Many a growing affection is nipped in the bud through the indiscretion of some of society's idiots, who are lacking in *savoir taire* as well as in *savoir faire.*

The day is winsome, and Miss Clavering wisely determines to enjoy it and put Lillian Fanshawe out of her mind. Is it not her duty to make all things as alluring to the owner of Brydone as possible? And so the guests assembled without trouble to Mr Glascott, and they set out by the land route towards the fisher village of St Oswin.

The church dedicated to St Oswin was a small edifice, built on a cliff nearly overhanging the sea-shore. So low was the cliff, that at the times of very high tide the little church and its encircling sea-wall often appeared to be entirely surrounded by the waves.

Huge gaps were apparent in the whole structure of the building, black, jagged, and hoary. Some ivy clung to the tottering, crumbling walls, which seemed to drag down the whole edifice, until it bade fair to fall into the midst of the masses of fern with which the burial-ground was literally choked.

A noble pall would be this wealth of the fern Osmunda Royal, — that queenly fairy cryptogam,

which adheres so persistently to the place of its birth
that it frequently refuses to exist when carried beyond
the reach of the particles of ocean spray from which it
draws its strength and its life.

Here, over and around, and through the cracks of the
dilapidated wall, which by a few yards only separated
the churchyard from the sea-line, this splendid fern
protruded itself in every stage of beauty—now bowing
its stately head seaward, as if in waiting for the spray,
anon waving and tossing itself backwards in all the
ineffable glory of the light.

The graves of poor humanity, which time and forgetfulness had alike pressed deeply into the mould, were
thus sprinkled by showers of water diamonds; whilst
the soft mantle of mother-earth heaped its rich texture
and warm colour alike upon the nothingness of the
dead, and the root and stem of the moving, living
frond.

Here was the repetition of the old story, life in
death and death in life! In all parts and places of
the earth time·chants the same requiem, and faithful
nature mutely rehearses the strain.

The ivy of the northern clime, and the rich parasite
vine of some of the islands of the tropical seas, both
thrive, and eventually bring destruction, upon the
temples raised by man.

The latter, as it grows and acquires strength, inserts
its tendrils till they penetrate the fibres of the stone,
and thus imperceptibly grinds its way, till, in course
of time, the masonry has crumbled to dust, and leaves

nothing but masses of bright foliage and trailing spandrils, raising themselves in tiers of coronals, and playing with the sunbeams upon the decay and ruin beneath them. The ivy, though it in a measure protects the stone, at the same time fosters damp, which permeates and turns to mould, and in the end is a most active agent in the destruction of what it was first planted to preserve. Life in death, and death in life !

Curiously enough, this little church, fast crumbling to decay, held within its walls, deep in the interior of the earth, a tiny chapel. This chapel was supported by two elaborately carved pillars, and all the subjects of the handicraft were figures allegorical of mourning and death.

The altar, stripped long, long ago of its original adornments, was plain in construction, and, owing probably to its being of marble, its solidity was very slightly impaired by time and neglect. There were also the remains of a very curious bronze lamp, highly wrought, and inlaid with delicate lines of beaten gold. This had evidently been surmounted by figurative ornaments, there being signs of chasing rudely torn away, to be carried off doubtlessly by the ruthless hand of devastation. The brown dust, thick, and made frowsy by the adhesive sticky strands of the spider's web, threw the pall of disuse over it, and over all around.

Many groups of red fungi were scattered in irregular patches upon the broken steps of the altar: it would almost seem as if the tears of those who had last wept there had turned to specks of blood. Who can tell?

There are living souls—God knows!—whose tears, falling from the eyes, are but the spray of the waters of agony which lie deep in the red caverns of the heart's life-blood.

We are well assured, in treating of those who have already passed out of life, that the majority of them have, at some time or other of their existence, drunk deep of the bitter waters of sorrow : let us then touch very kindly and very reverently on the sufferings of the dead.

A tomb stood in a corner : its size was so large that it filled more than half of the chapel. It was raised on three stone steps, but bore no inscription save the date A.D. 1470, and the single word, "Misericordia." This was cut on a lozenge pendant, on the slab which formed the eastern side of the tomb.

The Latin cross surmounted the whole, and seemed to appeal, in the name of the dear Christ of sorrow, to the sympathies of the living, in remembrance of, perchance, the broken heart that was at rest beneath it.

This chapel and tomb had been built up for a length of years by a wall of mud and sand. The flight of steps which had led down to it had been concealed by masonry, and there is no knowing how long, and for what purpose, this underground sanctuary had been shut off from the ken of man. No outlet from the place existed; and it had been at length assumed that the tomb was the sepulchre of the founder, who, being perhaps the last of his race, had desired to lie buried deep beneath the walls which his generosity had reared, and so pass away from human remembrance. An accident, some thirty years previous to the visit of the Brydone party, had revealed this underground chapel.

They were all examining the place with the greatest interest, and Mr Clavering had already begun to sketch the only window, which was a perfect Gothic in form, and high up in the wall, when the visitors were startled by the loud slamming of the outer door of the church. This was immediately followed by the sound of steps running round outside the building. The upper panes of the window were just on a level with the path, and Frank clearly descried feet and the heavy boots of wayfaring men as the sound passed by. At the same time the old fisherman who attended with the keys exclaimed—

" By golly ! Mr Glascott, sir—those two beggar chaps that we met have followed us here, and have shut us in !"

" But, Dobree, you surely never left the keys in the porch-door ?"

" I did, sir; and here we are for many hours, sure !"

END OF THE SECOND VOLUME.